The Shadows We Hide

The Shadows We Hide

Kassidy Caroline

Copyright © 2024 Kassidy Caroline

First edition July 2024

Cover Design © Carly Scott

ISBN 979-8-9909-1680-7 (Paperback)

Published by Kassidy Caroline

*To my own Dr. Shaw,
who got me through 6 hard years of my life.*

Soundtrack for The Shadows We Hide

"Silence" by Marshmello feat. Khalid
"Girl in the Mirror" by Bebe Rexha
"I Am Here" by Pink
"I Think I'm OKAY" by Machine Gun Kelly,
Yungblud, and Travis Barker
"This Feeling" by The Chainsmokers feat. Kelsea Bal-
lerini
"Weak" by AJR
"Show Me What I'm Looking For" by Carolina Liar
"Me, Myself, and I" by 5 Seconds of Summer
"Best Years" by 5 Seconds of Summer
"Dandelions" by Ruth B.
"Dial Drunk" by Noah Kahan
"Something Just Like This" by The Chainsmokers
"I Got You" by Bebe Rexha
"Doin' Fine" by Lauren Alaina
"Long Live (Taylor's Version)" by Taylor Swift
"Make it Sweet" by Old Dominion
"Dark Waters" by Tones and I
"Lighthouse" by Calum Scott
"Where I Want To Be" by Forest Blakk
"I Break Beautiful Things" by Robert Grace

*Some of the songs are listed with the chapters as I heard them
playing in my mind while writing certain scenes during those
chapters. I listed them with these chapters for you guys to hear
them as well.*

Days like this, when I can see my breath while waiting for the bus, are days when I wish for several things. That we didn't live in Minnesota. Or that I had friends with cars or just friends in general. Or that my mom would let me drive my bike to school already. And least of all, that I was still in Micanopy, Florida, as hellish as that was.

The sound of the bus sliding on the icy roads covered in snow wakes me from my daydreaming. We've been living in Forthsworth, Minnesota for a little over six months now. I remember how nice it was when my mom and I got out of the U-Haul and could smell the summer air. It was different from Micanopy. The air wasn't some humid monster hanging around, surrounding everything, and honestly just suffocating me. It's thinner and it flows in and out of my lungs easier than it did down there.

But Micanopy air was all I knew and I didn't realize how much I hated it until I left. And with that sentiment I set foot onto the prison on six wheels that takes me from something I've just started calling home, to a prison of another kind.

"Hey, jackass!". I hear the voice of my least favorite person as I make my way down the aisle of the bus towards an empty seat. Well, I guess uninterrupted peace was never going to last.

As I sit down, without even turning my head, I respond. "What do you want, shrivel dick?" It was less of a question and more of a statement. Reuben is the only person on the bus with that much energy this early in the morning to make me want to eat my fist.

He is a shrivel dick, I have that on good authority. "What do you want?" is the nicest way I have of saying that if he doesn't leave me alone, we're both gonna be in the principal's office first thing this morning. Me because I punched his teeth out and him because he's a little bitch baby who can't take a hit.

You see, the school counselor met with my mom during the first month of the school year to "talk about the issues Elleri has presented in her classes and around her peers." It was the nicer way to say that I, Elleri, something I loathe being called, was arguing with my teachers, cussed out many of my classmates, and punched a dent in three lockers. It was during this conversation between my mom and the principal that I was recruited by the one and only Coach Maddox, or as his doofus players refer to him as, "Coach Mad Dog".

They think it's a really clever take on his ACTUAL name, but I think it's a three out of ten at best. While I don't love the man and worship the ground he walks on like the other players, I do owe him for saving me from the school's version of community service. He also saved me from expulsion from the school since I'm a senior in high school and not worth the hassle, what with my being new and all. Don't know why he saved me, but now as far as punishment goes, I am now the starting center of the Forthsworth's Tardigrades. And please for the love of God no one ask me what those are because nobody knows and at this point, none of the students care enough to ask.

"What's got you so bitchy this morning?" Reuben pipes in out of nowhere.

"Ya know Reuben, it might have something to do with the 5'8 stuck-up egotistical asshat sitting across from me and interrupting *Love Grows*." Talking to Reuben always gives me a headache.

"Ryn, if you weren't so rude to people all the time, maybe girls would be your friends and guys would think you're hot."

"Reuben go fuck yourself." I respond while turning my music up to a deafening level.

"It'd be more fun if it were with you." As he retreats

to the back of the bus I gag and try to keep my breakfast down. I hear whispers that I know are about me. But I honestly don't care anymore. As I'm putting my Air-Pods back in I try to let the bumps and jolts of the bus as it drives me down the death road toward Forthsworth High School lull me into a sense of peace.

Lunch has never been my favorite subject. Being forced to navigate a sea of bland copycats and wannabes while everyone separates into cliques that will never really matter outside of the halls in this school never had any appeal. The only "friend" I have in this school attached herself to me and hasn't left me alone since she introduced herself on the first day of school. Don't ask me why she bothers with me– I really have no idea– and when I've asked her, she just laughs.

Liza Pennelli– flier on the cheer team, probably dating some big shot football player, mom and dad have been married for twenty-five years, basically gets everything she's ever wanted. But honestly, I don't know anything about her and I don't want to know anything about her. When I met Liza some asshole had "bumped" into her and when I say bumped, I mean he groped her and tried to excuse his behavior by being clumsy and not watching where he was going. I, being the way I am, punched him square in the nose then pantsed him in front of the whole cafeteria. Afterwards, I retreated to the fourth-floor stairwell in the Dockner building. It's abandoned for the most part, except for a few select classes. It was just my luck that Liza happened to have one of those few classes. She found me eating day-old Subway leftovers and biting my nails.

"You pantsed Jeremiah Hawkins in front of half the school," Liza remarked. Liza restates the obvious. I don't know why but it's more than annoying. Maybe she thinks it'll make whatever was said or is happening sink in further. Like that's actually necessary.

"See it's crazy, ya know, because I remember it like, oh I don't know, like I was there. Oh wait, that's cause I was." I kept walking away from her even as I responded. She followed me anyway. She either didn't care when I growled at her and threw murderous glares her way for stealing my food or she was strong enough to brave them silently. For some reason, even after that cold interaction, she still won't leave me alone. She finds all my hiding spots and even brings me coffee, which I have never asked her to do. While I still don't really talk to her she's still there. It drives me crazy. A small part of me thinks she might've been the one to sic Coach

Maddox on me.

"Here." Her eyes grow wide as I plop a package of fresh strawberries on the table in front of her and keep walking.

"Oh my god, Ryn! You brought me strawberries?" There she goes again, restating the obvious.

"Relax, it's not like I'm proposing." I respond, rolling my eyes.

Trying to avoid the cafeteria and anyone in it is like a military strategy itself. There's never anywhere to sit and the noise could rival that of a "Who" concert from the 80s. And while it's easier to survive the field when you have a place in it, Liza still insists on leaving her group of overly elitist friends to follow me wherever I'm going to lay low this hour. "Put on your coat, we're going outside today." Liza's like a puppy– she follows people blindly out of loyalty and we've already established that she has too much energy.

"Where are we going today?" I really wish she wouldn't chirp when she talks to me because it really makes it hard for me to not walk in front of traffic.

Spitting out blood usually isn't something people enjoy, but there's something so humbling to me when I get knocked into the glass so hard my vision blurs and the familiar taste of iron enters my mouth. Coach recruited me that day because he believed hockey would be a good outlet for me to release my anger in a productive and legal way, or at least that's the case he argued when he ambushed my mom talking with the principal. I just know that in that bright room with all the posters talking about helping kids with positive motivational quotes and the worried look on my mom's face, it was enough to make me accept whatever offer Coach was giving. I understand why she's worried. I'd be lying if I said I wasn't too.

"Knox! Get your shit together and get back on the ice! Stop playing around." I knew Maddox was mad whenever he called me Knox because he did it to piss me off.

"You know Knox isn't my name," I grit out under my teeth. It takes everything in me not to rush and slam *him* into the wall, no protective gear at all. I'd like to hear him call me Knox after that. The problem is, I'd be in jail and my mother would be broken and I'd have no one to blame but myself. What's worse is that when I skate back over to my position for the drill we're running, he almost looks proud of me for not giving him more hell for calling me that. That makes me more enraged than I already was, but instead of ending up in jail, I "put that negative energy into something productive" and body check my teammate as hard as I can into the wall on my way to the goal.

Once practice is finally over, I'm left to trek across town, unable to ride my skateboard through the snow or the work-in-progress I call my bike, to the one place that actually calms my nerves– the greenhouse on Swan Street. It's where I've been secretly working for the last three and a half months. I stumbled across it when I was out for one of my rage runs and stopped when I noticed a Sea Daffodil in one of the windows under the Ukrainian flag Mrs. Kahn, the woman who owns the greenhouse, hangs from the ceiling.

When I was younger, I had a teacher who spent

a lot of time trying to help me get my anger issues under control and she soon found that I was super into plants. So she started a garden at the school with me. I loved every second of it. I spent so much time there before and after school experimenting with new flowers and exotic plants. Honestly, part of the reason I loved it so much was because every day, when I came home and brought my mother a new flower, she had tears in her eyes from how happy she was. But now that I'm older, I realize that her tears weren't happy at all, and her tears weren't even for me.

As I walked into the house, the familiar smells of different wildlife and a world of possibility filled my nostrils. Mrs. Kahn was kind enough to offer me a job even though I was the strange girl lurking around her shop examining her plants. Not only that, but she caught me trying to steal the Sea Daffodil, a beautiful white cone-shaped flower with long skinny petals sticking out from the center cone. She didn't turn me into the police. And as far as the outside world, she was the only person who knew I worked here, and she didn't know anything real about me, so she didn't know I wasn't worth the trouble.

"Mrs. Kahn, that's too heavy for you to carry alone, let me help." As I rushed over to her to keep her from dropping one of the biggest Jade Vines– a plant that looks like a giant swiffer brush with petals that look more like turquoise peppers– we've ever had. Mrs. Kahn tried to shoo me away because, like me, she was stubborn. But unlike me she was short and didn't have the muscles of a high school hockey player.

"Ryn, I don't need you saving me every day around here. Buuut I will say I'm very grateful to have you around." Her thick accent comes through as she pats my arm. She also knows when to show gratitude to those she cares about. "So how was school? Still getting straight As?"

"Uh, yea." No. "Been studying a lot and asking for help when I need it," I don't ask for help, not now, not ever.

"That's good. And you wouldn't lie and tell me what I want to hear because you're afraid to disappoint anyone other than yourself?" She questions as she raises an accusatory eyebrow at me. She sees through me more than my own mother sometimes and that's because I have gotten good at hiding.

Yet I don't let her know she's right, "Why would I ever lie to you? I have no reason to."

"Hmmph." I sigh after she walks away and pray that those are all the questions she has for tonight.

"Why are you just getting home?" A light in the corner of the living room jumps on and I can't help but scream because I'd let my guard down. I wasn't thinking about how I was coming in. "Elleri Ryn Bradford! You'll wake the whole neighborhood if you yell like that."

"Mom, I'm sorry. I just wasn't expecting you to be up." Fuck, I've been spending too much time with Liza.

"I see that." She crosses her arms and I know that her anger comes from her being worried. Too many nights he would stumble in, alcohol on his breath. She thinks I didn't notice because I was little and was supposed to be in bed, but even then I didn't like rules very much. I hate that I remind her so much of him. "Stop thinking like that."

I purse my lips and my eyebrows knit together, "Like what?"

"You know what. We've been over this more times than I can count." She doesn't even have to say anything because we both know we're on the same page. This must be one of those times her "Ryn Bullshit Meter" is on high alert. Getting out of this isn't gonna be easy.

"Mom I'm not, I swear. I was just out with a friend and time got away from us that's all." Lying, lying, lying through my teeth.

"Really? What friend?" I can tell she doesn't buy my bullshit but I'm in it now.

"Liza." Fuck.

"Well maybe you should have this Liza over for dinner tomorrow. I think it would be really nice to—"

"NO!" If I had any sense at all, I would've held my tongue and let her finish her sentence. That way I could've acted like I was considering the notion only to counter back with the sudden remembrance of some made-up event she had. But now she knows I don't want Liza here.

"Ellie, I expect your *friend* to be here for dinner tomorrow. No ifs, ands, or buts." And just like usual, my tongue has kicked me when I'm down. Although, if I'm honest, I'm glad I didn't blurt out Reuben, because I'd rather attend my own funeral than invite Reuben anywhere near my house. "Now please go to sleep. You have therapy tomorrow and you can't afford to miss it." Therapy, a sadistic form of torture. One where I get to lie to a whole other person for an hour while they sit and try to figure out what's wrong with me and how to put it back together.

Forthsworth is different from Micanopy in more ways than one. For starters, there are thousands of more people because while it isn't considered a major city, it's still big enough to earn that title. Big enough for there to be three high schools, a university and sister-school community college, several Starbucks, and traffic on the busy streets. You would think I would hate the traffic and the noise it brings, but it's oddly comforting. Having to drive places was never a thing in Micanopy– everything was within walking distance and it was always nice enough to do just that. There's just something about the bustling life outside of the car that lets me fade away into the background.

My therapist says that that's because I use the noise of the outside world to escape the noise in my head. But that's really funny to me for two reasons. One, I'm pretty sure she's not in my head, and two, I didn't fucking ask. My well-known feelings about this woman still don't save me from my mom carting me off to her office once a week just for her to analyze why having string cheese at lunch means I actually want to hang myself.

I'm not suicidal. I'm not, really. Killing myself would be the cowardly way out. An easy out that I don't deserve. It still doesn't change the fact that she constantly nitpicks and whispers things under her breath while she scribbles in the notepad where she writes her true thoughts about my insanity that she's either too afraid to say out loud or she'd get fired for if she did.

"Ellie, did you hear me? God, your constant daydreaming is really starting to scare me. I don't like you so far in your head. It makes me worry that one day I won't be able to get to you." The way she says that last sentence makes me feel bad for being distant. That's why I even put up with the therapy. I know it helps her relax if she thinks that I'm not trying to put the weight of everyone's problems and the weight of the world on myself.

"Sorry. I promise you'll never lose me to daydreaming ma. I've always been a little spacey, you know that."

"I do, but you know this is something different. It's been this way since–"

"Don't", my tone is harsh and unyielding. She knows how I feel about this. I put up with all the shit from the school, her, coach, and anyone else who thinks I should do something, anything to "heal" myself. No one's ever stopped to ask me what I think I need to "heal" and you know what maybe I don't think I can.

But I can't say that.

"I'm sorry. I know how you feel about the subject. I didn't mean to make you angry, Ellie." And I know she didn't, which is what makes me feel like shit.

"It's fine– what were you trying to ask me, mom?"

"I was gonna tell you that Daniel and I would be able to make it to your game on Friday. He's really excited to watch you play." Daniel. I make an effort to be around the house as little as I can because even though my mother's husband, Daniel, is a nice enough guy, I can't bring myself to interact with him unless I have to.

"That's nice ma, but that wasn't a question." She gets sidetracked easily, always has.

"Oh right! Thanks, I thought I was getting better at that." She really isn't.

"Mom."

"Yes! Ok, so your friend Liza is coming over for dinner tonight and Daniel and I were wondering if you wanted a home cooked meal or takeout or pizza of some kind. We're fine with either option but we figured we'd leave it up to you two." Oh right. That. For a split second I'd forgotten about my inability to hold my tongue and the many consequences that come with it.

"Oh. Right. I'll talk to her." I wish this was a lie but once again I'm in the water too deep and if I don't swim a little I'll drown.

"Good." Her tone changes again, and she sighs, so I know she's gonna say something more serious. She's so in touch with her feelings and I guess she's had to be, but there are two types of reactions to what happened to us and I guess she got the healthier way with how the dice landed.

"I'm glad you've started to make friends. It gives me hope you'll be your old self again someday." I'm not sure I know what my old self would look like. I don't know if I've really ever been myself, always running from something. She's not looking at me, but as I look at her, I can see the tears she's holding back. I have to bite my tongue because I don't want to cry either. Instead, I slip back into daydreaming and lose myself to the traffic.

Dr. Shaw's office is small with sunlight filtering in through the windows outlining two of the four walls in the room. She's a thin woman who looks like she might break if the wind blows a little too hard. Sometimes, I wonder if maybe she has an eating disorder and has to sit in a different office and be analyzed the way she analyzes me.

But honestly, if we'd have met under different circumstances, just out and about in the world outside her office, I think we could've been friends. My mom chose her as my therapist because she said she saw a "spark" in her. Meaning she believes that Dr. Shaw has enough power and influence to see through me and knock me down a few pegs. I respect that cause not anyone can do that.

I have this whole fake first meeting planned out in my head of how I think we would meet, like the when, where, and why of it all. We're at some store somewhere. Probably a Target because even though I hate Target for being too lively and happy, it has things that I need that Walmart doesn't. But I prefer Walmart any day because everyone's miserable there, which almost makes me the happiest person in the building, and that's really refreshing. Anyways, we're at Target and we both reach for the last box of Cinnamon Toast Crunch. I like it cause it's always been my favorite cereal and I eat it like it'll be my last meal. She grabs it because she has four kids at home who go through cereal like it'll be *their* last meal. We'd then proceed to argue over who had it first and who needed it more and she'd go all mom batshit crazy on me because it'd been a long week and she was sick and tired of all the pushback from her kids that she wasn't gonna take any from a stranger in a Target.

"Ryn, I know you'd rather be anywhere else than here. That's no secret. But if you could at least try and pay attention when I'm talking to you, then that would give me enough grounds to stretch the truth to your mother and tell her you're making an effort." You see, Dr. Shaw and I have been doing this same old song and dance routine for five months. Which is why by now she's learned to gain information about my life from my mother and teachers and coach to use to her advantage. Next she learns from the behavior I present while I'm in her office, and then puts together her conclusions and understandings of what I'm feeling. I rarely talk in these appointments, at least not about anything important, and I don't intend on starting now.

"Let me guess, you were talking about how I'm closed off and guarded because of the "incident" and if I'm ever going to make any progress, I need to talk about what happened, accept that it happened, because only then will I be able to move on and live my life without being held back from my trauma."

"No, I was actually talking about how you needed to remind your mother to send in the bill for last month. But it is nice to see you pay enough attention in our sessions to learn and remember that." Damnit, I showed my hand. Therapy is like poker. Dr. Shaw wants me to fold or play my hand before she does– that way, she wins. Because even if I have the winning hand, showing it at all means I'm revealing too much.

"Oh."

"But I am curious about something." Here we go. "If you have been listening, and you have been taking in what I'm telling you and trying to get you to see for yourself, then what's holding you back from actually doing it and taking back your life?"

"I–."

"I'm afraid that's all the time we have for today, we'll continue this on Friday."

And just like that, she leaves me to stew with the question. I hate it when Dr. Shaw does that because when she does, she makes it very obvious that she knows the answer to what she's asking. Dr. Shaw just wants me to come to that conclusion and it pisses me off because I shouldn't have to come to the conclusion. My mom is busting her ass trying to pay for my therapy appointments where this woman is supposed to fix me and tell me what's wrong. But instead, she makes me figure it out, so honestly, can somebody please tell me what the fuck we're paying her for??

The worst part is, she *knows* it gets under my skin. I hop out of that stupid armchair and storm my way out of her office like a child, and I know I'm acting like one but I don't care. As I storm out of the waiting room and make my way towards the parking lot my mom rushes after me yelling for me.

"Ellie!" I don't turn around, I can't. "Ellie stop!" Still stomping to the car. "Elleri Ryn!" She's angry now. I finally stop and as I slowly turn around to face her she doesn't look angry, just sad. Sad and disappointed. But I guess that's what I do these days. I bite the inside of my cheek but it doesn't stop the angry tears bubbling up inside. I turn to the nearest car and just punch. Punch and punch and punch until my knuckles are bleeding. My mom is yelling my name but I can't hear anything. Just a high pitched ringing as the world fades away around me.

After what felt like an eternity, I'm pulled away from the car. I realize the security at the front of the building must've pulled me away. My mom doesn't ever dare get close to me when I'm like this. She's scared, I am too. I look at what I did and that just makes me more angry because just like that he wins. But instead of punching again I break down and sob. Slumping against the car. My mom sits down next to me and pulls me against her as I cry like the big idiot that I am. So we sit there and I sob and scream and my body shakes and we sit there for close to thirty minutes before I notice a man's shoes across from us.

As I look up from his feet all the way up to his eyes I see Daniel. He must've sped here as soon as my mom called. He doesn't look mad or scared or annoyed that his step-daughter just brutally vandalized a car that he had to be pulled away from work to come stop. Instead he just looks concerned. Concerned for me. At this point I'm tired of people looking at me so my mom walks me to our car as Daniel gives the poor old man whose car I dented an insurance card and handles the situation like the genuinely good guy he is.

Once I'm in the car my mom turns to me and takes my hand without saying anything. My knuckles are already bruising and they're splattered red from blood.

"Do they hurt?" That throws me for a second because I was expecting her to scold, yell, or be angry with me for breaking down like that but instead all she cares about is whether or not I'm hurt. I don't deserve her kindness. I don't deserve her.

"You're not gonna yell?" Her eyes search mine for a second or two before she looks down and just gently shakes her head and sighs.

"Ellie I can see you've already done a fine job of punishing yourself. I'm just more concerned about your hand for school and for your game." My game. Shit. Coach is gonna kill me. This is what he's been talking about in practice. *Think with your head, don't react with your body.* He's repeated this little mantra over and over to try and drill it into my thick skull but here I am reacting with my body. "Let's get you to a doctor and see what they say. I'm sure it'll be fine." Ever the optimist even when she shouldn't be. She chuckles to herself a little bit as she starts to drive.

"What?" For a split second my insecurities tell me she's laughing at me but I know she wouldn't.

"Ya know if you wanted to miss school *that* badly there were other ways to do it." With that I roll my eyes because I know she's gonna let this go because she knows I'm my own worst enemy and that I'll need someone in my corner when I beat myself up again.

"You say that but I've never heard you offering." She full on bursts out laughing after that remark and her laughter is just so contagious that it makes me chuckle a little myself. Her eyes crinkle at the corners and she looks truly happy. It almost feels like the way things used to be.

I2:OO P.M

Good news is my hand isn't broken but the doctor thinks that I should take it easy so I don't cause any more damage to my hand. The only problem with that is I have to play on Friday because much to Fox's chagrin, I'm a much better player than him because I'm a quick learner and spend the majority of my time at either the rink or the green house. It helps when the other team underestimates a girl player. My mom knows all this which is why she knows I'll still be playing.

"Just promise me if your hand starts to hurt at all that you'll get Coach to let you out."

"Mom, I'll be fine. I always am. Besides, I haven't been working this hard for months just to miss the first game of the second half of the season." Even though hockey wasn't my first choice or even on my mind to begin with, I don't hate it. Picking up skating wasn't as hard as it should've been or is for others but that's because back in Florida I was a two time state champ for skateboarding. And while I know it's not exactly the same, both sports focus on balance and quick movement so I was able to take my expertise in skateboarding and turn it into a basic knowledge of ice skating. Couple that with having no personal life and never wanting to be home and you've got a center starter who kicks ass and out performs the former center Hunter Fox.

Lucky for Hunter the team was in need of a right wing since I beat the last one into a bloody pulp during the first week of school. He then had to get a nose job and his shoulder relocated. If you're wondering why I beat him up it's because I overheard him talking about and showing his friends pictures of this girl he'd sexually assaulted. He was standing there in front of his locker bragging about it like he was a god. So I did what anyone else would've done.

"Are you nervous at all? Hockey's a big skip from skateboarding?" Small talk, refreshing.

"Nope. In fact I'm pretty sure I could run all the drills in my sleep." Except I was nervous. Not nervous that I would mess up or that we would lose. When it came down to it I didn't really care what the outcome of the game was. I was just paying off a debt. I was nervous that I would snap. That something would happen that would lead me to just lose my shit on the ice and take it out on someone. Coach had been spending the last month preparing me for the moment I stepped out on the ice for a real game. He had some of the players help him host a simulation of some kind where he gave them insults to call me anything ranging from how I played to the fact that I was a girl. Coach deemed his little experiment successful seeing as how we spent three hours doing this and I didn't hit/break anyone or anything and the only actual damage done was that I left Spitz, a junior on the team who plays second-string left forward, sobbing and begging for his "mommy".

He recruited me back in early December after the season had already started. There was a small two week break where there were no games for any teams (we still had practices though). I worked harder than anything during those two weeks. I watched reels and reels of past games and ran drills at the rink until I couldn't feel my legs anymore. And even though there were still games happening at the time he recruited me, he wanted to spend plenty of time training me and making sure I was prepared. And even though I had no obligations to him, I didn't want to let him down.

"Well I know Daniel's super excited to see you play. I am too but not as much as he is. He's going all out. All he's been talking about at the office is how his daughter is the only girl on her school's hockey team and that she's the starting center and she's only been playing a few months. I'm almost afraid of what he's gonna wear to the game," she ends laughing. But I'm not.

"I'm not his daughter."

"What? Oh honey, I know not biologically but he loves you so much. And I know and he knows that you're not ok with calling him dad but is it really so bad if he calls you his daughter to his coworkers and friends?" I can hear it in her voice how she's pleading with me to let him in. I don't want to, but I want to make her happy.

"Fine, just not in front of me." I still have to set a limit somewhere. My mom met Daniel at the supermarket in a neighboring town when we still lived in Micanopy. It had been a year since "the incident" and we were barely making ends meet. Even after everything she'd, no, we'd been through, (Dr. Shaw wants me to recognize that it's my trauma too), she still lit up like a Christmas tree talking to him. They fell in love hard and fast and after a few months of dating they got married on a particularly muggy and humid day in June.

It was hard on my mom to try and create a normal life for her and I, what with constantly feeling haunted and like at any moment we would be forced to confront the past. So Daniel being the stupid knight in shining armor that he is, suggested we move. He then told my mother about where he grew up, Forthsworth. He said he had family up here and that it would be a nice change of pace as well as scenery. That's more or less how I ended up here. The short version anyway.

Thankfully I was saved from this conversation as the sound of crunching snow and ice on a road traveled on before it could get plowed let me know we're pulling up to the school before I even lift up my head. As my mom stopped the car and threw it in park she looked at me and gave me a soft grin and for the first time in a long time I couldn't decipher what it meant. Was she mad at me? Feeling sorry for me? Seeing right through all my lies?

"What? Why are you staring at me like that?" My eyebrows furrow and I know I'm glaring and sizing her up like she's gonna attack me.

She chuckles before responding, "Nothing sweetheart," she shakes her head slightly and looks down and back up before continuing, "Just admiring how strong you are." Oh. I turn away and bite the inside of my cheek to keep from crying and just nod my head curtly. Why do I do that?

My lips draw into a small, tight smile and I barely glance at her as I say, "thanks mom." And with that I'm rushing out of the car and up into the school.

But even though I finally made it to school I don't plan on going to class. Instead I'll be busy committing a crime.

12:45 P.M

I don't remember when or where I was when I learned how to pick locks. But I can't say I'm upset that I did. That skill has come in handy on more than one occasion. And while I hadn't used it for too much evil, this takes the cake.

I keep my head down, hands shoved in my pockets. Thankfully there's never a whole lot of staff or admin roaming the halls during class periods. They're always too busy doing something else or being dragged to some class because some idiot is being difficult. However, just to make sure my ass is covered I'm not walking unarmed.

As I reach the first floor girl's bathroom in the Dockner building I look around me to make sure no one's watching and then kick the door three times. After about a minute of waiting I whistle four short whistles and the door swings open and I'm greeted by a puff of smoke. This bathroom has been taken over by the smokers and stoners. I think they've paid off a few staff members in this hallway to keep them in the clear. It's actually insane how corrupt the public school system is.

They've actually renovated it really well and turned it into some sort of clubhouse. There's a secret knock and code to get in and everything. One of the girls who hangs out in there stumbled across me in the stairwell one day and I don't know what it was about me but she handed me a slip of paper that had the code on it and just dipped. Seeing as how she reeked of weed it wasn't hard to track down where she'd run off to. I ended up going to the bathroom a few times to escape teachers trying to track me down when I ditched class and that's how I got acquainted with Julia.

"Well look what the cat dragged in." Her voice is raspy and low as she greets me and if her eyes are any indication, she is higher than this building. It's four stories.

"Julia, what services do you have for $50?" God this sounds like I'm trying to pick up a hooker.

"Depends, what are you wanting?" And I can tell that's what she thinks too. I roll my eyes and sigh.

"Look I need a hall pass.....I also need an alibi."

"That's worth a whole hell of a lot more than $50 and

I think you know that." She crosses her arms, raises a brow, and smirks. It's almost like she can smell the desperation on me because by now she'd have taken my money, shoved half into her bra and used the other half to roll joints.

I grit my teeth and ball my hands up because I can feel the steam coming out of my ears, but I'll be damned if I let her have the upper hand. "Fine, if you don't want the $50 I'll find another desperate stoner who's habits need funding. It's not like the school is scarce on them." As I turn around and reach for the door she grabs my arm. "Julia." My voice is low and unyielding. I don't like being touched.

"Sorry." She looks scared and I feel sorry for one second I've made myself so feared. Until she says, "I'll do it." Game on.

With the plethora of hall passes that Julia has stolen and then replicated means good business for her when kids want a safety net if they get caught in the halls. But for me, it's a cocky way to stick it to the teachers in this dump who I'm convinced have a club that targets kids walking the halls. They send secret emails detailing when they saw a kid walk past their classroom and then if another one sees it in time they can walk out in perfect time to catch them and scold them for not having a pass. It's a working theory but it's the only way I can explain the anomaly. After I learned of this super secret club I started watching the cameras and slipping around the doors and even got good at timing certain teachers' pacing-while-lecturing habits in order to sneak by at just the right times. Once I learned about Julia's little business I started paying for hall passes and stopped trying to be so sneaky so I could get caught and flaunt them around when I did.

Entering the counseling center I do a quick sweep of my surroundings. Just like I knew she would be, the secretary sits behind her desk typing away while she intermittently watches funny cat videos. Here goes nothing.

"Hey Ms. Kipper, I was wondering if I could use the printer in the back to make copies of this hockey flier talking about our game on Friday." This technically wasn't a lie because Coach had asked me to do this two weeks ago and I didn't.

"Sure thing Elleri!" She INSISTED on calling me Elleri. No matter how many times I corrected her she still did it. "Do you know how to use it?" She tilts her head and blinks at me and it makes me shift uncomfortably. She's always been too nice. Nobody's this nice, not even Liza.

"I'm a teenage girl living in the twenty-first century. I think I'm good." I do my best to look uninterested which shouldn't be too hard since I am.

"You are too fun Elleri, truly." I hate her.

After she's done laughing at herself and turns back to her cat videos I walk into the back room where the printer and copy machine is. Closing the door I make sure the sound is loud enough for her to hear the click but not too loud that it seems angry or suspicious.

Pulling out the paper I've been hanging onto I realize I really should've done this weeks ago because it's crumpled up with a few tears on the edges and a small Pepsi stain at the bottom. Well at least I made copies of it at some point and not never. I set the machine to one copy to start and it takes about 15 seconds. Which means that if I make the 50 copies Coach asked for I have about 12.5 minutes before they'll be done. I can't open the door while the machine is running because the noise will be too loud and Ms. Kipper will know that I opened the door. So instead I wait for the first sheet to slide out and before it even has I've turned the knob.

As it finishes printing, I carefully pull open the door and slip out keeping flat against the wall and pull the door close again, holding for a second for the copier to start so the click of the door will be masked. Three, two, one. The phone starts ringing right on cue. I told Julia I needed her to call Ms. Kipper and keep her talking so I could get to and from Mrs. Geller's office without being spotted. I get out a paper clip and credit card and start working on the lock.

I've had several meetings with Mrs. Geller since starting school here. Most of them have to do with my plans after high school. Each time I've told her I don't have a damn clue and that it's really the least of my worries. I sent out some college applications in November just to make her happy and get her off my back but that's all I've done since then. And if I'm being honest

I don't really want to go to college.

I told her that once and she just sighed. Like she didn't know what she was going to do with me. After that she went back into her collected counselor mode where she gave me a bunch of different pamphlets for future careers to look into that didn't involve college. Needless to say those were shoved to the bottom of my bag and remain crumpled there still today.

Mrs. Geller is always out of her office between 1-1:40 for lunch and since it's only 1:04 now, I'm not too worried about her being there. I look at my watch and see I have 7 minutes left. After what felt like forever I finally feel the lock turn and I quickly push open the door and get inside. Once I've closed the door again I rush to her computer. I'm praying that the file I need is digital and not physical because if it is then I'm screwed because who the hell knows where they'd keep those locked up.

But it's just my luck that her computer is password protected. Fuck.

Suddenly I'm searching through all the papers around her desk and digging through her personal things trying to come up with something that could possibly be this woman's password. It's a long shot but I try it anyway.

Typing in "IheartTomCruise", the computer unlocks and I see a giant picture of the man's face. It's the one thing Mrs. Geller actually talks about. It also doesn't hurt there's a picture of her on vacation wearing a shirt with that very phrase, and her mousepad dons it as well. I'm more mad at myself that that wasn't my first guess. My watch dings letting me know I've got three minutes. Since I'm in a hurry I've never been so grateful to be able to search keywords on a computer. After a few different ones I finally find what I'm risking my ass for. Liza Pennelli's class schedule.

As I'm sneaking back into the copy room I realize the irony of this whole situation. Me going all "Mission Impossible" to break into Mrs. Geller's office who is possibly the biggest Tom Cruise fan alive.

I grab the copies from the machine and head out the door.

"Oh! Bye Elleri!" I can't get out of here fast enough and away from that annoying, squawking woman. Walking through the halls on my way back to the bathroom where Julia is, I start looking through Liza's schedule and notice all the AP and Honors classes she's taking. It's weird to me that she's in these classes since I've had her pegged as an airhead bimbo cheerleader from the day we met. This would mean she has layers and that thought scares me and makes me uneasy because that would mean that maybe I was wrong about her and I'm not ready to admit that. Although she has been the only person willing to talk to me and occasionally stand up to me. I swallow because it's in this moment that I realize Liza might potentially be a friend. Maybe my only friend.

Once I get to the bathroom I barge in without doing the secret code because I need to get moving before I have to chase Liza to her seventh hour and beg her in front of people. As I barge into the bathroom I cringe and turn away as I apparently interrupted Julia making out with who I'm assuming is her girlfriend.

"Oh my god I am so sorry." Still facing the wall my eyes bug out of my head because holy shit.

"Ryn!! *This* is why we have the code. In case anyone on the inside is doing anything indecent." She huffs and as I turn back around she fixes her shirt and goes to the mirror to straighten out her hair.

"Again, sorry, but I'm in a hurry and I wouldn't even be back in here if you hadn't insisted on me bringing you this." I hold up the bag of weed that Mrs. Geller confiscated from Julia yesterday and toss it at her. "How'd you even know she'd still have it anyways?" I think it's super weird that a high school counselor was just holding onto a student's weed.

"She can never properly dispose of it until the end of the day and she tries to put it somewhere she doesn't think I'll find it but the problem is that come the end of the day, she's forgotten she ever had it." Impressive. I never thought Julia would put so much thought and effort into her business. I just assumed she would count her losses and move on.

Now that Julia has her stash back I pull out my phone and pull up the picture I took of Liza's schedule. It's almost 1:30 now which means that I have four minutes to get from the Dockner building to Eisenhower. Which is all the way across campus. Fuck.

Making it to the second floor of the Eisenhower building in four minutes feels like some sort of record and you would think that because I have to be in such a physical shape for hockey that it would be easy for me to book it across campus. However that is very much not the case. When I reach room 207 I'm panting and bent over with my hands on my knees fighting for my life. There's something supremely different between sports/any sort of working out compared to having to get to a class and not be late. It's like your body knows the stakes are higher so it takes more out of you because fuck.

I lean back against the lockers and kick my foot up behind me and cross my arms. But because the universe has some sort of vendetta against me the bell rings and I have to be prepared to grab Liza and haul her off to talk to her in private. God it sounds like I'm kidnapping her. Just then Liza makes her way through the door, her head down looking at her phone. She turns the corner towards me and I bend down a little and barrel into her causing her to fall over my shoulder. I grab hold of her, straighten up and start briskly walking away and towards a hallway I know will be mostly empty.

"Put me down! I've got mace on me! Help! Somebody help!" Of course Liza isn't making this any easier. She swings her arms and beats her closed fists on my back like a toddler trying to make an adult put them down in the middle of a tantrum. At one point I think she even pulled my hair a little bit. We get to the hallway and I set her down.

"God Liza," I sigh, "You're not being kidnapped, I just needed to talk to you and I didn't want to talk to you in front of other people." By this time she's visibly relaxed but at this her eyes start to widen then one of them starts to squint like she's going insane. "Are you ok–"

"NO I'M NOT OK!! I THOUGHT I WAS BEING KIDNAPPED! I WAS GONNA MACE YOU, YOU LUNATIC, NO YOU MANIAC!!!" I looked down at her hand that she had started to raise when she was yelling and see that she was in fact about to mace me and I was extremely lucky to put her down when I did.

How the hell did she pull that out of her bag while I was holding her?

"Could you stop yelling for two damn seconds." I whisper-scream at her and wonder where the hell this Liza's been, I like her. I swallow to try and clear the lump forming in my throat as well as quite literally swallowing my pride. Why is this so hard for me? Why can't I just tell her that she has to come to my house for dinner because I've caught myself in a lie with my mother and don't want anyone to know the truth. I don't want anyone to know the truth. The truth.

Liza looks down and then back up at me and I'm assuming she's a normal person and was able to use those two seconds to compose herself. Lucky bitch. She clears her throat and huffs, "Fine, what did you want to ask me." Her tone is mostly back to her normal chirpy and happy self but there's something else hidden there. Maybe a hint of annoyance? But that would be impossible, Liza Pennelli is never anything but a ball of shining energy. Right? Once I see her blinking at me I realize I've gotten carried away daydreaming and I clear my throat for what feels like the thousandth time today.

"I—uh. I wanted to—. My mom makes—." I groan and vigorously rub my palms over my eyes. I hate socializing.

"Spit it out, Ryn." There it is. That annoyance again, but this time there's a note of pity? No. It's not pity. I've heard pity enough times and this isn't quite it. They're similar and probably sound the same to someone who hasn't spent the majority of her teen years hearing it from everyone around her. I think... I think it's understanding.

I take a deep breath and play with my hands, "I wanted to ask if you wanted to come to my house tonight for dinner?" And just like that her eyes have lit up and her mouth falls open into a half smile, half jaw drop. Before I have the chance to stop it she throws her arms around me and I stiffen. She doesn't let go. In fact she just squeezes tighter. Finally I've had enough and I force her arms away from me and push her back into her space. "Is that a yes?" I'm less scared now after her reaction but I still need a yes or no.

"Of course it's a yes. I would love to meet your family! I want to know all about the people who make Ryn, Ryn." Well that's too bad because she'd really hate one of them.

I shove my hands in my pocket and pull my lips into a tight line and tell her that I'll need her address because I'll pick her up for dinner and we exchange numbers so I can contact her in the future without having to kidnap her. I turn and start to walk away before I realize I need to ask her what she wants to eat. "Hey my mom wanted to know whether or not you wanted pizza or a home cooked meal? She said she was fine with either but that she'd let us decide." For whatever reason Liza looks puzzled for a second.

"A home cooked meal would be great!"

"Ok cool, I'll text her and let her know, thanks." Before I even have a chance to take another step in the other direction she calls out for me to stop.

"Wait Ryn!" I try really really hard not to groan but a tiny one slips out because, more than anything, I just want to hide away and decompress from this whole event. I turn and look at her raising, my eyebrows to ask her "what" without having to say it. "Why didn't you pick yourself?" What? She must see the utter confusion on my face because she doesn't wait for me to answer and keeps talking.

"You said your mom asked you what we would want for dinner. Why didn't you pick yourself?" I'm still not really following so then Liza does what Liza does best which is state the obvious. "You asked me what I wanted." And now I get it. She didn't expect me to care about what she wanted. I never have before. God I'm an ass. Unfortunately I don't have an answer so I give a half-hearted shrug and turn around and keep walking. As I do Liza calls goodbye and I don't even need to turn around to know she's waving wildly.

Liza called me earlier to tell me she would be getting a ride to my house so I would only have to take her home and not pick her up. Ever since then I've been going a little crazy constantly checking the time and my phone to see if I had any messages from her. For the last hour I've been sitting in the living room on the couch rapidly bouncing my leg and chewing on my nails. Meanwhile I don't dare step foot in the kitchen because Daniel's cooking tonight and while Daniel is an amazing cook and that's the only compliment he'll ever get from me, he gets a little intense when cooking. It's not a bad intensity but he's very particular about the way he does things and if one step gets messed up he pours himself a glass of lemonade and curses Julia Child. So far he's had 12 glasses. He's been a little stressed about tonight along with my mother.

Just when I start to think Liza changed her mind the doorbell rings and Daniel screams a girly scream because he's not ready. Then he comes rushing out of the kitchen in his floral cooking apron that says "it's thyme to cook". To be honest Daniel is the perfect stereotype of what people think gay guys are.

"I got the door, I got the door!" He's running now and dusting his hands on his apron. Unfortunately for Liza he beats me to the door and throws it open. And instead of shaking her hand he immediately pulls her in for a bear hug and I facepalm because if this is any indication for the rest of the night I'm screwed. "It's so nice to meet you Liza." I can barely see Liza's face but what I can see is my new favorite thing in the whole world. Liza getting a taste of her own medicine. She looks beyond startled, face smushed, and very alarmed.

My mom comes into the room and pulls Daniel off of her and gives her a short, less aggressive hug and introduces herself, "Hi Liza, it's great to meet one of Ellie's friends." Shit. My eyes grow wide and I clench my jaw. Liza's eyes immediately jump over to me and she looks like she's gonna have a field day.

"Well it's a pleasure to meet you guys too. I'm really excited to meet the people who make *Ellie* the person she is today." My mom chuckles at that and before the conversation can go any further I interrupt.

"Ryn, my name is Ryn, only my mom calls me Ellie."

My mom gives me her best mom look because she thinks I'm being rude but then rolls her eyes and turns back to Liza.

"Well come in, come in, we don't want to keep you standing out in the cold." Daniel takes her coat, scarf, and hat and she takes her shoes off on our rug in front of the door in the house and then comes to sit on the couch. I perch myself on the armrest on the other end of the couch where I can see the entry to the kitchen as well as my mom and Liza who are starting to chat.

"Thank you so much Mrs. Bradford for having me." Wait, did she just say Bradford?

"Oh, it's actually Mrs. Torres. I took my husband's last name when I remarried." Shit.

"Oh I'm sorry, I didn't realize Ryn still had her dad's last name." Both of us tense up a little at that. But my mother being the saint she is brushes it off and politely answers.

"She doesn't, Bradford is my maiden name. She got it changed when he and I divorced." Well that wasn't as painful as I thought it would be. And as if the universe is trying to cut me a little bit of slack Daniel yells that dinner is ready.

As we're gathered around the table Daniel says a short prayer in Spanish and then encourages us to eat. Daniel is biracial, his mother is Colombian and came to the U.S from Colombia. Daniel's father is a French-Canadian who was doing work in Minnesota when he met her. The two fell in love and from that love came Daniel and six other siblings. Daniel gets his manners from his father. When his parents got married his father wanted to take his mother's last name so that her culture would carry into her kids even if it was just her name. All of the kids are fluent in Spanish, French, and English. My mom didn't stand a chance. Tonight he prepared his mother's recipe for stuffed peppers combined with his awesome chicken piccata with lemon sauce.

Surprisingly, dinner goes smoothly. My mom is sweet and caring, but Daniel steals the whole show. The man's apparently lived a lot of life. But what I find the most interesting about the night is that not once does Liza look like she's not enjoying herself. Even when Daniel tried to get her up and dance. Or when I snorted lemonade out of my nose from laughing so hard. Or when my mom, much to my chagrin, showed her some of my baby pictures.

After Liza and I help clean up the table my mom shoos us away so we go upstairs to my room. It's the biggest in the house and it connects to the attic which I've turned into a secret hideaway of sorts, but I don't show her or tell her that. She's learned enough about me tonight.

"No fucking way." My head snaps her direction and she's looking over my books and I can see which she's picked up. It's a book Mrs. Kahn gave me when I first started working at the greenhouse. I've highlighted the crap out of it and there's so many different sticky notes and page markers. My mouth opens a little because this feels too personal. It's one thing that she's been thrust so deeply into my life tonight but this is something for me. I'm not ready to share it. I rush over to her and yank it away. She grabs at it but I'm quicker and so she just ends up falling into my nook of pillows and blankets. She turns over and looks at me curiously and concerned. "Pushed too far didn't I?"

"Huh?"

"I pushed you too far. For information. To let me in. It's fine though. I knew we were gonna hit a wall at some point. There was no way you were gonna do a complete 180 in one night." Her words just now were like a punch to the gut. Did she think I was cold and closed off? Would she be wrong if she thought that? No. She wouldn't because I am. I work so hard to push everyone away. But she's also right. I let her in a lot tonight, I don't need to do it all at once.

"No, I'm sorry I just–. This is just something really really personal to me and I'm just not ready to let somebody know why. I have other books you can look through though." I offer her that much so that she knows I really am sorry and that I'm trying.

With that thought I plop down on my bed. I'm trying. Huh. That's weird. I'm brought back from my daydreaming by Liza calling my name. "Earth to Ryn? Can I borrow this book? I've always wanted to read it and I saw that you annotated it like your other books so I thought it would be cool to see what your thoughts on the book were without you having to actually tell me. If you don't want me to, that's ok, I'll just get it from the library." A simple gesture. Not a big deal at all.

"Yea. Sure, go ahead." She had grabbed my copy of *The Great Gatsby*. She continues to tour my room and look over things. She's not analyzing me though. She's just curious. She's taking it all in like it's water and she's dehydrated. I sit on my bed unaware that I'm hugging my pillow to my chest like a child waiting on her to give me her assessment and tell me what's wrong with the room and make fun of the silly ridiculous things I have like a 3D printed version of Miljonir, Thor's hammer. But she doesn't. In fact when she gets to the hammer she puts her hand through the strap and starts to pull up on the hammer. But she doesn't pick it up. Instead she pretends she can't lift it all. She looks at me to see if I'll say anything but I don't. I just keep sitting and watching. I feel like prey and I hate it.

As if she can sense my unease, "Hey, I think I should get going. I got some homework to do and I don't wanna be up too late."

"Ok, that's fine. I can take you home."

We spent the next five minutes in silence after Liza said goodbye to my mom and Daniel. The only sound in the car is the low volume of the radio, the faint sound of our breathing, the tires on the ground, and the low hum of the engine as I drive. It isn't until we're in the heart of the city before Liza speaks.

"Are you excited for the second half of the season

tomorrow?" In all the insanity and absurdity of the day I'd kind of forgotten about tomorrow. To be quite honest I kind of expected the world to end with all of this going on. Like my life just couldn't take any more shaking up so it would just implode.

"Uhh, yea I guess. I mean I haven't really been thinking too much about it. It's just a game." Because it is. It's not a chance for me to prove I'm better than him. That I can control myself, that I'm not a worthless piece of shit that's destined to repeat his life. I may be a girl but I'm a bigger man than he ever was.

"Oh c'mon I've seen you play. You're great and–." She's almost talking too fast for me to catch what she said but I still do.

"Seen me play? What do you mean you've seen me play?" Suddenly I'm gripping the steering wheel like a lifeline, and my knuckles are turning white. The foot that isn't controlling the car is bouncing uncontrollably. If she's seen me play that means she's seen me at some of my most ugly moments. Definitely not my worst but still not moments I've been willing to show anyone at school.

"Um yea. Shit. It slipped out. Your hockey practices are open so people can come into the stadium and watch you guys. I usually come at least once a week. I thought it would be nice for you to have someone cheering you on even if you didn't know they were there. Plus I knew if I told you you would try to ban me from going. But I guess that cat is out of the bag."

She blows out air and turns towards the window.

"You don't have to be so closed off all the time. I know you're afraid of what people will think if you let them in but not all people are the people who hurt you. And you may think I know nothing about you but we've been friends for practically four months now and I'm not blind. I don't know what happened or who your father is but not everyone is him." That last bit pissed me off even if it shouldn't have. I *know* everyone isn't him. I'm not worried about other people being him. I'm worried that *I'm* him.

"Whatever, come to the practice, don't come to the practice but don't bring up my father." I can tell she feels sorry she brought him up, but she looks happy that I said she could keep coming to the practices.

"You're gonna do great tomorrow. Your mom invited me to sit with them. We're gonna be your biggest fans there." Dear god they're gonna embarrass the crap out of me aren't they. That thought makes me chuckle though because it's been a long time since I've worried about my mom or anyone embarrassing me because they're proud of me. It's mostly just me embarrassing me.

"Just promise me you won't let Daniel bring his megaphone." She bursts out laughing at this and it feels like maybe things will be good between us. Like maybe Liza might actually be my friend.

11:00 P.M

Once I finally get home, instead of going in the front door like a normal person, I climb up the drain pole until I get to the one window I always leave unlocked in the attic. After stumbling through the window and pushing it closed I walk over to the other side of the room careful not to trip on anything seeing as how to anyone else it may seem cluttered. I get to the stairwell entryway and flip on the light and just like that the attic looks like New York City with how bright it is. I've spent the last six months after getting settled here gathering different plants and have created my own little greenhouse up here.

It's the perfect environment for tropical plants since there's not a whole lot of circulation so it stays pretty humid even in the winter. The only downside to that is I have to be careful of mold growing. Mrs. Kahn let me buy fancy lights that substitute the need for sun on the greenhouse credit card.

As I check on my plants and wander around the room cleaning things up, I see the very faint glow of the downtown city lights out of my window. I walk over to the window and look out of it.

We live in the suburbs of Forthsworth which places us a nice distance away from the traffic and business of the heart of the city, but still connects us to it and doesn't feel anything like a small town. Looking out the window, I feel small. Like a little pawn in the grand scheme of the world. There've been only a few times in my life where I've felt small. When I was a child at Disney World, when I first fell off of my skateboard and twisted my wrist, and at the time of the incident. Those feelings of feeling small felt like a weakness. But this one, this one feels like a strength. I don't know why, but this one is comforting.

7:30 P.M

The entirety of the day was pretty uneventful. There
was a bit of awkwardness between Liza and I at lunch
but it quickly went away because Liza has never been
one to stand for any awkwardness. She soon started
babbling on and on about this amusement park that
comes to the city at the end of every school year for the
seniors. When she first said that I snorted my Pepsi
because I just couldn't get the final scene from Grease
out of my head. When I explained to her why I was
laughing she started laughing too and we fell back into
our regular groove. Me, somewhat brooding, and her
carrying the conversation while I intermittently inter-
jected with some snarky or smartass comment.

The only thing that was different than today was the

stupid pep rally the school held at the end of the day. All the hockey players were expected to be there and would be showcased like prized possessions the school obtained. Meanwhile the cheerleaders would do their little stunts and cheers and get the crowd insanely riled up all for it to end with Coach giving a speech/toast to a great season and a great game.

I spent the entire rally with my AirPods in and used my long hair to shield anyone from knowing I wasn't paying attention. No one expected a whole lot from me anyways because I had a reputation. I knew I did but these days I'm seeing the consequences more and more. Everyone's afraid of me and thinks I'm this mega asshole who'll cut a bitch for crossing me. While the last part of that isn't entirely untrue I don't consider myself mean on purpose. But I can see how my lack of trying can be perceived as that.

As of now though I'm sitting in the girl's locker room by myself staring down at my helmet. I run my fingers over the scuffs and scratches earned from one too many nights on the rink. As I gather the long strands of my hair and wind it into a loose bun at the back of my head, I take a deep breath and splash some water on my face. Right as I turn to look at the clock, Coach pounds his fist on the door and yells to me to meet him in the boy's locker room. I grab my helmet and awkwardly walk towards the door in my skates. Coach has been so worried about the other team knowing I'm a girl but when on the ice with my helmet on and skates on I'm a bulky 6'2 so I don't really look like a girl at all.

Pushing open the door to the boy's locker room the guys greet me with a nod and a few "Hey Bradford" of different variations. Once Coach sees me enter he gathers us round to huddle up so he can give us one last pep talk before the game. I'm leaned up against a locker next to Spitz and Duke Ballinger. Duke's the captain of the team and he's always been welcoming to me so I feel safe enough to hang around him without actually communicating with him. He's the goalie and a damn good one at that. I'm our best shot; let's just say we both give each other a run for our money.

Spitz –and I'd never tell him this– is turning into something like a little brother to me. It's why I give him such a hard time. He's got these big eyes that are always so full of life and curiosity and I feel it's my duty to prepare him for the real world which is often cruel and unfair. Which is probably why he doesn't know that I actually do care for him and think he's an alright kid. He's second string so there's a good chance he won't be playing tonight. Yet he still stands here looking like he'd kill a man, or at least try, if Coach asked him to. I look at him as he's listening so intensely to Coach. I purse my lips and feign feeling sorry for him as I pat him on the head like the good little puppy he is.

Duke's watching me and he gives me what I'm sure is supposed to be a playful shove, telling me to leave Spitz alone, but instead I glare at him not to touch me. He throws his hands, pretending to be caught, and shakes his head. All of our attention is turned back to Coach though, when he has us huddle up and throw our hands in the middle. The next few minutes are kind of a blur. All I remember next is skating out on the ice while everyone in the stadium cheered and screamed for us. We all skate over to the bench and wait as the announcer introduces the starting players for the other team. Then the lights dim and a spotlight starts sweeping over the ice. Music starts to play and our fan section starts to roar. I keep my head down even as my teammates start to slap each other on the back and encourage the crowd to get more intense.

Starting with Duke, the announcer starts calling out the players on our team who are starting. I sit in the middle of the bench, head down and drowning out all the sound. This moment kicks off the event that determines the rest of my year. I've been telling everyone that I'm not nervous but the incessant beating of my heart is proving me wrong. There's no backing out now. They've announced the last player and now it's just me sitting on the bench with the others out on the ice with ones not starting, creating a line on both sides for me to skate down just like the other starters. Then the announcer finally brings me to the moment I've been dreading.

"And now for your starting center. A senior coming in at 6'0, 180 lbs of pure muscle and an icy glare that could kill," Coach wrote these introductions, guess he thought that glare line would scare the other team, "number 13," his voice is booming and dragging out the last syllables of my jersey number. "Ryyyyyyyynnn the Ice Queen," dear god. I cringe because I didn't agree to that nickname, "Bradfordddddd!"

At the mention of my last name I lift my head with a wicked smirk because I can't say I don't enjoy the hype. I stand up and skate to my teammates and smack my head into Spitz at the end of the line and chest bump Jet, a 210 lb defender, so hard he stumbles back. All the players on the other team are staring at me with wide eyes. A few of them even look scared.

Oh yeah. This is gonna be fun.

8:00 P.M

Spitting out blood is not anything new for me. But my mother seeing me spit out blood is not something I'm proud of. I want to punch that bastard's face in. It's one thing to call me a bitch, but it's an entirely new thing to bring my parents into this.

Your mother must be a real dumb cunt if she let her daughter play hockey.

That alone was enough for me to grab him by his jersey and lift him up off the ice and skate him into the wall where I pinned him and steam shot out of my nose and ears. But the final blow was this.

Or maybe it was your father. Was dear old dad not around enough to be the man in the house? You had to step up and do it yourself?

Before I could even stop it I was beating the shit out of him. At one point I ripped his helmet off and head-butted him so hard I even saw stars. Duke was pulling me off of him and it was only when I heard my mother, Daniel, and Liza at the glass begging for my attention, pleading with me to stop that I did. Suddenly it was like I was coming back into my body, into my sanity and I let Duke drag me away. But he didn't get me far enough away before that jackass is pulled up by his teammates and uses everything he has in him to shove me in the back with his stick. I lost my balance and knocked into Duke and we both fell. Except when we landed my lip got sliced on his skates and blood filled my mouth. Now there's a ringing in my ears and every-one's voices are muffled.

Which brings me back to the spitting blood. This time I'm seeing red. No. I'm not seeing at all. My vision is black. I push myself up off the ice and as I stand up I make a concentrated effort to spit blood at his feet. I know I must look terrible because my mother is cry-ing and covering her eyes while Liza comforts her and Daniel's doing what I can only assume he could do at this time. He's calling Dr. Shaw. With my head angled down at the ice, I lift my eyes up to this jackass, and without breaking eye contact I smile. He wants a psy-chopath. He'll get a psychopath. I'm sure my bloody smile and tilted head is a sight to see because suddenly he looks scared. But before I have the chance to fulfill his fear I'm grabbed from both sides and am being hauled away by two of the defenders while I twist and squirm in their arms. But it's no use because I'm not getting away. And it's a good thing too. Because I'm not sure what would've happened if they hadn't stopped me. I think I might've killed him.

8:15 P.M

I'm left sitting in the locker room by myself while Coach, my mom and Daniel, and Dr. Shaw do their best to clean up my mess. And while I know I should be grateful for people not letting me kill him, instead I'm angry. And I don't even know why or at what or who. For the first time in my life I think he might be right. Tears start to stream down my face but I quickly wipe them away as the door to the locker room swings open and Daniel storms in followed quickly by my mother.

"Dammit Ryn. What the hell was that?" His tone isn't angry but it is demanding. "Your first game, your *first game.*" He wants answers and that's fair but I don't feel like I owe him anything and since I wasn't able to beat the living shit out of the kid I still have anger I need to misdirect.

"No. You don't get to come in here and demand answers. I don't owe you an apology, I don't *owe* you anything." There's ice in my voice and I'm really living up to my name.

"You're right Ryn. You don't owe me anything. But what you do owe is that kid an apology. And you owe your mom an explanation. You can't just lose control out on the ice like that. You can't lose control ever like that. You're lucky that Dr. Shaw was able to convince his parents not to press charges. And cut a deal with the schools to only suspend you for two games." He's not backing down and his voice is just as unyielding as mine.

"You don't think I don't know that?!?!" I scream back at him. "My entire life right now is about not losing fucking control! But you know what *Daniel*, I don't need you to tell me that because everything I do, everywhere I look is a constant reminder of that! You aren't my parent, and you aren't my father–"

"You're right I'm not your father." His voice is low and soft now. Almost like he's realized what's more important here, but this next part his voice is filled with venom. "Your father is a sorry excuse for a man who didn't deserve anything good he got in his life. And I'm not gonna lie to you that if I saw him I could and would want to kill him. To end him right there on the spot." His eyes are searching mine and he's slowly started getting closer to me.

"But then you and your mom would be alone. And I would be no better than him. I would say that I know what you're going through is hard, but I don't. So it wouldn't be fair to you for me to pretend that I did. But I can tell you that if you'd let me, I'd listen. Your mom would listen. And she's the closest person in this situation to having gone through what you did." Finally he's standing right in front of me and he looks me in the eyes. No pity in his. Just a want to understand. A want to be there. "Ryn, what happened?" Before I could stop it the floodworks begin and I'm sobbing uncontrollably.

He wraps me in his arms and for the first time I don't fight it. I'm tired of fighting. I start to collapse on the floor because admitting that to myself causes my body to stop pumping adrenaline through my veins and insisting I carry on. The weight of all that just happened catches up to me. I start screaming because the pain from my lip just hits me like a truck. My fist is throbbing from punching and my skull is throbbing from all the emotions and the fact that I used it as a weapon to headbut the kid doesn't help either. But Daniel stays holding me up. Supporting my weight and stroking my hair as I sob.

After about fifteen minutes of sobbing I start to come down. Choking on my words a little and sniffling back snot I decide to come clean about what happened. "Your mother must be a real dumb cunt if she let her daughter play hockey."

"What?" My mother's voice is quiet and unsure and I'd forgotten she was here for all of that.

"That's what he said. That's what made me drag him over to the wall." Reliving it was just as hard as the first time. Except this time it wasn't because of his words but because of the way I acted.

"Wait. Drag him to the wall? What do you mean? That's not what made you punch him to begin with?" Daniel interjects and I can't tell if I wanted someone to catch that or not.

"Yea. I almost had myself calm and was gonna walk away but right when I started to loosen my grip on his jersey he just chuckled and then said 'Or maybe it was your father. Was dear old dad not around enough to be the man in the house? You had to step up and do it yourself?'" We all sit in silence for a few seconds till the one person I didn't expect to break the silence does.

"No, fuck that, I'm gonna beat that little prick myself."
"Mom!"

"Honey she's already done a fine enough job of that herself. Let's take a minute to just cool off ok? Remember Dr. Shaw said she would talk to them about suspending him as well? Let's let her handle it and focus on Ryn." Ever since my mom met Daniel he's always been the voice of reason. But I can't focus on anything else because now the world is going black again but for a much different reason this time.

"Ellie?" My mom noticed first.

"Ryn? Ryn, are you ok?" Daniel's frantically holding my face and looking me over.

And even though I don't know when she slipped in here, the last thing I hear is Liza's voice as she says, "Oh my god she's going down." And then I hit the floor.

10:00 P.M

Waking up to the sound of machines beeping and white noise everywhere was a little alarming at first but was less so when I felt a hand on my forearm put there to calm me down. Liza was sitting in a chair by my bed and two others were on the opposite side. I recognized the beeping machines to be the hospital.

"They just went to get some food." She knew my question without me asking it. I nod my head slightly and then lean back on my pillow. Her hand lingers a second too long before she pulls it away and now my arm feels cold because it's no longer there.

"What happened?" My voice is dry and rough so I clear it and she hands me a cup of water from the side table.

"Well seeing as how we were all distracted by other things happening and you had seemed to be fine, we'd all forgotten that your lip was sliced open and you passed out from the pain and blood loss. You didn't lose too much but just enough to make you faint. They gave you a pint once you got here and ever since they've just been monitoring you and giving you pain meds through your iv. But you've been out cold the entire time. They took you for a CT scan to check your head and thankfully you don't have a concussion. And I'm sure you feel this but you do have five stitches in your bottom lip. The top one came out mostly unscathed in terms of severity but you're gonna have some scratches and scabs." Wow. I'd really gotten a number done on me. I look down and see that my other fist is bandaged up so now it looks like I'm going boxing.

Liza breathes in when she sees me looking at them and shakes her head slightly, "Yea you got really lucky and didn't break your hand....again. I think your sub-conscious made you punch with your left hand so you wouldn't further injure your right and potentially ruin your whole season."

"How's the other guy?" Don't know why I'm think-ing about that asshole but I am.

"Don't know. He's at some other hospital. We didn't want to take you to the same one." On the off chance that I lose it again. She didn't say it but I know that was the next part of her sentence. I don't blame her though. I can't. She saw me out there firsthand. Saw the angry demon that lives in me.

This next part comes out harsher than I mean it to because she cringes as I say, "Why are you here?" She takes it in stride though and looks at me when she answers.

"Because Ryn. You're my friend. I care about you." I scoff when she says that.

"I'm a monster. Monsters don't deserve friends."

"You aren't a monster. You just have issues you have to work through. We all do. It's a part of being human. You just have to work on not letting your issues overpower who you are. I know you think you're this angry person who can never change and is destined to always be the bad guy but you're not." She pauses for a beat before continuing, "Ryn what happened with your dad?" Her voice is quiet and sounds fragile, like she has an idea but wants me to confirm it.

"I'm not ready to talk about it yet." My voice is low and on the verge of breaking. I have to clear my voice before I continue, "But I want to be." Because I do. I don't know what it was about tonight but I'm tired of fighting. I don't want to do it anymore. I finally realized what Dr. Shaw meant when she asked me what was holding me back.

It's me. I'm holding myself back. I'm scared of what will happen if I don't. And I've been scared enough times in my life that I don't wanna be anymore. But I won't have much of a life if I don't let myself be scared. Maybe being scared means I can move on.

After I said that Liza smiles, "Good, I'll be here when you are."

My weekend was pretty uneventful after my night in the hospital. Liza stayed until about 2:00 in the morning. Then she realized what time it was and figured she should get home and get some sleep. I was in and out of sleep due to pain and the uncomfortable fact that I was in a hospital bed and not my own. Daniel was up most of the night with me and after about two hours of awkward silence between us, the next time I woke up and was given pain meds Daniel offered to play blackjack with me. So we did.

I don't really know how much sleep he got but I do know that every time I woke up he was awake. The way he treated me that night made me feel bad for the way I'd been treating him for so long. I can see why my mom cares for him. I just still don't know why he cares for me. Mom bought me a teddy bear from the gift shop and slept most of the night. The only time she woke up was when the pain in my lip got so bad that I was moaning in pain and crying loudly. She crawled into the bed with me and stroked my hair as I cried. A nurse came in and pumped more drugs through my iv.

Now I'm sitting in my first hour back at school after what happened Friday night. The game had to be postponed due to what happened but that doesn't erase the fact that the first 30 minutes happened and almost the whole school was there to see it. Those who weren't there saw it plastered all over social media and shared so many times people from Illinois would have seen it. I can feel the eyes of every kid in the class on me. When I go to chew on my nails I hit my lip and curse under my breath. I hear Reuben snickering to himself and I have to clench my fists because I don't want to let my anger get the best of me. Instead, for the first time since learning them, I try one of the coping skills that Dr. Shaw tried teaching me in the first few sessions we had together.

Five things you can see.

The chalk sitting on railing of the board. The ceiling fan about two feet away from me. The glow of Mr. Cutler's phone as he receives yet another text from his mother about some household chore he has yet to do.

The light in the back of the class that flickers twice every five seconds. And finally the steaming coffee cup sitting on Mr. Cutler's desk.

Four things you can hear.

Grace sitting about two rows back from me furiously typing on her computer since she still hadn't finished the essay assigned three weeks ago due at the end of class. Mason's heavy breathing because it's almost 9:00 and like clockwork his asthma flares and he has to use it on the hour every three hours. The tapping of my foot as I try to calm down. Nathan's pencil as he scribbles notes on the chapter everyone's supposed to be reading and taking notes on.

Three things you can touch.

My scabbed knuckles. The satin-like pages in my history textbook. And the cold desk with scratches from kids carving stupid messages into them for as long as the desk has been in the room.

Two things you can smell.

The flowers on Mr. Cutler's desk that he got for his birthday on Monday that are starting to wilt. Joseph Carlile's obscene amount of cologne.

That kid sits in the back of the room and he still can be smelled all the way in the first row. Maybe he's the reason Mason has to use his inhaler so often. And there's gotta be something else Carrie sees in him. Or maybe she's just been with him so long that her sense of smell has died.

The further down the rabbit hole I go concerning why Joseph does anything that he does keeps me from realizing that the last fifteen minutes of class are gone because before I can finish the thought that maybe he bathes in the cologne every morning, the bell rings. I'm startled out of my daydreaming and I realize it worked. I calmed myself down. I calmed myself down without it ending in tears and blood. And I don't know if it's sad that that thought makes me smile but it does.

Liza's waiting for me outside of my class and I honestly have no idea how she got here so quickly considering that her first hour is in the Plotner's lecture hall. But all the same she's outside the door bouncing like a little child with news she's excited about. And to be honest I feel like I might kind of match her energy for once. Don't get me wrong it's nowhere near the level her's is but I'm still riding the high of not dislocating Reuben's shoulder.

When she sees me her excitement turns into the nervous kind and she rushes over to me. "So how was class? Nobody said anything to you, did they?" She's been worried about the same thing I was. I may not be super active on social media but she is. I mean she has to be considering how involved in the school she is and all of the friends she has. I'm sure she's seen more recaps than I have and it's playing on a constant loop in my head.

"Well no one technically said anything but I could practically hear their thoughts. And Reuben snickered when I tried to chew on my nails but couldn't because of the stitches." She frowns and for the first time she looks angry. I've never seen her angry and I just gotta say while I don't ever want her to be angry in life because I know it all too well and it consumes you and eats you alive, it kinda does something to me. I've never had to calm anyone down in any situation so I try something my mom has done for me a lot. I tentatively reach out and hesitate as I put my hand on her shoulder and pat. I throw in a smile but once I do she starts squinting at me and raising her an eyebrow.

"Are you ok? You look like you're having a stroke. Maybe you do have a brain bleed." When she says that I yank my hand away and glare. I roll my eyes before continuing.

"You looked angry and that's my thing so I was trying to calm you down. I don't know, it was stupid. My mom does that sort of thing to me all the time." At this she laughs and I roll my eyes and cross my arms. "Yea, yea laugh it up." I turn on my heel and start to walk away but she calls after me and after I don't stop she jogs to catch up to me.

"Hey I'm sorry but you seriously looked like something was wrong. Maybe don't try to comfort me unless I ask," she smirks a little and adds, "you're not very good at it.

"I'm a big girl and believe it or not I've been through my fair share of crappy life experiences to know how to cope. Besides, my anger isn't my problem and I'm allowed to be angry that Reuben's being an ass. You should be too. You just have to learn to control how you react to that anger." I huff because I hate that what she said makes sense. "Certain amounts of anger are *healthy.*"

"Ok well I'm tired of talking about my *feelings*," I shiver at that, "change the conversation." And being the good friend I'm starting to realize she's always been, she does.

So I spend the next five minutes as we walk towards our classes listening to Liza go on and on about the newest episode of "NCIS". Her and her mom watch the show a lot and everytime a new episode airs she tells me about it the next day. After a while I drown out Liza's talking and think about how different my life seems just from last Monday. I finally consider Liza a friend and I was able to calm myself down from an episode. I know it's just a start but maybe life will turn out ok?

Lunch was a little more trying today because I had the brilliant idea to try and eat lunch in the cafeteria and not in some weird hidden location. Liza invited me to sit at the table with her friends that she waits for me at, but that's a little too bold for me today. Instead we sit where the overflow of people sit, on the stage scattered about. I like this better than sitting at a table because I can trick myself into thinking we aren't in the actual cafeteria where everyone can look at me and whisper about me. I know they do that anyways but at least when I'm not there I can pretend they aren't.

Today's lunch consists of the usual Pepsi but this time accompanied with two jumbo slices of cheese pizza, a corndog, a cup of popcorn chicken and a side helping of grapes.

Liza was having a cheeseburger and strawberries that I'd brought her again. She was also reading *The Great Gatsby* and had already made her own annotations and notes in the margins right alongside mine. And for some reason watching her read made me feel like sharing.

"You know the first time I read that book was when I was nine." At that she looks up at me and lowers the book from her face.

"Wait," she shakes her head and looks skeptical but intrigued, "but these notes seem a lot more sophisticated for a nine year old?"

When I laugh everyone in a ten foot radius' head snaps to me and it occurred to me that no one had ever heard me laugh. They probably didn't think I was capable of it. I cleared my throat and turned my attention back to Liza to try and drown out the awkward and embarrassed feeling that filled me when their unwanted attention fell on me.

"Yea well I didn't write these notes when I first read it. I wrote them about two years ago. I was going through something and thought rereading my favorite book would be a good idea. But when I started reading it I started noticing little things that I didn't the first time. Little connections and hints to things that happen later in the book that I didn't pick up on the first time. It distracted me when I needed it." I have to look down because the look she's giving me is too intense and I'm not sure I like the way it makes me feel. "Anyways every year I reread it and sometimes I see new things that I make note of, other times I just like being reminded of how the book saved me when I needed it."

Instead of reacting the way I thought she would, Liza proceeds to tease me, "That is WAY more sentimental than I ever thought the Elleri Ryn Bradford would ever be." I glare and clench my jaw at the use of my first name. "Does Reuben know? Maybe you two could go to a poetry reading together." At that I burst out laughing and end up snorting. That catches the attention of the entire cafeteria but it doesn't stop me because the image of me at a poetry reading with Reuben is the funniest thing I've ever heard. I can see it so perfectly. He's up at the mic in a black turtleneck and matching beret while he reads this overly obnoxious poem he's written about every girl who's ever rejected him and everyone would be asleep by page 15 out of 1,000.

"Like I would ever be caught dead anywhere voluntarily with Reuben." This makes her giggle and she takes a bite of her burger. "So how's a flier on the cheer team eat like she's a linebacker on the football team?"

"Ohhh so that's how we're playing it?" She acts mock offended and wipes her mouth with her sleeve. "You're really one to talk. I mean the amount of food you have in front of you is enough to feed a starving village."

"Hey! I'm a growing girl, I need food if I want to grow big and strong like Reuben some day." We both get quiet for a second before laughing again because

I already am bigger than Reuben and always will be. The kid comes in at 5'8 to my 6'0. Not to mention my muscle to his twig.

"You're right, you're right, what was I thinking of course you have to bulk up."

"Ok but back to my original question. Don't cheerleaders have like a strict diet they have to follow?" I rip off the top of my corndog with my teeth and ask the next part with a full mouth. "I've seen you eat. Most girls would kill to eat like you and look like you."

"Look like me?" By the way her face turns the color of the strawberry she just popped in her mouth I think I embarrassed her.

"I– I'm sorry, I uh, I didn't mean to–." Thankfully she interrupts me and puts me out of my misery.

"It's fine. I uh, guess I've always been on the small side. That's the best answer I can give you." She ends with a shrug and turns back to her food.

I chuckle to myself but it's more of the self-deprecating kind and less of the kind involving genuine humor. I reach out and tilt my popcorn chicken cup towards her and she smiles and then grabs one. But instead of eating it like I thought she would, like a normal person would, she chucked it at me giggling.

And I played along. Feigning being hurt, I dropped my jaw open and I gasped and pulled my hand to my chest. That made her giggle harder and it was nice to know she wasn't mad at me.

"So have you been doing cheer just in highschool

or were you on one of those peewee cheer teams as a little five year old Liza?"

"I actually only started cheering last year." This throws me for a loop because the way she interacts with the other girls on the squad seems like she's been part of the team since freshman year.

"What made you start?" She looks down and messes with the strawberries I slid in front of her at the beginning of the hour.

"I wanted to impress my parents, make them happy." My brow furrows because why wouldn't her parents be happy? Liza's one of the kindest people I've ever met in my life and while I mostly know terrific assholes, I still know she's better than most.

"I," She pulls her bottom lip between her teeth and swallows. Suddenly there's a darkness behind her coffee colored eyes and it doesn't belong there. Darkness lives behind my eyes, not hers. "Let's just say I'm not as perfect in their eyes as I am in other people's."

And because I'm so used to wanting a subject change I can suspect that she wants one now so I do.

"You ever seen Scrubs?"

4:45 P.M

Coach wasn't making me sit out practice and I don't understand why. I was suspended from playing so it wasn't like I needed to be on my A-game. However when I mumbled about it on the ice Duke skated up and told me that a) my mumbling isn't as quiet as I think, and b) that the reason I still need to practice is so that I'm still at the ready and don't lose any skills come time after my suspension's up.

I was wearing a fancy mouth guard the doctors provided so that I would be less likely to rip out stitches. They didn't want me playing at all with them in, but when they told me that my mom started hysterically laughing.

"I– I'm sorry." Giggle. "*You think that if she won't listen to– to her own mother."* Snort. *"That she's gonna listen t–to you?"* Full on hysterics again.

Let's just say the doctor was not happy my mom was laughing at him but was still nice enough to make a custom mold with a little extra protection. He then proceeded to drill it into mine and my mother's head that if I did rip my stitches out or make my injuries worse that the hospital was in no way responsible since I made the decision on my own even after being informed of the consequences.

The weird part about practice was my teammates checking on me. We never really talked outside of practice or even during practice unless it was strictly during a drill or play. Spitz was the first one on me when I walked into the rink. He kept asking me if I was ok and told me that even though he's not a fan of violence he was sure whatever I did to the guy was warranted. And I'm not sure what's funnier to me about that. The fact that Spitz is a smaller than average guy playing *hockey*, which is considerably one of the most dangerous sports, or that he tried to lie to me and tell me that my almost killing that guy was completely warranted.

After unenthusiastically thanking Spitz and skating away from him as quickly as I could, Jet came over to me and bumped me with his shoulder.

"Not that you ever need backup in a fight, but me and Cliff," he points to Cliff over by the net talking to Duke, "we got your back. If you say we're fighting, we're fighting." Before I can say anything he's skating off and I'm left standing with a very confused look on my face because from the way these guys are treating me it's almost like they didn't see the same fight that I did. I know for a fact that if I hadn't seen what I had in my life and been through what I'd been through I would be running scared from me. If I were Coach I would've thrown myself off the team so fast. I actually wanted to quit but he wouldn't let me. Neither would my mom and Daniel. Instead it just feels like I'm being rewarded for losing my shit.

I see Duke massaging his knee and I realize that he got knocked down that night too. I'm guessing he hit his knee wrong on the ice. Or maybe even twisted it. Point is he texted to check up on me when I was in the hospital and I haven't given him a second thought.

Fuck I really am the biggest asshole.

"Hey Duke!" I yell across the ice and start to make my way over to him.

"What's up Bradford?" Duke starts taking off his helmet. He does that whenever he talks to any of his teammates. I think he thinks it makes him less robotic or hidden and more human. He's so considerate of others it tends to make me angry but I'm trying to focus on the fact that I'm trying not to be an asshole and to not be an asshole means to not get angry at someone for being nice. God why is this so hard for me.

"How–uh, how's your." I stop and point to the knee he was just massaging.

"Oh!" He seems genuinely surprised that I'm asking

and once again for the infinitieth time in my life I realize how big of a dick I am. "It hurts a little but nothing a good ice bath and stretching exercises can't fix."

"Good. Good, that's good." I pull my lips into a tight line and then turn sharply on my heel and skate away.

"Thanks for asking!" Hate that he yelled that across the ice. Gives people the idea that I care about feelings. I don't and the day that I do I give someone permission to shoot me.

"Shut up about it." I yell back which I realize now only draws more attention to me and the situation so instead I grumble under my breath and start my warmups.

Once practice is over Coach whistles to me and waves me over to him. I come skating in fast and grab on to the wall and finish gliding over.

"You did good."

"Excuse me?" C'mon blood, not now. You don't need to boil.

"Friday night. You played well but the way you handled yourself after that situation was admirable." What.

"Coach, I handled that situation terribly. I almost killed the guy." And I'm afraid I would've if Cliff and Jet hadn't pulled me off of him. What is with everyone acting as if I did some admirable thing that night. Why is everyone babying me like I'm just gonna break if they tell me what they really think of me? Why can't one person just tell me what they really think of me?

"But you didn't. And I saw you start to walk away from him before he shoved you and you tripped and fell. That's progress." The more he says the more angry I get.

"I don't care if you think that's progress. Any progress I might've made went straight down the drain the second I stood back up and *smiled at him* with blood pouring out of my mouth." I know that, he knows that, the whole damn stadium that night knows it.

"Ryn I don't know why you're picking a fight. I'm trying to tell you I think you're doing a good job. You're always gonna have moments that are gonna try you or maybe even set you back a few steps but as long as you keep pushing forward you'll get where you're trying to go eventually." I know he's right. Dr. Shaw often talks about the ups and downs of someone's healing journey. She often compares it to a rollercoaster or bumpy road. It has its smooth and peaceful moments but it also can whip you around and spill your drink on your lap as you try to take a sip.

But I'm not quite ready to listen to reason.

"Look Coach, I don't need you to tell me if you think I'm doing a good job. I don't need your approval and I don't need you coaching me on my trauma. I've got Dr. Shaw for that even if I don't want her. You may call the shots here in this rink but in my outside life you don't. So I would appreciate it if you let me keep that outside the rink." I know that's harsh and he doesn't deserve it but hey I'm only trying to heal it's not like it's done yet.

"Fine. But either way, whether you want me to say it or not, I'm proud of ya Bradford. You're one hell of a center and one hell of a person." He gives me a sad smile like he knows what he just said is gonna make me pissed at him. I just don't understand why he does that if he knows I'll get mad.

But either way I take off towards the locker rooms without another word between us. He may think I'm improving and becoming a better person but everyone acting like Friday night wasn't as bad as it was is only fooling themselves. I lost control. And I lost it bad. No matter how big of a prick that kid is or how much I've grown, there's no excuse for the way I acted that night. I've seen what happens when people lose control. Families break apart. Relationships end. Marriages crumble overnight. And little girls are left without a dad. And while I don't know much in my life, I know one thing. I don't want to be mine.

Mrs. Kahn was out at the store getting stuff for the house when I got there today. I went to the back and put on my apron and checked up on my Philodendron Pink Princess –a regular Philodendron with pink splotches on the leaves– that I worked hard to get for the house. I spent hours searching the web for a legit seller and when I finally found one I got caught in a bidding war over it. We ended up spending $2,000 on it.

I think it's more than worth it. It's another rare plant we get to add to the greenhouse and work on multiplying. We won't let it be sold until we've got at least five more growing. That's what we do with all our plants. If they ever get below six different starts then we take them off the market until we grow more. We still keep them out in the greenhouse for people to see and look at since the greenhouse is also a place for people to come and see pretty plants. We just don't sell them.

I hear the bell attached to the front door ring meaning a customer just came in. I dust my hands on my apron since they're covered in dirt from me digging in the soil of my plant. Coming out from behind the curtain in the back of the house I see the customer that walked in and I wish more than anything that Mrs. Kahn was here.

Duke.

He hasn't seen me yet and I'm wondering if it would be terrible for me to slip into the back and pretend I didn't hear the bell. But before I've made up my mind he looks up and sees me. When he does, a puzzled look comes across his face and I sigh because now the world's gonna know the tiny tiny soft side I have for plants.

"Ryn? You work here? I didn't know you liked plants." He has a kind genuine smile on his face but mine is a set line and a slight glare.

"Yea I do." I cross my arms and lean against one of the tables covered in plants.

"I can tell what you're thinking." Yea right. "You think I'm gonna tell people I saw you here." He raises an eyebrow basically asking if he's right.

"Well, are you?" I'm not into beating around the bush.

"No." He laughs as he says that. But when I squint

further he stops and gets serious. "Ryn it's not any of mine or any of the school's business what you do in your free time. Plus I think it's kinda cool that you've got layers to yourself. Everyone does." My arms are still crossed and I'm still a little tense but I can feel that I'm a little less threatening. "Help me find a plant?" Right here right now is another choice that I feel is gonna determine whether or not I take a different path than my father. I can choose to ignore him and go back to my plant in the back. Or, the much, much, harder choice, trust him.

I must've been staring at him for a little too long because he clears his throat either out of discomfort or because he was trying to get my attention. I unfold my arms and straighten up.

"What are you looking for?" He smiles wide and runs his hand through his messy brown hair.

"I'm getting a plant for my mom. Her birthday is in a week and my dad seems to think she likes plants enough for me to get her one. What do you have? Anything that would fit that description?"

"I mean yea. Most of the plants we sell are sold to mom's or housewives. You've got your occasional botanist wanting to grow their collection. And then the guys who come in wanting a plant as a gift for their partner, mom, or aunt. Basically every plant in here is meant as a gift to someone. Even if that gift is yourself. What does your mom like?" He's staring at me after my long spiel and I don't like it.

"In general or having to do with plants?" He's being smart so I glare at him. "Ok, ok I'm sorry I won't make jokes." He throws his hands up in mock surrender and shakes his head. "Well her favorite color is lavender and I think her favorite flower is an orchid. She also really likes big leafy plants. We have like five in our living room."

"Ok well that alone gives a bunch of different options. But I do have a few in mind she might really like. Do you know which 'leafy plants' she has currently?" He looks like a little kid that's just been given a pop quiz because he goes pale and scrunches his forehead and his mouth keeps opening and closing. "Relax, I don't expect you to know the names. Just point to the ones you recognize being in your house." I gesture to the big and vast room containing so much nature and greenery.

I follow him around the house as he occasionally points to different plants that he's seen his mother take care of. By the end of it he's pointed to a Chinese Evergreen, a Ponytail Palm, a Stephanotis, a Yucca Cane, and a Peacock Plant.

"Ok so I have a few ideas." He looks at me hopeful. Like just having to identify the plants has exhausted him. "There's this plant we have called a Purple Passion plant. It's this fuzzy leafy plant that has purple tips that on some climb the edges of each leaf." He nods slightly and gestures for me to continue. "There's also this nice one over here," I talk while walking and he follows me over to the plant I'm talking about now. "It's called a prayer plant. It has purple veins that run through the leaves and at night they fold up and look like hands praying." He sees a plant in the nearby area and he runs to it.

"Oh my god! This one! It's perfect." As I round the corner I see the plant he's deemed as "perfect".

"Duke, I don't think that's the plant you want."

"What, why? It's a giant green leafy thing in the shape of a heart!" I guffaw at his lack of plant knowledge and am offended on behalf of the plant.

"First of all, it's not 'leafy'. It's a succulent, it has leaves but they aren't the typical ones you're referencing. They're fleshy and thick. Second of all," my tone gets softer because this plant holds a lot of meaning to the people who generally buy it. "It's called a Hoya Heart. It's a plant that people usually give out of love, romantic love. It's known as the most romantic succulent there is. Mrs. Kahn has a lot of customers come in here and get them for Valentine's Day. And while you could get her a heart shaped plant that is a symbol for romance, you could get her a plant a little more suited to the other things she likes. Like a purplish color, orchids, and the leafy plants you pointed out."

"Oh. Damn. Yea, you're right. What else did you have?" I'm surprised he gave in that easily. I expected more of a fight, more push back.

"Wait, that's it? You're not gonna fight me on this?" He looks like I just asked a dumb question and after reading my face he laughs because he realizes I don't get why it's a dumb question.

"Why would I fight you when you very clearly know what you're talking about?" Oh. He...he trusts my opinion. He trusts my advice. He trusts me. Huh.

"Oh." I must be blushing because I can feel the heat from my face. "Well we have this other one that between the other two I showed you would be perfect. It's called a Rex Begonia. The spiral of blues and purples on the leaves feel almost like the 'Nightmare Before Christmas'. It's a leafy plant but also has the purple color she loves."

"Wow. It's beautiful." He stands and stares at the plant with awe and I take a few steps back and check on some of the nearby plants to see how they're doing and whether or not they need watered. "I think this is the one!"

He doesn't know it but this is technically my first sale. Mrs. Kahn is the one who deals with the customers. I'm almost always in the back or tending to the plants while she walks with them and educates them. She also entrusts me to bring new plants to the house. She says she likes the eye I have for rare and exotic plants and wants more of them. And while it isn't the first time Mrs. Kahn has left me alone in the house, it is the first time a customer has come in.

"Great." I smile. I'm proud of myself. I made a sale and I may have even made a new friend. "I can ring you up over here." I point to the small desk and counter with our register on it over by the east wall. After I check him out and send him on his way I go back to my plants in the back that I'm working on seed improvement. Which is one of the few fancy ways to say "plant breeding".

When Mrs. Kahn finally did get back to the house she came in with a few common houseplants and a shit ton of dirt she yelled for me to come carry. When I came out of the back to help her she screamed.

"Oh my god what?! What's wrong, are you ok?" Panic filled my voice and my eyes were wide as I searched her for signs that she was hurt.

"You." Me? "Your face. What happened to your beautiful face?" Oh. That. She rushed over to me and cupped my face. I flinched a little and she apologized thinking she hurt me. It didn't hurt. I just don't like being touched. "What happened to you!" She goes from being concerned and sweet to smacking me on the arm.

"Hey!" I feign hurt even though this small old woman could never hurt me. I'm also just a little surprised she smacked me. "It's nothing Mrs. Kahn." I try to muster some amount of believability into my statement as I stare at her. "I just got into a little sports accident." She knows I play a sport based on my build and the fact I'm always hungry and sweaty when I get here but she doesn't know which one or why. I'd like to keep it that way.

"How can you say this is nothing! You've got a black

eye to go with those green ones and your lip has thread coming out of it!" She takes a step back and puts her hands on her hips. I'm just glad she doesn't know what my hands actually look like since she only ever sees them covered in dirt or wearing gloves.

"Mrs. Kahn I went to the hospital and got all checked out as soon as it happened. I promise I'm fine." After spending a minute looking me over, up and down, squinting her eyes at me occasionally, she finally huffs and walks away spewing what I'm sure is profanities in Ukrainian.

Once I finally got home from the greenhouse I laid in my bed and stared up at my ceiling. I wasn't tired and couldn't sleep. I had an appointment with Dr. Shaw again today and my mind was trying to play out how exactly that would go. I didn't really want to think about that so I decided to shoot Liza a text. To be honest I didn't expect her to be awake but almost as soon as I'd put my phone down it dinged.

> **Liza:** *Why are you up?*
> **Me:** *well that's no way to say good morning*
> **Liza:** *Fine, good morning. Why are you up?*
> **Me:** *couldn't sleep*
> *why are you*

Liza: Homework. AP classes suck.
Me: still can't believe you're an ap student
Liza: Why's that?
Me: idk. stereotypes

The only light in my room right now is the glow of my phone over my face as we text.

Liza: Well I hope you're realizing that your first impressions and assumptions of others aren't usually right.
Me: yea well i'm not entirely convinced that's true
Liza: Wanna see my dog?
Me: see this is why you aren't getting work done. you're too focused on your dog
Liza: Can't believe you're calling yourself a dog

Now the only sound in my room goes from my breathing and the soft vibrations from machines in the house to my laughing.

Me: woof

She sends different symbols that I assume are supposed to be a laugh-crying emoticon and I can see her sitting in her room, books laid out in front of her, hair pulled back in a ponytail, laughing at my jokes. And that makes me proud. That I can make someone as kind as Liza laugh. And not make her scared. She ends the conversation a lot sooner than I'd like though, and says she really needs to finish up her homework. I put my phone up and try to get some sleep. Sleeping through therapy is not a lecture I want to receive.

8:00 A.M

Walking into Dr. Shaw's office today feels different than the last. There's something in the air. Probably all the things unsaid, not only from what happened at the last appointment, but what happened the following night at the hockey game. She may not have seen the fight but I'm sure seeing the aftermath was enough to know the deep shit I was in.

We sit there in silence for two minutes before I clear my throat. She looks completely dumbfounded that I was the first one to break the silence. Well what I'm about to say next is really gonna shock her.

"I messed up." She raises a brow at me and gives a slight nod for me to continue. "I– I lost control." I swallow because I desperately want to keep it together.

"The kid, the kid said something about my mom first. I got angry and dragged him to the wall. He– he called her a cunt." My voice is more of a breath on that last word. Dr. Shaw looks at me sympathetically but doesn't say anything.

"After having him pinned against the wall for a minute I calmed down. I started to let him go, I was loosening my grip on his jersey." I swallow again but this time a tear escapes and starts sliding down my cheek. "But then he brought up my dad." My voice starts to break and I look up at the ceiling and blow out air. Gripping the fabric of my jeans, I continue, "Accused him of not being around. That I had to step up and be the man of the house." I laugh bitterly. "But that wasn't the problem. No. The problem was that he was there too much." I start to bite the inside of my cheek but grimace because it hurts my lip.

Dr. Shaw takes this chance to speak, "I know you've known this for a while. Or at least I suspect you did. So why are you talking about it now?" Her tone isn't mean or accusatory. It's her tone she uses to get me to come to my own conclusions.

When I answer, more tears come to my eyes and my voice, for the first time in a long time, sounds small and like a child. "I'm tired of being angry." I take in a shallow breath and this next part is when the tears really start coming. "And I *don't* want to be like him." There's a fire in my eyes. I can feel it. But it's not malicious. No, I'd like to think it's determined.

Dr. Shaw smiles. "Then let's work on that." A small weight but a weight none the less feels like it's been lifted and I smile a genuine smile at her. "What happened when you went back to school on Monday?" She looks hopeful for the first time in all of our sessions. This is probably the most I've ever talked to her.

"It actually went surprisingly well. Nobody came up and said anything to me directly. I could feel their eyes though." I pause a beat before continuing. "There was a moment during my first hour that I got frustrated at this one kid. Reuben. He's always causing problems for me. I chew my nails, it's a nervous habit, or so I'm told." She chuckles a little at that which confirms my suspicions that she is fully aware of my quirks and habits. "Feeling everyone's eyes on me made me nervous and I went to chew on my nails but it hurt because, well," I gesture to my stitched lip and continue. "When I cringed and pulled my hand away he laughed to himself. It pissed me off."

Before I can continue she interrupts. "Why?"

"Why what?" I furrow my eyebrows and stare at her. She sighs and rubs her head. "*Why* did it piss you off."

Oh. Why did it piss me off? "I mean it was Reuben. Reuben's always doing things to piss me off so it could've just been the fact that it was him."

"I think it's more than that." She crosses her arms and leans back in her chair raising an eyebrow at me. I sit there for a few minutes thinking about what more there could be to it. I kept coming back to the same thing. It's Reuben. Reuben is the class dick. He spreads gossip and cracks jokes about everyone. Why wouldn't his laughing make me angry? Apparently she thinks I've had enough time to think because she clears her throat to get my attention back and speaks again. "You and Reuben aren't close right?" I scoff at that and she continues, "You two don't really know anything about each other outside of your interactions at school." My brows furrow again because I have no idea where she's going with this. "Reuben only knows you for what you present yourself at school. And if we're being honest, you present yourself as a mean, violent, and closed off person." She's right.

"Reuben doesn't know me. He doesn't *know* me. He doesn't know my story or who I am or why I am the way that I am so he doesn't get to laugh or judge me." I take a deep breath because I believe I just angrily came to the conclusion she wanted me to reach. "It's not because he laughed. It's why he laughed. He thinks I got what I deserved." I look down because I don't want to see her face but she forces me to look at her again with her next question.

"Do *you*?"

Liza offered to hang out with me to pass the time before the hockey game. It was an away game tonight and even though I was suspended I was expected to be there and support the team. I was stressed out and worrying about whether or not the other team had heard of what happened last Friday. So in true Liza fashion, she invited me over to her house before the game. My mom wasn't home from work yet so I snuck my baby out of the garage and revved the engine before taking off to Liza's.

"Sorry that I can't make it tonight." Liza apologized a few times but this time she does so while shoveling Cheez-its into her mouth and laying strewn across her bed.

"It's ok Liza. I didn't expect you to come anyways. Especially since I'm not playing." I reach over from the spinning desk chair I've been shoving myself around the room in.

She laughs at me as I stretch my arms out to reach the box on the bed without leaving or moving the chair closer to the bed. "You are such a child!" She swats at my arm and hugs the Cheez-its to her chest and I do something I haven't done since I *was* a child. Pout. Her reaction isn't quite what I expected. She bit her lip. I started blushing and coughed a little and went back to spinning in the chair.

"So uh, how long have you lived here?" Instead of waiting for her to change the subject I do it myself because whatever this tension is it's putting me on edge and I don't like it.

"Four years." Now she's laying on her back looking up at the ceiling. That surprises me because for some reason I was so sure that she lived here her entire life. I spin to face her.

"Wait what? Where did you live before then?" I lean back in the chair and the family cat jumps into my lap and from her snicker I realize I look like the stereotypical villain in any old Hollywood action movie. I pull my lips into a tight line and squint at her and in response she sticks her tongue out at me. "But seriously, I– I want to know about you. I mean that's what friends do right?" I'm almost sure that for a split second she looked upset but I don't know why and almost as soon as I saw it it was gone.

"Right. Uh yea, well I lived in this town a few hours from here but moved four years ago." It felt like she was dodging my questions but I know what it's like to want someone not to pry into your life so I don't.

"Hey wanna see something cool?" She perks up and I smile because her attitudes are all so contagious.

"When would I not?" I laugh and shove my feet on the ground and propel myself backwards in the chair and the cat jumps off and sprints out of the room. "Whatcha got?"

"Ok stay exactly where you are alright?" She giggles and nods. "I'm gonna open my mouth and I want you to throw a Cheez-it at me ok?" She raises a brow and nods.

"Are you just gonna catch it in your mouth?"

I gasp and bring my hand to my chest and blink at her. "*Just*? Ye of little faith Pennelli." I do my best to look disappointed and shake my head at her. "I don't *just* do anything." I pause for a second before throwing in a very poorly executed wink but either way she blushes and my brows furrow and I tilt my head at her. Before I can assess the situation further, she chucks a Cheez-it at me and it hits me square in the head. "Woah woah! I wasn't ready!" I throw my hands up in the air in mock surrender and stare at her, mouth agape.

"Ok, fine, fine. I'll throw another one. You ready?" I hunch my shoulders and put on my game face. I nod and she throws.

As soon as the Cheez-it leaves her hand I watch it

glide through the air with hawk-like precision and just when it reaches directly above me, I scoot the chair back just enough to use my socked foot to chuck the falling Cheez-it back into the air and reangle myself so it lands right in my mouth. Like a game of food hacky sack.

"How the hell did you do that??" She looked at me, incredulous. I couldn't help but burst out laughing looking at her. My laughter must be contagious because she joins in and there's an easiness to this that I haven't felt in a long time.

"I guess when you spend so much time hiding out in your room you learn some cool tricks to keep yourself occupied." We both go really quiet at that and I would physically kick myself if I could for making it awkward. "I'm sorry. I didn't mean to be a buzzkill."

"It's alright. Don't ever feel like you need to apologize for things like that. I *want* you to tell me about that kind of stuff, that is if you want to." She stutters at the end and I smile because it's nice to have someone who cares, even if I used to think that that was annoying.

I spent the next hour and a half at Liza's house before the game. We watched a bunch of youtube videos and ate probably way too much food for teenage girls. But to be honest I don't really remember much about what we watched because I couldn't stop looking at her. I was mesmerized by the way she laughed at almost everything. It was intoxicating and terrifying.

Truth is I only ever had one girlfriend. It was before we left Micanopy.

I met her at the skatepark I used to practice at every-day after school. One day I wiped out pretty badly and she was there. She laughed at me for a few minutes and I dusted myself off and was ready to find a completely new park somewhere far away from that one and pray I never ran into her but before I had the chance to skate off into the distance with what little shred of dignity I had left she called out to me and introduced herself. She offered to buy lunch in an effort to apologize for laughing and I figured I might as well get a free lunch out of it. I didn't really want to go home anyways. We hit it off immediately and I found myself spending all my time hanging out with her. Including occasionally skipping school.

Everything was perfect in paradise until I lost regionals and with it, lost my temper. I lashed out and yelled at her. Called her names I'm not proud of. But she wasn't entirely innocent either. She told me she'd cheated on me a few weeks prior and then shouted at me to never speak to her again. So I didn't. I turned fifteen a few weeks later and the next year of my life went by and suddenly I had too much going on to think about anything other than surviving. Another year passed and my mom met Daniel and well we know how that story goes. Fourteen and I was already jaded, bitter, cynical, and any other word you could use to describe a broken and hopeless shell of a person. I hadn't even had any real feelings for another girl since her. Looking at Liza though, I'm starting to suspect that maybe that's about to change.

The hockey game was pretty uneventful for me since I spent it sitting on the bench. I smack talked to the other team's players as they came by our bench, but that was about all I did. We won 3-2. After the game the team was going out to celebrate but I just headed home. I figured I'd just be sitting there in silence while they all talked and chatted like old friends which they were and talk about the game they just played that I didn't. Saturday was a little rough for me because once again I lost my temper. It wasn't to any dangerous extreme but I did break the glass of a vending machine in an arcade Liza and I went to. I didn't damage my hand any more than it is, because this time instead of punching, my subconscious told me to kick.

We had been going for a relaxing day of fun but a little kid started taunting me at a Crossy Road game. We ended up competing and the little shit beat me and after hearing the kid gloat and dance and make fun of me for what felt like fifteen minutes, I stormed off to the vending machine for some sort of snack to distract me. But once again because the universe has some sick vendetta against me, after I'd paid for my Peanut M&M's, they got stuck and didn't fall to the bottom like they were supposed to. I'm not proud of what I did next but I proceeded to stick my arm through the opening at the bottom and try to reach them that way.

When that didn't work I shook the machine, shoulder bumped it, smacked it while yelling, miserably thumped my head against it, took a running start and crashed into it, but none of that worked. Finally, I was so frustrated that when I went to just kick at it my anger had built to an "I don't know my own strength level" so when my foot made contact with the glass it shattered.

They kicked us out pretty fast and I left Daniel's number with them to pay for my mess. That's what he's told me to do if I get myself in trouble. Just leave his number and he'll take care of it.

"I don't know why I do that." It was pretty quiet for the most part on the drive home but I still felt like a child waiting for her punishment for acting out. Recently it seems like I only ever feel like a child.

"Do you want to talk about it?" I sat there for a few minutes before answering her.

"I'm still not ready to tell the full story but uh, my dad, my dad is a prolific asshole. And before my mom left him he said I would be just like him. And every day I feel and fear that's becoming more and more true."

"Ryn the fact that you know that he was an asshole and that you don't want to be him, is enough to know that you won't be like him. Plus you have so many people in your life who aren't going to let you repeat whatever cycle you think you're destined to repeat." I didn't say anything after that and neither did she. Instead I let the sound of traffic lull me into a peaceful state until she dropped me off at my house. *"I had fun today, even after you assaulted a vending machine."* She giggled when she added that and I laughed a little too at the absurdity of the situation. I assaulted a vending machine. It is pretty funny when you think about it.

"Bye Liza. I'll text you."

"You better." She gives me a serious look before pulling out of my driveway and heading across town back to her home. And to be honest her threat gives me a weird, warm feeling that spreads through my body and makes me feel fuzzy and I realized I was smiling like an idiot to myself when I walked inside my house.

The weirder part of that day was Daniel and my mom not being as upset about the situation as I thought they'd be. I mean sure they were annoyed I'd broken a vending machine that they'd have to pay for but they didn't seem disappointed that I'd lashed out at it in the first place.

However they did tell me that today, Sunday, we would all be going over to Daniel's parent's house and I would be meeting my "new family" whether I wanted to or not. For the six months we had lived here I somehow managed to weasel my way out of ever having to meet Daniel's family. My mom and Daniel go over there pretty frequently but I was always able to come up with an excuse or to be deemed not in the right headspace. But let's be honest when have I ever been in the right headspace for anything.

Today was different. There was no getting out of it. I was being dragged into a family of Daniels whether I wanted to be or not. And as my mom so delicately put it, I would be dragged there kicking and screaming if she had to.

So now I'm in the backseat of the car while Daniel drives and he and my mom casually chat. I, instead, have my AirPods in and am listening to Five Seconds of Summer to destress. Daniel has a big family. Seven kids, five of them married, four of those five with kids of their own. So not only do I have step grandparents, aunts, and uncles, but step cousins too. Daniel is the oldest of the bunch at 39, my mom bagged a younger man. The rest of his siblings are Penelope, age 38, Ben, age 36, Owen, age 33, Ruth, age 31, Beatrice, age 29, and the baby of the family Carina, age 24. According to Daniel she's a miracle baby their parents didn't think they'd have. I'm pretty sure that's just a polite way of saying she was an accident.

I'm the oldest "grandchild" of the group. Penelope is married to Gavin and together they have 8 kids. Ingrid who's the oldest at 15, Zara the second oldest at 12. Next is Rylee who's 9 and then Vivian who's 8 followed by Fiona who's 7 and Leah who's 5. Karmen is 4 and the baby of their 8 girls is Mya who's 2. Penelope swears that Mya is the last one and that the only reason they keep trying is so that maybe they'll have a boy. But she says that 8 is enough and that her and Gavin just weren't meant to have boys. I'm fully expecting baby number 9 within two years.

Ben married a very loud woman from California, Bianca. Bianca and Ben have three children. Charlie, 9, William, 6, and the baby girl Quinn, 3. Thankfully for me they live out in California close to Bianca's family and to my understanding, won't be here today. Owen is married to Kimberly, a supposedly very sweet woman from Georgia. They don't have any kids yet and I say yet because according to my mother, Kimberly is a very motherly woman and they've been trying for 3 years so it'll happen someday.

The last married Torres is Beatrice. She's married to some big shot business man, Arthur. They met when they were both vacationing in Cabo. Arthur is originally from Manchester, England, but moved to the states to be with Beatrice. They got married just as quickly as my mom and Daniel did and started building a family right away. To my horror, they have been married for five years and have five kids: Everly and

Evan who are four year old twins, Rebecca following not even a full year later at three, Madison and Max once again not even a full year later at 2 and their most recent addition Gus at just 5 months old. And unfortunately for me they do live here and will be at this gathering from hell today, which means a screaming baby as well as many screaming children will be making me want to end it all.

Ruth and Carina are the only ones who aren't married. Not for lack of trying. Ruth's been married and divorced twice and is currently dating a construction site manager and hinting at husband number three. Carina on the other hand spends her time traveling the world. She's a free spirit and wild child all at the same time. Has a bunch of tattoos, piercings all over, hair's dyed bright red. To be honest I'm pretty sure she's gonna be my favorite. However it's kind of a mystery whether or not she'll be at this oh so joyous family gathering. She never RSVPs so no one really knows if she's gonna show up or call from some Botanical Garden in Singapore or some fancy five star cafe in France.

If all of that information confused you, good. I'm still not entirely sure I have that right.

I'm brought back to reality when the sound of gravel underneath the tires fills my ears. Daniel's father is some big hotshot real estate agent and worked hard enough for him and Daniel's mother to retire in a giant mansion-like house in the rich suburbs of the city. Meanwhile I'm in dirty ripped jeans, my hockey jersey covered in various stains, and my muddy Converse sneakers. I start to bite my lip and even though I'm met with searing pain I keep biting because I'm about to be thrown into a world that I am almost positive I don't belong in.

The first step I take into this giant house feels like it might be my last purely from all the chaos that's hidden behind its beautiful eggshell walls and palace-like doorway entry. Daniel brought three dishes filled with empanadas and while I originally thought that would be too much food I realize now I am dead wrong. All of the grandkids are tearing through the house screaming and yelling. There's loud laughter and chatting coming from the right side of the house where I'm assuming the kitchen and living room are and from there also comes a heavenly smell of what I can only assume is a beautiful feast of all kinds of foods.

Before we can even take another step inside the house we're bombarded from all sides. Daniel begins hugging his siblings and even gives one of his brothers, Owen, a noogie. His sisters swarm my mom and give her hugs and they all start chatting about kids, life, and clothes. I'm left standing in the doorway feeling invisible and while I prefer it that way something this time feels off about it. But before I have too long to sit and stew in my own emotions, I'm interrupted.

"They all can be a little much sometimes right?" I look to my right and have to look down at the tiny, wrinkling, old woman standing next to me. I have no idea how long she's been standing there because apparently unlike the rest of her family she moves like a cat.

"Oh, um," I cross my arms over my chest and continue, "I– I guess. Do I know you?" She chuckles to herself a little.

"No you don't, but I know you." She squints and jabs me in the chest and smiles. "You are my beautiful new grandbaby!" Oh. This is Daniel's mother? I don't know why but for some reason this woman next to me already doesn't fit the idea I had in my head. I was picturing a tall confident woman who commanded the room with her presence and has just as much personality as her children. This woman already wasn't like her children seeing as she was hanging in the background and was the only one to notice my existence.

"Oh, I'm– I'm not your 'grandbaby'." She frowns and swats my arm.

"Don't correct me." I was about to laugh a little but she looked so serious it was kind of scary.

"Sorry." I respond quietly and look at the floor while rocking a little on my heels.

"Follow me." She turns on her heel and starts walking away without even waiting for me to answer or see if I'll follow. But I do because how could I not. "It's Ryn right?" She looks back at me while walking and I nod. She leads me into the kitchen and it smells even better in here than it does in the foyer. "Hold this." She hands me a tray of food and pushes past me as she opens the oven and pulls a different tray out. I stand there confused and frazzled and she snaps her fingers and motions towards the oven at me. I walk over and hand her the tray. Running my hands through my long brown hair I look around the room and see a feast of food. "My kids really know how to eat. Annnd from what I hear about you, you do too." She winks at me and once again motions for me to follow her. As she leads me into the dining room we pass through a hallway, family photos adorning the walls. Entering the dining room she walks over to the table and picks up a plate and adds a knife, fork, spoon, and napkin to the plate and hands it to me. I stand there blinking at her for a few seconds before she sighs and points to the end of the table wanting me to set it down there.

Once I do she holds out another set and we continue doing this until there are enough place settings around the enormous table. She starts to walk towards the giant windows in the dining room and slides open the glass door leading to the back porch. Without her even having to tell me to, I continue to follow her around. When we get outside she whistles at the kids running around in the snow and immediately they stop and look at her. When she turns around and goes back in the house the kids come running through the yard and traipse into the house. She stops each one when they get to the door, handing them a towel to dry off and taking their wet snow clothes and throwing them in a hamper that's sitting in the corner of the room.

This woman hasn't said a word in minutes and still everyone knows exactly what she's trying to say to them and doesn't have to repeat herself. So when Daniel and Ben come tearing into the dining room yelling and arguing over something trivial, what I could catch from it was Ben beating Daniel's old Dance Dance Revolution high score, and all she had to do to break it up was clear her throat and tilt her head and shake it slightly, I was fascinated with the woman. Even though she wasn't what I imagined, she still commanded a room. Just without yelling to make herself heard.

Just as everyone starts to pile into the room and find seats around the table, a man I can only assume is Daniel's father walks into the room. He's so bright and full of energy. The entire room feels like it lit up when he walked in. And Daniel was his spitting image. He jokes with his kids and is so comfortable around him. It made me feel a little bad because that's exactly how Daniel tries to be with me and I constantly push him away.

Everyone spent the next hour and a half sitting around

the table eating like there were holes in all of our stomachs. Even after all the food was gone everyone stayed seated at the table and chatted and shared stories. Daniel's mother eventually stood up from the table, patted her husband on the back and gave him a kiss on the cheek and continued walking out of the room. I pushed my chair back and left the table to follow her in the kitchen. I wasn't having any conversations at the table and I didn't figure anyone would notice if I left. I was right. Life kept moving as it was before.

Continuing to follow her through the house at what I thought was a safe distance for three or four minutes until she spoke unexpectedly, "Stop walking so slow. If you're gonna follow me, walk next to me. I don't have time to pretend no one is following me." I stop dead in my tracks and stand there opening and closing my mouth because I'm startled she knew I was there. Apparently I was standing there too long for her liking because she turns around and wildly gestures for me to catch up to her. I take long strides to catch up to where she is and we start to climb the staircase in the foyer of the house. It's a sideways staircase that zigzags diagonally till you reach the top.

Once we did she took me down a mostly dark hallway and then she opened a locked door and went in. I hesitated for a second to follow her because for a split second I thought she was going to kill me. This time when I hesitated though she didn't yell after me and tell me to keep coming. She left the decision up to me and that made me even more nervous. And to be honest if I thought about my death, I never really envisioned it being by a tiny Colombian woman who I'm related to by marriage.

Entering the room I was met with a beautiful fragrance from a candle she'd just lit and shelves and shelves of books. I spun around in a slow circle taking the room all in and was filled with a thousand questions.

"Your mother tells me you like books." It was less of a question and more of a statement. Pouring herself a glass of whatever was in the decanter on the rolling cart by the door, she takes a seat in a leather cushioned chair by the big open window. After I was done spinning and taking the room in in all its glory she pointed to the rolling cart. "Go ahead and pour yourself a glass." My expression turned to stone and my blood started heating up. I'm 17 and that's no age to be drinking even if I wanted to.

My voice is dark when I respond and I can't say I don't mean the venom that comes out because I do. "I don't drink."

She huffs and rolls her eyes which pisses me off further and I have to remind myself that my mother likes this woman and that I should try to behave if not for myself, for her sake. "Relax, it's Pepsi. It's my favorite soda. And I don't drink either." She pauses before continuing and I open the decanter and take a whiff and my nose is filled with the sweet and tangy smell of Pepsi. "But I get the feeling my reasons are different from yours."

She leans back in her chair and takes another sip of her drink. I pour myself a glass because I figure she's gonna try to have this conversation with me and I'm gonna be forced to behave so I'm gonna want something to sip on as a distraction. I clench my jaw and lean on the wall by the door waiting for her to continue because I'll be damned if I start the conversation myself. "You can unclench your jaw, I'm not your therapist. I'm not gonna make you talk about it." The more this woman talks the more she's growing on me. I chuckle a little and push away from the wall and start to browse around the room and look at the different books. "You know I used to be an English teacher." I look at her when she says that. I don't know what I thought she did but it wasn't that.

"Oh, um, why'd you stop?" She laughs and raises a brow.

"I retired early to help take care of my grandkids. Life got pretty crazy around here, what with Penelope popping out kids like they're shits." I burst out laughing at that and she gives me a small smile. "I love my grandkids but they can be a lot sometimes. Hell I love my *kids* but they can be a lot sometimes. I come up here when I want to escape. That's why the door's locked. I don't want anyone getting in and messing with the small ecosystem I've built for myself." She has a greenroom. Not a literal greenroom filled with plants but a room that has the same meaning and value as my greenroom in my house does for me.

"I know the feeling."

She sighs and continues, "I could tell you were feeling a little out of place down there."

"A little? Was it that noticeable?" I play with my hands and continue to scan the books on the shelves and not look at her. But even though I'm not looking at her I can feel her eyes on me.

"To me." We sit in silence for a while after that. Her reading her book and nursing her glass of Pepsi, me pulling out various books and skimming them. Finally, after about 30 minutes, she breaks the silence. "Come sit down. I want to play a game with you." My brows furrow and I frown slightly. She rolls her eyes. She seems to do that as much as I glare. "Just sit down, I'm old, I don't have time for this." I walk over and take a seat across from her. She takes the end table between the two chairs and moves it in front of us. Then she gets up and crosses the room to a trunk on the far wall away from the many bookshelves and windows. She opens it up and pulls out a wooden chessboard and walks back to her chair. Placing it down on the table she begins pulling out the pieces and placing them on their corresponding spots on the board. She looks up at me and asks, "Know how to play?" I nod slightly and sit up, interested to see what she has planned if anything. "Good. You can be white." She lets me begin the game, my first move is to bring my knight forward, and as the game continues our pieces dance around each other. Blow after blow she continues to defeat me and again we set up the board and continue playing. Finally I feel like I have her beat. Two queens on the board and all she has is her king and a knight.

In two moves she calls checkmate.

I growl and push away from the table and stomp over to get myself more Pepsi.

"You leave your king unprotected."

I turn quickly and look at her, my answer exasperated and breathy with a sharp and quick edge, "What?"

She points to the board and continues. "Your king. You often focus on your other pieces almost like you forget he's there. You spend all your time moving your pawns and upgrading them to better, stronger pieces, you neglect your king." I study the board and consider what she says. I try to think about the last few games and the moves I made. This is bullshit. She set me up. I don't know what point she's trying to prove but it's just causing me to want to flip this board and break the king right in her face. "Continuing to ignore the king, no matter how useless you believe him to be, will cost you the entire game." At that she pushes back her chair and starts to leave the room. This time I don't follow her. I grab the king, the muscles in my arms bulging and my jaw tightening as my wrist squeezes the piece. And my breathing quickens as I imagine smashing it to pieces on the corner of the table.

11:37 P.M, Wednesday

In order to boost morale and raise money for the team, Coach came up with the stupidest idea I've ever heard of, hockey Valentine's. Hockey Valentine's are these stupid pucks with custom messages on them and a bag of candy if the hopeless sap giving us money so chooses. I don't know why they're such a hit every year, but I hear that the team sells enough for an entire season's worth of new gear. Coach sets up a table at lunch and delegates different players to man the table. Today he's stuck Spitz, Duke, and I at the table. Duke looks all too happy to be here and Spitz is using his bar mitzvah calligraphy lessons to write the messages on the puck.

He brought colored markers and everything. And while this isn't the first time I've wanted to shove Spitz into a locker, I'm starting to realize I might need to protect him because c'mon, all of the cards are against him. Meanwhile Duke talks to the people and collects the money. I'm just sitting in the middle of them wearing my jersey and holding a stick to attract attention. Not only do we have to sell the damn pucks but we have to deliver them in a week and half on Valentine's day by shooting them into the classrooms to hit the feet of the sad fucks receiving a hockey puck for Valentine's day instead of a real gift.

My day goes from bad to worse in seconds when Reuben's sorry ass walks up to the table.

"Interested in buying a Valentine's Puck?" Duke's cheery voice drowns out my growl and glare.

"If I was interested in buying a puck for every girl I'm involved with I'd be broke broski." I scoff as Reuben answers and try to keep my lunch in my stomach and not on the table or his face. Although seeing it on his face would be pretty funny.

Duke continues on conversing as I imagine vomit all over Reuben's face and I start smiling widely and probably look like I'm insane. "Well then what can we do you for Reuben?" My eyes do some weird eye aerobics. The left eye squints while the right eye becomes impossibly wide and I stare at Duke because he sounds like an old man.

"Just wanted to make sure Ryn wasn't feeling depressed because she won't have any Valentines this year, or any year if she continues not to wear any makeup." He ends with a pout and pitying look. "It's ok Ryn, you'll find a great guy one day, even if you have to pay him." I bite my tongue and roll my eyes and glare at him.

"Wait isn't Ryn–." I slap my hand over Spitz' mouth before he can continue and the kid's eyes grow wide like saucers and Reuben looks at us suspiciously. I know if I want him to go away I'm gonna have to play into his game just a little bit.

I sigh and look up at the ceiling before speaking. "You're right Reuben, how could I ever forget that I'm so hopeless and unfuckable and will be lonely for the rest of my life unless I take your advice." I throw in a fake cheery smile to really seal the deal and Reuben makes a childish face at me before leaving and I make one right back. After he's gone I still have my hand on Spitz' mouth and he lets me know it by licking my hand. "God, you're a fucking child." Cringing, I wipe my hand on his shirt and punch him in his shoulder.

"I'm really confused. Why didn't you tell him you're gay?" God Spitz really is a clueless, helpless, little bird.

"She's messing with him, Toby." I dramatically wave my arm over at Duke letting Spitz know he's right. "But to be honest, how does he *not* know you're gay?" Duke adds while counting the money we've made so far today.

"Because he only ever pays attention to himself." I see a freshman walking by with a corndog and I call him over and grab it off his plate when he's close enough. "Go on, scat!" Shooing him away and taking a giant bite of corndog and proceeding to talk with my mouth full, I continue. "Honestly though, messing with him is the most fun I've ever had. So I don't plan on ever stopping. I'm almost convinced that if I do get a girlfriend and he sees me physically kiss her in front of him, he'll chalk it up to us just 'sharing chapstick' or just 'being roommates' or some other oblivious homophobic excuse."

"Speaking of girlfriends, I've noticed you've been spending a lot of time with Liza Pennelli recently. Not just hanging out with her at lunch now huh?" I tense when he brings up Liza.

I pick up a puck and start spinning it around in my hands and swallow. "What about her?"

"I just thought it was," He drags out the "s" and waves his arm around a little before changing his mind. "Uh, nevermind. Forget I said anything."

"No no, you were saying something." I'm daring him to continue, just trying to pick a fight, and at this point I'm already angry with him for bringing her up in the first place.

"Ryn you don't scare me." To make a point I reach forward and grab hold of the table we're sitting at and squeeze. When I pull my hand away there's a dent in the shape of it. Duke swallows and holds his head up higher, probably trying to convince himself more than he's trying to convince me. I raise my eyebrows at him and tilt my head. "I just thought that maybe you were interested in her, that's all." I dart my tongue out and pull it back in as I bite the inside of my cheeks and my eyes flare with fire. I don't want Duke inserting himself in my business with Liza. Besides, he doesn't know what he's talking about.

I take a deep breath, "Shut. Up." And, as if the universe was trying to protect Duke or trying to keep me from doing something stupid that I would regret later, another lovesick teenager walks up to the table to buy a puck. I don't know why he would bring up Liza. It's not like she's into girls. Bringing her up when he should know that's just cruel and I really thought we were starting to get along. But then he says something that throws me off of any game I may have or be on.

"You should go for it. She might be into you too. She talks about you a lot."

I whisper-yell at him after the kid leaves. "*What?*" He chuckles a little and shakes his head looking down.

"We have AP Calc together. More and more it's starting to seem like the only thing she wants to talk about is you." I bring my nails up to my mouth and start chewing. "I brought you up the other day in class and she blushed immediately." He pauses and looks at me, "It wouldn't hurt to try Ryn. To let people in. Otherwise Reuben'll win and you'll be bitter and alone for the rest of your life." And after he drops that bomb on me the bell signaling the end of the lunch period rings and Spitz and Duke stand up and start cleaning up the table. I however remain seated, arms crossed, opening and closing my mouth like an idiot. What if he's right? The thought makes the cold that usually resides in my chest warm just slightly.

Fuck.

6:45 P.M

Today Mrs. Kahn forced me to take a day off for the first time in the months I'd been moonlighting at the greenhouse. Something about it being good for mental health and stability and yada-yada. I stopped listening. I didn't really know where to go after practice. Liza was busy with plans she'd made with other friends and for some reason, it stung to think of her hanging out with other people besides me. I know she has other friends and is pretty popular, and before a month ago I didn't care if she hung out with other people. But recently I've been letting her in more and it's been throwing my entire ecosystem I've built for myself off the rails.

So now I'm sitting in the living room on the couch after being home for dinner for the first time in forever.

My mom and Daniel are whispering about me in the other room. They think something's wrong with me because I'm home at this hour instead of god knows where. I can't keep fidgeting on the couch like an animal being investigated or a criminal on trial waiting for the verdict.

Instead through a last ditch effort I text Duke and ask him what he's up to tonight. I don't know how long I expected him to take before answering but it definitely wasn't two minutes.

Duke: Basketball
Me: ?
Duke: You should come. It might be fun. Spitz and a couple of the other guys from the team are here. It's a home game too so no unfamiliar turf.

I leave him on read and spend the next few minutes contemplating my options. I don't have any. Guess I'm going to a stupid basketball game.

When I got to the school and tossed my skateboard into a bush by the doors, I found out that the basketball game hadn't even started yet. People were just sitting around in the stands watching them warm up. I guess people do the same thing with hockey but I never really noticed how weird it is until now. It's like a mini pre-game where you can see if certain players are doing well and when which ones might suck. That's not nerve racking or anything. Tonight I'm wearing an old ripped up leather jacket and I've got my hands shoved into the pockets. Muddy Converse sneakers are on my feet and I'm wearing ripped jeans.. Scanning the stands for any sign of Duke or Spitz I get bumped into and am turning around, ready to try and find some hideout place, somewhere in town to spend the night. But Duke calls my name from the stands, spotting me before I could see him. I groan and turn back towards the stands to see him waving wildly and Spitz shoveling popcorn into his mouth. Rolling my eyes I duck my head and make my way through the crowd and take the bleachers two at time till I reach where they are.

Jet and Cliff are here both with their girlfriends, Hunter's here too along with two other girls I don't know either.

As I sit down next to Spitz and Duke, Duke starts introducing me to the unknown girls, including Jet and Cliff's girlfriends Amber and Hannah. The other two girls are Spitz's sister Natalie, and a girl who goes to a different school but who has been friends with Duke since pre-k, Sloane. Hunter sits slouched back on the bleachers a step down from Duke, Spitz tossing skittles in the air to him while he attempts to catch them in his mouth. When one hits me on the head I clear my throat and he turns around slowly, eyes wide knowing he hit me.

"Sorry?" He offers a skittle and I take it but chuck it at him instead. I give a small smile and turn back to the game and can physically hear him relax. Scanning the court and unwillingly searching through the cheerleaders, I'm interrupted by Duke leaning over and whispering to me.

"She doesn't cheer during basketball season." My

head whips toward him. "Were you looking for her?" He asks, a smug look on his face.

"Huh?" I can feel my face heat up. "I'm not." I wasn't. Not on purpose. My eyes search his face for any hint of trickery or plans to embarrass me and I find none. I realize now I've given myself away and he never said what cheerleader. I might as well commit and ask what I want to know. "Why do you know so much about her anyways." That question comes out harsher than I meant it to and I cringe a little internally.

He shrugs before continuing, brushing off my venomous tone. "We met freshman year during P.E. Believe it or not we were both super awkward and shy so we kinda gravitated towards each other. We became friends and have been friends since. We're not ridiculously tight like you two are or even like some of her and her other friends but we confide in each other and get along." I'm silent after his response because I don't know what to say to that. "Where is she tonight anyways?" I choke on the popcorn I was stealing from Spitz and everyone in a 5 feet radius turns and looks at me which makes me red and probably look skittish. Cliff leans down and pats me hard on the back and as I'm gathering myself I give him a thumbs up to lay off.

"I don't know. I'm not her keeper. Plans with friends or something." Duke lets the conversation go and I'm grateful because it's one thing to talk to him about Liza when it's just him or just him and Spitz but we're in a very public setting with other teammates surrounding us and I don't want them that deep in my personal life.

Hunter chooses now to join the conversation. He jumps up and turns to us and looks like he's about to give a grand speech. "Ok guys it's that time of the night. We've seen both teams warming up, we know the stats of their seasons, who's placing a bet tonight?" I sit up straight at this because Hunter just got a hell of a lot more interesting to me.

"Wait," I shake my head out quickly, "you guys place bets on these games?" Hunter raises a brow at me while taking money from Amber who thinks we'll win.

"Want in?" I bite the side of my tongue for a second and a mischievous grin spreads across my face.

"What's the bottom amount?" Hunter sits down still facing me and counts money he's collected.

"$20 minimum. But if you want you can place more. It gets put into a pot and the winners split the money."

Natalie jumps in before he can finish, "yea and whether he wins or loses Hunter takes a 'collectors debt' from it."

"Hey it's only $30 and I gotta make a living somehow!"

I take a second assessing the teams and Sloane lets me borrow the little pamphlets the school makes with information about the players and give it a glance over. "Ok, I want in." I hand Hunter $50. "We're gonna win." He looks so smug about that and I'm guessing he bet against the team.

"$50?! You just carry around that much cash?" Normally no, I don't carry around a lot of cash but I figured I might as well bring enough for snacks, admission, and anything else I might decide I want. But instead of answering I just wink and let him think I'm loaded and cocky. Might as well, everyone already thinks one of those things is true.

To my surprise, being at the game was pretty fun and I didn't hate hanging out with the guys from the team, plus the other girls. There were a lot of stares and whispers when I got heated over a play one of the refs made and Duke pulled me back down into my seat. At the end of the game though I'd just doubled the money I'd bet since Duke, Amber, Natalie and I bet we'd win and in a buzzer beater shot we won 78-77. Walking out of the stadium I was prepared to start making my way back home but Jet called out to me and everyone was headed towards the same car. My brows furrowed and I shouted back confused and Spitz waved me over. Taking long strides to close the distance between us I made my way over to them.

"Wanna come get pizza with us? We never go home right away after a game and tonight Cliff and Jet want to go to this arcade down on Beale St." Duke nods in the general direction of the arcade even though it's blocks away.

"Oh, uh."

"You don't have to if you don't want to." Hannah interrupts and offers.

I take a deep breath and think about my mom.

About how happy she'd be that I'm trying, really trying to make friends. That I'm not sitting at home being cynical and miserable, and that I'm trying to move on. "Yea sure that sounds great." Everyone looks a little surprised that I agreed to come and so I start walking towards Natalie's SUV that we're all gonna cram into forcing them to turn and follow me instead of standing and gawking. "I call shotgun." I start sprinting towards the car and everyone else does too and I'm startled for a second when I hear a foreign sound coming from my mouth. Laughter. Open, happy, free, laughter.

The rest of the night I played games with people who were starting to become less afraid of me even when I had to take breaks to punch the living shit out of the Boxer Punch Machine because I'd gotten too competitive, lost a game, and was fuming. I kept setting records on that machine. There was one time that I accidentally hurt Spitz and felt like shit because of it. We were playing air hockey and he kept beating me and I got so mad that it transferred into one of my shots and the puck flew off the table and hit the kid square in the forehead. I muttered an apology and went off to sulk after that. Spitz finally found me and brought me a Pepsi Slushee from their food concessions.

"I'm ok ya know. Not the first puck and certainly not the last that I'll take to the head." I chuckle at that and apologize for laughing. But he laughs too.

We gorged ourselves on all the pizza we could eat but I was deemed "winner" of food for the night since

I put away the most slices and still wanted to order more food. Duke and Natalie competed on the Dance Dance Revolution machine and Natalie absolutely crushed him. Duke dancing looked like a baby deer learning to stand up for the first time. Sloane ran into some people she knew from school and everyone said hi to them but I stayed focused on the game I was playing and didn't want to Converse with any more new people tonight and thankfully no one made me.

Hunter challenged me to an arm wrestling contest and after about 3 minutes of me pretending to try my hardest and us being at a standstill, him with his veins popping out and me looking perfectly fine, I put him out of his misery and slammed his hand into the table. He wanted a rematch but everyone complained and Cliff dragged him away to play a two person shooter game with him.

When Natalie finally brought us back to the school and we went our separate ways I waited around a random car for everyone to leave before I dug my skateboard out of the bushes and went off into the night.

"I made friends." I blurt it out so fast that Dr. Shaw can only look at me bewildered, mouth agape. After a few seconds of processing what I practically just yelled at her in the first few minutes of the appointment, she answers.

"That's good." She smiles and her eyes light up. "It seems you're pretty happy about this development too." I nod and play with my hands. "Tell me about them."

"Do I have to?" She rolls her eyes and folds her notebook closed and blinks at me.

"I guess not but I thought that's why you brought it up?" She has a point. I don't talk about anything and when I do it's never just small talk or to fill the silence. If I don't want to talk she knows I don't care about the silence.

"Sorry. I'm not ready to talk about it, I just wanted to tell you. I know you report stuff back to my mom. Telling her how I'm doing, any progress I may have made. I just thought you could tell her I made friends." She puts her notebook on her desk and leans forward and puts her elbows on her knees, hands folded peering at me over her glasses.

"If you want your mom to know why don't you tell her yourself?" Truth is I don't really know why I don't want to tell her myself.

"I don't know."

"That's alright not to know. Don't you think your mom will be happy you made friends?"

"I mean yea, that's all she's wanted for me since we got here."

"Is it possible that you don't want to be the one to tell your mother on the off chance that you disappoint her?"

"But why would she be disappointed?"

"I don't know Ryn. I can't tell you how you're feeling. I can only try to lead you to the answer." I huff because of her answer but it seems to be the only definitive one she ever gives me.

My voice raises as I answer her, "I don't know!" I rush out.

"Maybe I'm worried that she won't like the friends I chose! Or maybe I think that I'll fuck it up like I always do! Or– or maybe I think that these people that I think like me for who I am will go running the opposite direction when they finally figure out I'm not worth the trouble. And I don't want to be the one to tell my mom that I'm never gonna have friends because of the prick who calls himself my father!" I'm panting when I finally finish and Dr. Shaw looks like she wasn't fully prepared for me to react the way I did. If I'm being honest with myself neither was I but here we are with a thick air hanging between us now that I put there with my outburst.

"He has a name." I slowly lift my head up from where it was angled down at the floor, my eyebrows furrowing and my eyes widening. I can feel my eye twitch for a second but she doesn't look alarmed by my reaction at all. In fact she just looks pleased.

"What." It's not a question, I'm daring her to continue.

"Your father. He has a name." She draws her mouth into a line and looks at me cluelessly like she doesn't know why I'm reacting this way. But I know that she does and that it's just an act. And then she decides to really piss me off. "Say it." I clench my jaw and my teeth grind involuntarily. My voice is low and quivers without my permission when I speak.

"No." She leans back in the chair and crosses her arms.

"You can't keep acting like he doesn't exist. As much as it may pain you, he does. He exists and he's a part of you. Pretending that that's any less true than it is is only hurting you." I grip the edge of the chair and my eyes start to water. I don't want to think about him. He doesn't deserve to be the center of so much of my pain but I don't know how to force him from it. I hate him and it's a red hot burning hate but that makes me hate myself because that's exactly what he wanted. It feels like a never ending cycle that I'm imprisoned in. Dr. Shaw sighs, bringing me back to the present and I look at her. "Touching on what you said though, you aren't going to push them away. And no matter what your brain is telling you, you do deserve friends. And I'm not gonna let you become your father. On that note, that's all the time we have today. We'll pick up on where we left off later."

I've never been to Liza's when her parents were home. Which in turn means I've never met her parents. At this point I'm starting to feel extremely creepy just pacing on her porch debating whether or not I'll knock, ring the doorbell, or text Liza telling her I'm here so that she'll come down and let me in. But the universe decides for me because right as I start to raise my hand to knock on the big white door it opens and my eyes widen.

An average sized middle aged woman with long curly hair similar to Liza's stands in front of me.

"Can I help you?" She tilts her head slightly and looks at me with a small smile. Her eyes however, tell me she's trying to decide whether or not I'm a threat to her and her family. "You've been standing outside my house for the last," She looks at the watch on her wrist, "eight minutes."

"Aunt Arabella, who's at the door?" Liza calls from the other room as she rounds the corner coming towards the door. She speeds up when she sees me. "Ryn. Hey!" She looks thrown off and I realize now that I was so nervous about being here when her parents were home that I forgot to tell her I was even coming in the first place.

Before I can apologize for not giving notice that I was coming, her aunt, who I didn't realize lived with her, says, "This is Ryn?? *The* Ryn?!" She looks at Liza with some kind of look that I don't quite get. Liza's eyes grow wide and she clenches her jaw and gives a slight shake of her head to tell her aunt to knock it off. Her aunt just smiles a wicked smile and her eyes twinkle like she's just stumbled across the greatest secret ever. Liza pushes her into the other room and they whisper back and forth to each other while her aunt tries to push back and get a good look at me. I feel a little like a caged animal so I start fidgeting with my hands and rock back and forth on the balls and heels of my feet a little.

Liza makes her way back to the door and holds the edge of it and smiles at me. "What's up?" She sounds exhausted from fighting her aunt and she looks a little flustered. She catches me assessing her appearance and even though she blushes, she smirks a little.

I cough before answering and look at my shoes. "I uh, I wanted to show you something." I pause for a second before considering and glance up at her and now she looks more relaxed and a little intrigued at where I'm going with this, "It's kind of special to me. No one else really knows about it. Well no one else but Duke and that's not because I showed him voluntarily, he found out by accident but anyways I really wanted to show it to you too." My rambling got quicker and quicker as I went on and I didn't even realize that she'd slipped on her shoes and was putting on her coat out on the porch waiting for me to be finished with my speech.

When I finally stop and look up and see her she gives me a slight smile.

"Well come on. Let's go." She waits for me to start walking towards the car and then follows me. She's purposefully letting me be in charge of this even though she knows how to walk to a car and knows which one I drive.

We spent the next 30 minutes making our way across town, casually talking about whatever, when I finally turned down the greenhouse's street. As soon as I did I wasn't very chatty and instead my stomach was a ball of nerves. I didn't realize it at the time but I was gripping the steering wheel so tight that my knuckles started turning white.

"You ok?" Liza looks at me concerned and glances from my face to my knuckles and that causes me to look at them. I ease up on my grip and breathe out.

"Yea I'm fine." I swallow because I know now that she sees right through me and knows that I'm lying. But she doesn't push or pry, she drops the subject and we ride the rest of the way to the house in silence. When I pull into the parking lot Liza looks over at me quizzically and looks me up and down then turns back to the house.

Getting out of the car I take her through the back entrance where I've been growing and cultivating different plants. She stands in the middle of the room slowly spinning in a circle, taking it all in. After a minute she starts to move around the room, reaching out, running her fingers along some of the plants. I stand over by the wall, ready to make a full break back to the car in case this goes wrong. I let her wander the room inspecting different plants and finally she stops and it takes me a second to register where she is in the room. I swallow because I know I'm gonna have to explain myself.

But she doesn't speak when she turns around. Instead she runs over to me, grabs my face and kisses me, hard. For a second I stand there completely still but then my brain turns on and I'm kissing her back and pulling her closer. The kiss is electric, something I feel down to my toes. Her lips taste like rainbow sherbet chapstick and I can't help but lose myself in the kiss, my hands gripping her waist as I hold her against me. When she finally pulls away it simultaneously felt like we'd been kissing for an eternity as well as much too short of time. She rests her forehead on mine and we're both a little breathless. Maybe that's what Duke meant.

"You grow strawberries for me."

11:03 A.M

Three months ago I was running late to dragging Liza somewhere random and secluded in the school for lunch. When I finally got to the cafeteria and started to drag her away from her table she cursed and dragged behind. It turns out that in my haste I had caused her to spill the strawberries she'd grabbed for lunch. As we kept walking she continued to mumble angrily under her breath. I don't think she realized I could hear her.

"The last fucking carton of strawberries and now they're on the floor. Now for the next five or six months, no strawberries for Liza, because why would she ever get anything she ever wanted."

There were a lot more curse words and unsavory name calling before she got it all out of her system.

But by the end of it I realized a few things about her. She loved strawberries, she was beyond pissed at me for causing her to drop them, and even though she was beyond pissed she would never tell me. I learned one thing about myself that day. I don't know who made Liza think that she shouldn't get anything she's ever wanted or what made her feel like she never would, but I wanted to make sure I did everything in my power to *never* make her feel like that and to do my best not to ruin anything she wanted. Because I know what that's like.

For the next week I sulked around whenever I was near her because I felt like I wasn't good enough. Like I was gonna single handedly take away what she loved. I started working at the greenhouse soon after that, and I realized that this crazy and unusual city had brought something I loved back to me. So I wanted to do that for her. One of the first plants I started working on in the house was that strawberry plant. Finding one that already had flower buds as well as some baby formations of the berries took a hot minute but I searched all over for them and finally found a seller in California.

Come mid-January the plant started producing ripe berries and even some runners, I started putting them in these little packages I bought for the greenhouse in case we ever wanted to sell the strawberries. As soon as we were back in school I started bringing her some every day at lunch. At first she was skeptical of how and where I'd gotten strawberries at this time of year in Minnesota, but she stopped questioning it after a while.

Standing here now, holding her in my arms while she beams because of something I did has to be the best thing I've ever felt. Maybe even the best thing in the world. I kiss her forehead and start to push away from the wall. Taking her hand I guide her through the house and through my workshop describing the different plants, their origins, how much they cost, what's so unique about them, and anything else I can think of.

To me it felt like I was talking for only thirty minutes tops, but then Liza's phone rang and her aunt was calling to see how long she'd be out and I had a chance to look at the clock. It was 2:30 P.M and she spent all that time listening to me and letting me drone on and on about plants. I can't imagine it was as entertaining for her as it was for me and my cheeks heat up as I realize I've probably been boring her with botanical nonsense.

After she hangs up the phone and walks back over to me I clear my throat and look at the floor before speaking.

"I'm sorry for talking for so long. I guess I can kind of get caught up in all of this," I motion around the house with my arm and draw my lips into a tight line and continue, "I just really wanted to share this part of me with you." She walks up to me taking my hands in hers and places a soft, gentle kiss on my lips. "You know I could get used to you reassuring me like this instead of with words." She laughs at that, throwing her head back and I smile wide, ear to ear and it almost hurts because I haven't used the muscles like this in so long.

"Thank you." My face screws up and I'm about to question her when she interrupts, "For being you. For thinking about me. For sharing this part of yourself with me." I blush and try to look away but she grabs my face with her hands and forces me to look at her. "You, Ryn Bradford, are an amazing human being." My eyes start to well and she can tell I'm panicking from the display of emotion my body is giving so she lets me wander away a little to compose myself. Once again Liza being Liza, she changes the subject for me, "What got you into," she pauses, "All of this?" She waves her arms around and trails her hand gently along the petals of a cupcake blush cosmos flower.

I swallow and realize now is the time I have to start letting her in. If not all the way at least a little if I want to keep her. "Well, if you can, try to imagine an angry baby Ryn." I joke, trying to lighten the mood as much as possible. Thankfully she rolls with it.

"Ah yes, balled fists, lots of tantrums, and beating up school yard bullies." She gestures for me to continue and I chuckle because yea, she's pretty dead on.

"I was eight when I first lashed out at a teacher. I don't know why but I was just so angry and pissed off. The world seemed to be gray when it used to have color." I sit down on the edge of one of the tables and

Liza walks over and leans on it next to me. The table is up to her waist so jumping on it wouldn't be so easy for her. My legs just barely are able to swing gently back and forth, my feet sometimes skimming the ground. "All she had to do was take away the book I was trying to read and it sent me to a dark place. I started screaming at her. Her face showed her shock and concern. Like I had shapeshifted in front of her. I felt like a different person too."

I pause running my fingers through my hair. "She took me outside and gave me a talking-to and asked me if I was alright. By the end of her lecture though I'd zoned out and blocked the world out enough to calm down." Liza still doesn't say anything, just keeping quiet and letting me tell my story. "We went outside for recess right after that and some kid pushed my friend down the slide. There was no reason for me to be as mad as I was but as soon as he put his hands on her I yelled and lost it. I just lost it."

I shake my head and sigh, "I dragged the kid over to a tree and pinned him up against it. There was just so much adrenaline and anger running through my veins. I screamed in his face and the kid looked terrified. I found out later that he actually peed his pants out of fear. But as he was pinned to the tree I wound my tiny little fist back and slammed it into his stomach. The teacher pulled me away right after that and I spent the rest of my day in the principal's office while my parents were called and the school social worker was brought down to talk to me about my 'feelings'."

Liza doesn't say anything after I stop talking. Instead she just grabs my hand and squeezes. She lays her head on my shoulder and I start to tear up again. Thankfully she's not looking at me so I don't try to fight them. "When my mom walked in she didn't look angry or mad. She looked worried. And I don't know if she was worried about me or for me. But it was easy to forget why I was so angry in the first place when she came through those doors. I sat there in her arms and cried while the principal explained what I'd done. She just stroked my hair and held me while nodding at the principal as he spoke. I was relaxed and completely calmed down. That is until he came in."

My breath shudders and my voice breaks. "My father came in those doors looking –to most– like a concerned father, exuding patience and understanding. But I knew what was behind those eyes. I was fidgeting the second he stepped in the room. And suddenly I remembered why I was angry. My mom felt the change and held me tighter. She cooed in my ears to soothe me. It worked back then." I turn my head and look at her now because for some reason I want to look at her when I say this. After feeling me move she lifts her head and meets my eyes. I want her to really truly know what she's getting into. "I get my anger from my father. And my father is a terrible excuse for a man. When we left he told me that I would be just like him.

That a red hot rage was inside of me and it would come out whether I wanted it to or not. I was 16." I sniff and bite the insides of my cheeks because even though I've already cried a little I don't want to outright sob. Liza pulls me into her arms and puts her chin on my head as I, against my mental will, cry softly onto her shirt. After we sit there like that for a few minutes I start to speak again, my voice slightly muffled from my head being in her shirt.

"And I look *just* like him. I'm his fucking spitting image. So I'm always reminded of him when I look in the mirror. Not only that but no matter what she says I *know* that when my mom looks at me she sees him." That brings a soft sob out of me. Liza sensed I'd shared enough trauma for today so she brought the conversation back to plants.

"Is that what led to the plants?" Her voice is quiet and smooth. She's confident in her question and not at all worried I might lash out at her. God she's a saint.

"Yea." I sniffle and sit up and begin playing with my hands. "I had this teacher, she taught English, and she for whatever reason, thought I was a good kid. Even after I punched the kid on the playground." I chuckle softly and shake my head because to this day I still don't know what she ever saw in me. "I spent a lot of time in her room after that day. She came into the principal's office and offered to help me work on my anger and try to get to the root of it. The entire school staff knew I would never talk to the social worker. But everyone knew that Ms. Dugan was my favorite. I read at a way higher reading level than any of the other kids in my class. And it was thanks to her."

"So every day when other kids were at recess, I was in her classroom trying different techniques and activities to manage my anger. We painted, did crafts, played games like checkers and chess. It wasn't until she'd bought a new plant for her classroom and I asked so many questions about it that she found the perfect activity for me to relax. Botany. After a month of filling her classroom full of different house plants and flowers and eventually not having any more room for more, she was able to convince the principal to let us build and grow a garden at the school. Every day I brought home my mother more and more flowers. She was so happy that I'd found something that I loved so much."

"One of the saddest days of my life was having to leave that elementary school and in consequence leave Ms. Dugan and the garden. But mom let me continue my garden at home. So I did. I kept it up until we left that house. Then I didn't think about plants until I came here. I stumbled across this place on a fury fueled jog. I was pissed off at Reuben and kicked our mailbox out of the ground as well as putting a few dents in it. I passed the house on my jog and saw a Sea Daffodil." I pause and take a second to point at the plant across the house. "It's one of my favorites and I always wanted one when I was little, so naturally," I stand up and laugh at the irony of what I'm about to say next. "I tried to steal it." Shoving my hands into my back jeans pockets and shrugging at Liza's guffawing I lower my head and roll my eyes while smiling. "Thankfully, instead of turning me into the police, Mrs. Kahn offered me a job. I don't know why I decided to take it. I think I just really missed all of–," I gesture around the big and vast room filled with different greenery, "This."

Once I'm finally done speaking Liza just stares at me gently biting her lip while smiling. Her eyes are lighting up like they do when she's happy, so bright it's like they alone have the power of the sun. I swallow because I feel like there's something I've said or done that she might be silently mocking me for. That something I said or did was funny.

She takes a few steps towards me but instead of closing the space between us she just looks me in the eyes and speaks. "You will never cease to amaze me." Her voice is so sincere that suddenly I don't have mine. So she speaks for me. "Ice cream?" She holds out her hand for me to take and without hesitating I take it and a small smile finds my face that turns into a full on grin when she bounces on her heels thinking about what flavor or combination she'll get.

As we're walking to the car I notice a feeling I've never felt before, or at least not one to this extent. I can't say I hate it.

Liza directed me to this little mom-and-pop ice cream shop that she and her aunt came to one time after she'd first moved here. Apparently her aunt is one of her best friends and strongest supporters. I wanted to know more about her and about their relationship but I couldn't bring myself to press because this just officially started today and I didn't want to send it crashing back down before it fully left the ground.

What was nice about the shop and something Liza seemed to really enjoy was their experimentation with flavors and the variety they had with them. If you thought Baskin Robbins had a lot of flavors, it had nothing on Klippers' Kreamery.

I ended up getting three scoops of their Blueberry

Graham Cracker Crunch flavor. Liza spent seven minutes deciding what she wanted, causing me to even offer to get her multiple different flavors just so she wouldn't have to choose. Watching her run her hands through her tight brown curls every time she saw a new flavor she might want, and sigh, was like injecting drugs straight into my veins. The best part of it all was I got to touch her. I walked up to her and put my arm around her waist and assured her we were in no hurry and she could take her time. I don't think I realized how badly I wanted to do this until I got to and now just like drugs I'm addicted and can't stop.

She finally decided on Cinnamon Toast Swirl and I died a little when she got some just outside her mouth because she stuck her tongue out and swirled it around the ring of her lips to catch what escaped.

Now we're lying on the hood of my mom's car looking up at the stars, a blanket thrown over us mixed with the warmth of the running engine below us keeping us from freezing our asses off in the mid Minnesota winter. The moon isn't full but the light that's coming off of it makes her olive skin shine and I'm not even looking at the stars as Liza points out which ones she knows and what the constellations mean. I feel bad because I'm only partially listening but fully thinking that this must be heaven.

Days like today are some of the ones that suck the most. A new kid transferred to our school and ended up in one of my classes. First thing that happens is the teacher doing a roll call. Most people wouldn't have given the extra name a second thought, or even hear it at all.

"Jack."

One word and I'm a kid again. One name and I feel like the helpless little girl I was back then. My head whipped in the direction of the kid whose name got called but when I turned and looked I only saw *him*. I felt sick and ran out of the classroom. I didn't come back to school for the rest of the day.

At lunch I texted Liza that I wouldn't be there.

When she asked if I was ok I didn't know how to respond. I tried but nothing would come out. Every letter and every word I tried to type just didn't show up. I felt bad not answering her. A few days in and I was already trying to damage the one good thing I had going in my life.

Spending the rest of the day sitting on the ledge of a billboard overlooking the town, I cried and yelled and threw rocks as hard as I could at the sign. My voice was hoarse from the shouting and after I'd missed practice and decided I wasn't going to the greenhouse today, I had 50 missed calls from my mom, 25 texts from Liza, calls, texts, and an email from Daniel, all trying to reach me until I finally went home.

Walking through the front door of my house you'd expect I was walking into a family being told their relative had died. My mom was sitting on the couch crying while Daniel stood over her comforting her and simultaneously calling different people. Once they heard me come in relief flooded their faces but was soon overtaken by anger. Everywhere I go anger follows me. Just like he follows me.

"Where the hell were you?" My mother speaks first and she's tired of my bullshit. I can hear it.

"We were worried sick about you. Liza was worried sick about you." Daniel joins in the chorus and I just stand there quiet. I have nothing I can or want to say. They're looking at me. Wanting some sort of reaction from me, anything. Instead I say I'm tired and start to head for the stairs.

"No! You do *not* get to just walk away. You are my child and you left school and no one could reach you! I thought you'd gotten yourself hurt, or kidnapped or dead! I've had this conversation before and I *refuse* to have it and put up with it from you. So, I'll ask again." She grits her teeth as she continues, "What. The. Hell. Happened."

I take a deep breath and all I can muster, all I can give her right now is this.

"Him." With that I turn and walk up the stairs to my room. I close the door and head to the bathroom to start getting ready for bed. Walking in there and looking in the mirror I don't recognize the person staring back at me. I don't know who she is. I don't know who I am. Going through my nighttime routine I open the mirror and take one of the antidepressant pills Dr. Shaw wanted me to try and go to close the mirror. But when I do it's his reflection staring back at me.

I bite my lip and my breathing quickens and gets heavy. I start crying and sobbing and yelling. I kick at the walls and pound at my head. Out. Out. I want him out. I look at the mirror again and he's still there like he's taunting me. So before I even know what I'm doing I rip the towel rod off the wall and smash it into the mirror. And even though it shatters on the first hit I keep swinging over and over until Daniel busts in and yanks the rod out of my hands. I struggle with him over it but he wins because I'm exhausted and am so tired. Tired of everything. Slumping to the floor against the sink I continue to sob and pull at my hair. My mom slumps down next to me and pulls me into her arms and pets my hair.

"I keep seeing him." Today wasn't the first day. A few months ago I was walking past this shop downtown and my reflection made me do a double take because I swear I'd seen him instead of myself. I didn't say anything and I thought it was a fluke but then on Christmas morning when we were standing at the window looking at the fresh falling snow, my eyes honed in on my reflection in the mirror and suddenly I wasn't looking at myself. And it just kept getting worse. "Everytime I look at myself I see him."

"What?" My mom pulls away and her eyes search mine. "Baby when did this start happening?" She's concerned and her eyes start filling with tears but I can see she's fighting them for me.

My lips quiver and more tears start falling from my face, "A few months ago." I'm clenching my jaw so tightly that my teeth feel like they're gonna break any second. But my mom just pulls me back into her arms and starts rocking with me. And to my surprise she starts singing me a lullaby she used to do when I was a child. One she'd sing when it was a particularly bad night. I think she sang it to calm us both. But she was singing it just for me this time. I don't remember falling asleep there on the floor in her arms but I know I did. Yet I still woke up in my warm bed with my blankets. Daniel must have carried me in. Why couldn't I see him when I look at myself. He's been nothing but good to us, to me. I may not be able to see Daniel when I look at myself, but maybe I can let him in. Because I don't want to see *Jack* anymore. I want to see me, I want to see Ryn.

Getting up earlier than normal and dragging myself out of bed to trek across town to Liza's house before school was something I felt I had to do. I hadn't talked to her since I'd texted her yesterday telling her I wasn't going to be at lunch.

Walking up the porch steps and ringing my hands out psyching myself up to knock on her door was once again foiled by her aunt.

"Oh, hi." She seems happy to see me which I'm guessing means Liza didn't tell her about yesterday.

"Is Liza still here?" I sound like a little child asking her parents for a puppy. A desperate plea in my voice.

"Yea she is, she's finishing up getting ready but she's up in her room if you want to head up there and talk to her. I'm on my way out for work."

I bite my lip and nod then thank her as I walk in. She steps out and closes the door behind her and I'm left alone in the big house knowing Liza is up in her room. Now I just have to get there.

The creaky stairs give away my presence and Liza steps out of her room calling for her aunt. "Arabella I thought you were leaving –oh. Hi." She looks mad and she deserves to be.

I start speaking before I can back out or talk myself out of it. "I owe you an apology. What I did yesterday was," I pause trying to find the words, "Unacceptable, to say the least. There's no excuse for the way I treated you and even though this next part is gonna sound like an excuse I don't want you to think that in any way that it is." She crosses her arms and leans against the wall and raises her brow at me to continue. Her sass for some odd reason makes me feel a little better and a little more confident that I'm doing the right thing, "Something happened yesterday that triggered my problems with my dad and I spun out. I didn't handle it well. Or at all. But the point is, I'm sorry. I understand if I fucked up our– whatever this is." I gesture between us, "I just felt like at the very least you deserve an apology."

We stand there in silence for a few minutes and I've had enough of it so I turn around to leave. She stops me though by gently laying her hand on my arm because she knows the sudden touch while I'm not looking could spook me. I tense a little but relax almost immediately. Turning around she looks at me, brows raised and lips pursed.

"I'm not letting you walk away that easily, Ryn. You did worry me. And hurt my feelings a little bit." I frown at that and she takes her fingers and pushes my frown into a smile and I'm sure I look deranged because she laughs. "You know I'm here for you if you ever need me right?" I nod slightly. "C'mon, we gotta get to school. I'm not letting you skip today because I've grown dependent on your strawberry deliveries."

I chuckle a bit at that and follow her down the stairs. And since I don't have my own car (and my bike isn't quite ready to drive passengers) and only ever use my mom's, Liza drives us to school.

The entire way there we sang songs of all kinds of genres ranging from Lady Gaga to Five Seconds of Summer to Taylor Swift to 2000's Indie Pop. I make fun of her driving and she threatens me in Italian. Which I gotta say is very, very hot. At one point I make a game out of creating fake conversations of the people in cars next to us. This old couple in a Mini Cooper is having a baby via surrogate so that they have someone of blood relations to take care of them when they can't perform bodily functions on their own. That made Liza cackle.

A douchey looking business man is trying to pay a blackmail threat regarding the pictures of him fucking the office water cooler after getting too drunk at the New Year's party. Liza came up with that one and I gotta say I was impressed. Normally I'm the most fucked up one in the room but I think that out did even me. I pretended to crown her queen and she gave a fake wave and teary eyed speech and we laughed some more. Today was looking promising.

All that fills my head right now is the sound of the blades from our skates meeting the ice and our sticks smacking the ground and pucks sliding around. I know there's music playing from the speakers in the stadium and noise as parents, students, and fans of high school hockey enter the stands. But I don't hear any of it.

Tonight's my first night back playing on the ice since I bashed the kid's head in. As much as I hate to admit, I've been nervous as hell the entire week. And that just makes me see him more. It hurts but I've been dealing.

Liza took me to a rage room yesterday. She kept referring to it as our first date and that made it really hard to have anything to rage at. But she told me to channel all my hate for my dad into destroying the room. We got fancy hazard helmets and a bunch of different weapons and items we could use to break things. Liza looked adorable in her helmet. It was way too big for her head and was constantly trying to fall off. All in all the day was really fun and it felt like for the first time in my life my destructive ways were productive and didn't cause any damage. At least not any damage it wasn't supposed to. Watching Liza struggle with the sledgehammer is something I'll always remember because it was hilarious as it almost pulled her over when she swung it over her head. Afterwards we got pizza and I downed over half of a large pitcher of soda because of the pit in my stomach. Liza ate what I didn't and teased me every time I went in for more.

I snuck her into the rink after that. She wanted to go ice skating but every place that we could we'd have to pay to get in. All the players have passes we can use to swipe in and out of the rink for practices and whatever else we may need. I figured I could get us in, hook up my phone to speakers so that music would be playing, and find skates her size somewhere in storage.

Turns out she wasn't as good as she remembered being and fell on her ass a lot. I had to help her find her balance and she skated bent halfway over with her arms straight out and her legs straight and unmoving. We talked a lot that night, somehow the conversation kept steering to my father and how therapy is going.

We stayed out a lot later than we probably should have and by the time she dropped me off at my house it was 1:30 in the morning.

This afternoon I took Duke up on his offer to go running sometime and we did. Running usually clears my head and I figured if I had someone with me I wouldn't run off and never come back. He wasn't terrible company either. We were constantly pushing each other to work harder and run faster and longer.

Afterwards he invited me to get a smoothie to rehydrate. Apparently getting a mango banana smoothie is a pregame ritual he always does and thought it might be good bonding and good juju if I joined him. Duke is a definite mama's boy. He calls every woman around him ma'am no matter how old they are, and he praises his mom any chance he gets. Apparently his dad isn't around a whole lot because of work but his mom has always done her best to be two parents for him. I guess in that way we're similar. I didn't tell him that.

He's the middle child of his family which is somehow shocking but makes so much sense all at the same time. He has an older brother, Miles, who's off at college at the University of Minnesota, and a little sister Piper who's in 6th grade. What shocked me the most was him talking about living in his brother's shadow. Duke has never struck me as the type of person to feel any sort of resentment or frustration towards anyone he cares about. It's honestly an emotion I didn't think he had.

But while we sat at Smoothies Sipway and talked I realized there's layers to him I didn't see as well. His brother was like some sort of legend and perfect child growing up. Perfect grades, great at sports, even plays the violin. It put a lot of pressure on Duke to follow him after that. And while Duke has his own successes he often worries about putting that same pressure on Piper.

He also worries about the pressure his mother must feel to show all three of her kids the same amount of love and affection for two parents while their dad is away. His father is a hotel travel reviewer. It was great when they were kids because it meant the family got to go on lots of cool vacations around the country and sometimes even around the world, but the older the kids got the more obligations and different interests they had and things to do meaning there was a lot less time to jet off across the world. So Duke's mom stayed home with the kids whenever his father had to rush off somewhere. While Duke understands his father's job and wishes he could see him more he's ok with the situation and doesn't blame him for not being around. But apparently that's not the case with Miles.

Miles started to become closed off around their father during his teen years and would often close himself in his room during the family's regularly scheduled skype calls with their dad. Miles and their parents got into a huge fight one night and everyone said some things they regretted. But it ended with Miles saying that their father didn't love them because if he did he would find a way to be around.

After that Miles left for college. Duke is still in touch with him and he FaceTimes their mom occasionally but he rarely speaks to his father.

This afternoon when I walked back home from the smoothie shop I had a new profound respect for Duke. All that going on at home and he still manages to look out for others. I guess it makes sense. He's been having to do it his entire life. Looking out for his mom, his brother and sister, and in a way trying to look out for his father by subconsciously trying to be the man of the house that they all feel missing. He does it for the team too.

Tonight was the first night that I decided to join the team for a pregame ritual where they all gather at Coach's house for a home cooked meal and hangout before the game. When I showed up at Coach's door everyone looked like they'd seen a ghost. And I suppose that they had. However after the initial shock Duke, Jet, Cliff, and Hunter welcomed me with open arms and everything felt easy for once in my life. Like maybe I was where I was supposed to be.

Tonight we're facing the Kitsbury High School Killer Sharks. It's a mouthful I know. They're a rival high school about 20 minutes from Forthsworth. It's not just a big deal for me tonight but for everyone on the team.

Our record this season so far was 2-0. We were supposed to have played three games by tonight but thanks to me our first one was postponed. Kitsbury high is our number one competitor for state champions every year. Coach gave me literal books and binders about our high school's statistics and past seasons that I had to study and learn if I was gonna be on the team. If we wanted a good spot in the playoffs we needed this win tonight. So did they.

Spitz had been nervously chatting and talking excessively. It had been three minutes that we'd been running a drill together and I already knew about the in depth details of his life from the day he was born to age six. I really wish I didn't know how hard it was to potty train Spitz. Or the fact that he couldn't pronounce his "r's" for the first three years of his life.

At one point I took a shot and sent the puck flying right past his head as a warning shot for him to shut up. Coach had his switch drills after that anyway so Spitz got lucky to be removed from my earshot.

Before I can take another run at the crossfire in the slot shot drill the buzzer sounds and both teams have to skate into the locker rooms for one last pep talk and then skate out onto the ice to play.

I look around the crowd as I'm making my way to the locker room and spot Liza, Daniel, and my mom in the stands. Liza made a big sign with glitter and our school colors on it and I roll my eyes and blush when I see it. She didn't tell me she was doing that and I know why she didn't. I would've told her no if she did. And no amount of pouting would've made me change my mind. Daniel of course bought a foam finger and to my embarrassment brought his megaphone. I groan audibly and grumble to myself as I make my way into the girl's locker room. My hair's in two Dutch braids tonight and I pin the ends to the bottom of my head so they'll fit underneath my helmet. I shove my custom mouth guard in even though I got my stitches out on Tuesday, just to be safe. When I look in the mirror I see my father for a split second and take in a sharp breath.

Gripping the edge of the sink I look down and take a deep breath. *I can do this. I'm not him. I'm my own person. And I am better than him.* I look back up in the mirror and see myself. Just as I release the breath I didn't realize I was holding Coach pounds on the door and calls for me to meet him in the boy's room. I hear imaginary boxing bells in my head going *ding ding ding.* I do my best to school my features. I can't help that if the grin on my face borders on devilish. Round two.

7:56 P.M

I bang on the glass of the penalty box as the ref makes another bogus call against our team. Coach is screaming about something and I'm guessing it was at me because the ref turns towards me, puts one hand in a fist and lays his other hand over it and pushes it up and down signaling another penalty. This time for unsportsmanlike conduct. The first was for elbowing. But I only elbowed the jackass because he cross-checked me into the boards and nobody said a damn thing. No, instead I get in trouble for jabbing him in his soft gut.

I groan and grumble under my breath because my time was almost up in the box but now I've got the last 29 seconds plus two minutes for my new penalty.

Natalie, Liza, and Sloane start bounding down the steps and bleachers towards the penalty box to talk to me.

"What's going on out there? I've been learning as much as I can but that guy totally did something illegal to you first right?" Liza half-shouts over the loud noises of the game and crowd.

"Yea he did." I grumble back.

"Hey don't pout, you're playing great out there!" Sloane adds in an attempt to make me feel better. With my helmet in my hand I use the back of it to wipe sweat off my forehead.

Natalie joins in singing my praises, "You really are. First goal of the game, you're a beast Bradford." She smirks and raises her brow at me and nods as if saluting me.

My attention is brought back to the ice as the buzzer for my confinement sounds signaling my freedom. Liza kisses her hand and puts it up to the glass and the other girl's "oo". I slightly shake my head as I put my helmet on and skate back onto the ice.

9:01 P.M

Sweat drips off my forehead as I skate back towards the locker rooms, holding my helmet in my hand and avoiding talking to anyone.

We may have won the game but that doesn't stop me from analyzing every little thing, every little move, pass, play, whatever. The final score was 2-1. And while I scored one of those I still feel like I wasn't playing at my best.

In my head I just keep hearing over and over again that I could've done better or that we didn't win because of anything I did. I keep my head down and I've torn the crap out of my lip because I keep chewing and pulling at it with my teeth.

I can hear the guys behind me yelling and cheering

because all in all the truth is tonight was a big deal for the team. Beating our rivals solidifies our reputation as a team. And while that should make me happy, instead I'm leaning up against a locker in the boy's room while everyone else skates in waiting for Coach to tell us we did good, waiting with a sour expression on my face.

There's one play in particular that keeps replaying in my mind. It was right before halftime. I had the puck and had the chance to score and was about to take my shot but got slammed into the boards before I could. I was supposed to be open. I don't know where that player came from but I shouldn't have let myself be so blindsided.

Coach doesn't give me any more time to dwell on it because he just marched into the locker room so we all snap our attention to him and whatever he might say about the game and about the way we played.

"Well done boys..." he pauses and looks at me then nods and continues, "and girl. You put up a good fight tonight and you should be proud of yourselves. However, we're gonna need to put in a lot of time on the ice if we're gonna keep playing the way we have been and if we expect to make it far in the playoffs, which I do. I'm proud of you guys. And you should be proud of yourselves." I can tell this next part is directed at me even if he doesn't name names. "The refs didn't do us any favors tonight either." Most calls made against the team tonight were aimed at me even when it wasn't my fault. These refs were obviously misogynistic assholes but hey, what else is new?

When he's done talking to us I start to make my way to my locker room to get changed and go home to do absolutely nothing with Liza.

He follows me out of the locker room though and pulls me aside before I get to the girl's room.

"Hey Bradford!" I stop in my tracks and turn around and raise a brow at him. "Stop punishing yourself." This makes my brows furrow and I frown because now I don't know what he's talking about. "There was nothing you could've done to keep from getting checked. He broke free from Cliff and took off after you. You couldn't have seen it coming and there wasn't enough time for you to react and get away with the puck. So stop beating yourself up about it." I swallow and turn around to go back to my locker room because I don't know what to say to that. I'm surprised he knew I was over analyzing it and dwelling on it instead of celebrating a well deserved win. Why do I do that to myself?

When I finally get home Liza and I hang out in my room and we do absolutely nothing. This isn't like those times where we sit in the back of her car and make out like the horny teenagers we are. There's nothing heated about this. It's gentle. Domestic.

She's half sitting up on my bed while I lay down next to her with my head on her stomach and arms wrapped around her waist and I can feel her heartbeat under my cheek and everything feels like it's going to be ok. She's reading out loud from a book she grabbed off my shelf and I'm only half listening. Here and now I feel something close to what I haven't felt in probably seven or so years.

"My family wants to meet you." It's so quiet that I almost miss it. My brain starts going a thousand miles a minute and I think she knows that because she quickly interrupts them. "You don't have to if you don't want to. But they keep asking questions about you and speculating and they're just really excited and happy for me." I can hear how much she wants this and I don't have to look at her to know that. I relax instantly and bury my head further into itself on her stomach.

"Ok." I can feel her sharp inhale because her lungs and chest jump upwards. "I want to meet them too." She relaxes after I say that and I kiss her stomach through her clothes. I love her.

Oh my god, I love her. I love her and I'd do anything to make her happy. I love her.

With that thought and the fact that she started petting my hair while reading, I'm no match for the sleep that consumes me.

Today is the first time in my life that I truly feel like a girl because I've changed my outfit six times. My nails and lips must look terrible from the constant chewing I've been doing out of nerves. I'm meeting Liza's family today. I'm meeting Liza's *parents* today. For some reason I really, really want them to like me. I want them to *trust* me.

I'm redoing my hair for the third time in ten minutes when my phone chimes probably from a text from Liza. She's supposed to be picking me up and taking me over to her house instead of having me just come over there by myself. I think she wants to prep me. God I hope she wants to prepare me because I have never felt this nervous before in my life. At least she met my parents before we were dating. But now I'm their daughter's girlfriend and not just her friend so that's a hell of a lot more pressure.

Liza: Almost to your house, be there in five.

After reading her text I bound down the stairs and make my way to the kitchen. Daniel's cooking my mom breakfast while she goes on a cleaning frenzy around the house. I know she won't but part of me worries that today's the day she'll decide to go up to the attic to clean and discover my mini greenhouse forcing me to explain myself and probably my job.

"That smells delicious." Daniel is very much in the zone when I say that because his tongue is sticking out of the side of his mouth and his face is scrunched as he prepares the creme fraîche for the coconut pancakes he's making, paired with bananas and said fraîche.

"Don't touch that." I don't know how he does it because he isn't even facing me and I only started to move my arm a split second ago but he snaps at me keeping me from sticking my finger in the pancake batter he has sitting by the stove.

"How do you do that?" I walk around the island and face him with an incredulous look on my face.

"Ryn." He stops and looks up at me, stone faced, serious expression. "Ryn, Ryn, Ryn, Ryn, Ryn, Ryn, Ryn." He's shaking his head, angled down towards the counter again before looking back up at me with that same expression. "I've said it once. I'll say it again. I am a wizard, nay," He holds up a finger correcting himself, "A god, in the kitchen."

I just blink at him and one of my eyes squints as my mouth hangs open, too stunned by his absurdity to even speak. I hesitantly reach over and grab a banana and back out of the room, never taking my eyes away from him as he continues to throw himself back into his cooking. I will never understand that man.

Saturday mornings like this are some of my favorites. Standing in the archway between the kitchen and the living room I can hear the sound of my mom vacuuming the stairs. The sizzle of the stove as Daniel starts to make his pancakes. The low hum of the tv that Daniel put on and started to watch before the house was thrust into happy chaos.

It almost feels like a perfected dance that the two of them perform. Gliding back and forth between their respective spaces while I stand in the middle of it, not there at all. I used to cherish it because it meant I was invisible. No one saw me. No one saw the mess that is me. And while it's still true, I'm not really seen, it doesn't have the same comforting feeling it used to. I still feel that magic of the household ecosystem moving around me, but it just feels different. That's the best and really only way I can describe it. It's comforting for a different reason.

Before I had a social life I usually spent my Saturday's either skateboarding around town when the weather was nice enough or hiding up in my room and occasionally sneaking away to my greenhouse in the attic, or hiding in the garage working on my motorcycle that my mom swears is a death trap. I'm only realizing now that I really didn't have much of a life. If I could even call it that. More and more I'm realizing that Liza really is the best thing to ever happen to me.

I chuckle to myself at that because the irony of the situation is not lost on me. At the beginning and even at the middle of the year she annoyed me. She annoyed me though because she represented everything I wasn't. A happy, smart, girl, without anger issues or a dark, haunting past, and her constantly hanging around me was a persistent reminder of that fact.

And now I'm waiting on a Saturday morning for her to come pick me up so I can meet her family and I desperately want them to like me. If I had time to go on a run to get my nerves out I would. But Liza will be pulling into the driveway any second now.

Magic. I'm literally magic. I can hear the gravel in the driveway crunch under the sound of Liza's 2014 Radiant Silver Metallic Cadillac ATS. I'm pretty sure her dad bought it for her when she first learned how to drive. It's got a dent in the bumper from when she first tried to reverse the car and instead drove right over the curb of a parking lot and right into a tree. Luckily it wasn't an aggressive hit of any kind and she mostly just rolled into the tree and tapped it. But it was still enough to leave a dent and she didn't let anyone pay for it to be fixed because she thought it gave the car character. In a way it does.

She named the car Oatmeal. One night, she offered to drive home a girl from a party she reluctantly went to who was ridiculously drunk. The girl threw up oatmeal all over the car and thus the car earned the name Oatmeal. It may be a gross memory but she says that that night she realized a few things. One, never let yourself be dragged anywhere or to any event you don't want to be at, and two, never offer the drunk girl you're driving home some leftover oatmeal you had at breakfast so that she has something in her stomach no matter how kind the offer may be.

Now I'm sitting in the passenger seat sorting through the playlists she's created on Amazon Music. She listens to everything. And I mean everything. Anything from songs from the 60s to R&B in the 2000s and the soundtracks to musicals and Broadway plays. Her playlists reflect this range of music and most contain a variety of each. I pull up her playlist full of feel good songs like Summer by Calvin Harris and On Our Way by The Royal Concept.

Usually my go to is "oldies" and songs that are from the 60s to 80s. Liza however has expanded my music taste and I'm starting to enjoy songs from all varieties of music. Except for country. I don't do country. Never will do country.

The first song that comes up when I hit shuffle is "Rockstar," by A Great Big World, and as we drive

down the suburban roads and start to get on the high-
way that runs through the city and makes the drive to
her house quicker, the outside world fades to a blur.

Pulling up to her house I'm sure Liza looks a lot like I did when I first took her to the greenhouse. She doesn't usually bite her lip, that's my thing when I'm nervous, but right now she is. When she puts the car in park she abruptly turns in her seat to look at me. Her eyes are big and wide and she looks like a scared animal that could run off with any sudden moves. My eyebrows knit and I reach for her hand and rub my thumb over it to try and calm her down.

"Hey." My voice is softer than I've ever known it to be. "What's wrong?" I search her eyes wondering for a split second if she's having second thoughts about me meeting her family. But that doubt melts away when she gives me a small smile. She takes a deep breath before speaking.

"I want to prepare you for something before we go in and meet everybody. First off, my family's crazy and very energetic. I know that when we first met you thought that *I* was bad but they are *so* much worse." I'm sure I look crazy because my eyes are wide and my mouth is slightly open because she's right and I can't believe she knew that. "Also, my par–," Before she can finish the sentence or even the word I'm yanked from the car by these big strong arms that I'm sure are her fathers.

For a solid three seconds my body goes rigid underneath him as I panic but he doesn't even notice. His entire body has me up in the air bear hugging me and swinging me around like I'm not a buff 6'o girl made of pure muscle. As I recover and loosen up, he swings me around like I'm a rag doll. After putting me down her aunt, Arabella, pulls me into a lung crushing hug and kisses both my cheeks.

"Mr. Pennelli! It's so nice to meet Liza's father." Everyone got really quiet and the man I called Liza's father grew red in the face and shifted back and forth on his feet like a child. I sink into myself and swallow hard and stare at the ground. I don't know what I said that was wrong but I'm sorry I said it.

"We'll let you two talk." Arabella looks between Liza and I as she takes the man's arm and they make their way back towards the house. I run my tongue quickly across my lips to wet them and try to keep them from cracking. It's also a nervous habit I've picked up over the years. Liza leans against the car, folds her arms, and sighs.

Without even thinking I walk up to her and she opens her legs enough for me to stand between them. Her arms go around my neck and my hands lay on her waist. It's a move we've done only a handful of times but it feels more than natural to us. I kiss her forehead and stay there for a second before pulling back and looking at her.

"What did I say?" I'm looking down at my feet now because I don't want to see her disappointment. But she doesn't let me stay looking down because she takes one of her arms and nudges my head up.

"You didn't say anything." She pauses and looks like she's looking for the right words. Ironic and a bit scary since she's never had a problem searching for the right words before. "I was trying to explain this before my uncle pulled you from the car." Uncle? My eyebrows furrow and I start to open my mouth to ask but she interrupts me and doesn't let me finish. "Roughly four years ago I came out to my parents. I was a month into my freshman year of high school and there was this girl who showed me around the school and immediately I felt differently about her than I did any other guy I had talked to.

"I didn't understand these feelings so I went to the school's GSA club and learned about sexuality and everything involved in it. Once I finally came to terms with my own sexuality I decided to tell my parents." When she takes a second before continuing I absent-mindedly rub my hands up and down her sides. She pushes away from the car and moves out of my arms and stands in front of me swaying back and forth on her feet. I lean up against the car this time and shove my hands in my jacket pockets. It's early March so the weather goes back and forth trying to decide if it wants to try and be spring or blizzard and pull us back into a cold and dark winter. But that's just life in the Midwest apparently.

"I remember coming home from school that day nervous but excited to finally share this part of myself with my family. My mom was working from home that day. She's a fitness instructor and sometimes she teaches online classes in her decked out gym in the basement. When I came in she had just finished teaching a spin cycle class so she was in athletic pants and a tank top wiping sweat from her forehead and chugging water in the kitchen window. Like a perfect clock ticking without any problems, I hopped up on a barstool at the island and she came around, kissed the side of my head and started pouring me a glass of iced tea. While I was nervous I didn't think too much about it but I still wanted to just put it all out there so I did."

Her face looks sad and I'm worried about what she's gonna say next. "She was appalled. Started yelling at me in Italian. Next thing I knew she was calling my father, shouting at him to get home," Her voice starts to break.

When she looks up at me her eyes are watering and her jaw is clenched and she looks angry. Maybe not angry at her parents, maybe not angry at herself but with God and the universe itself. "She said, 'something's wrong with your daughter'. Not our daughter, I was no longer her daughter. She didn't elaborate more than that. Instead she hung up, looked me up and down, and then scoffed and stormed out of the kitchen. I didn't move for the entire time that it took for my dad to race home. Could've been hours, could've been minutes but I don't know because it felt like time was standing still or at the very least moving in slow motion.

"When he came in he was screaming and my mom was crying and I just sat there frozen. They spent hours debating what to do. From sending me to a camp to pretending the conversation never happened, they went through it all. Finally they decided that there wasn't anything they could do. When I heard that I felt relieved because I thought that they came around and didn't care and loved me anyways. But even though they decided they couldn't do anything they did agree they didn't have to put up with it." At this point she looks me dead in the eyes, tears slowly flowing down her face. "I was to be out of the house before dawn."

All of a sudden I felt something wet on my hands and it startled me at first because I didn't realize I had started crying too. I gently walk towards her and hold her tight as she buries her head in my shoulder. She sobs lightly and I stroke her hair and shush slightly. She lifts her head, clears her throat and starts talking again.

"I'm so, so lucky that Arabella was willing to bring me into her home and was so ready to accept me. She had always been my sweet escape from the strict life and rules my parents made for me. I sat outside the stoop of the house till 2:30 a.m before she made it. She ran out of the car and threw her arms around me and told me it would be ok while I broke down for the first time since coming out." She swallows and looks at me so seriously it scares me. "My point is Ryn, that we all have shadows we want to hide from the world. We all have dark pasts and things we wish to lock away from the eyes of everyone watching us."

And it's at this moment I feel like such an asshole because she's right. I walk around constantly acting like I've got the throne and only keys to the kingdom of pain and trauma but I don't. And here she is, feeling some of that pain, pain of her own and I've always had the wrong idea about her.

As I stand there and hold her though I start thinking about what she said, about shadows. Shadows. That's what Duke has regarding his brother. It's what Liza has with her parents, and it's what I have with my father. A shadow.

Once Liza had composed herself she put her hand in mine and we headed up towards the house. I was a little less nervous now and a little more protective. I know Liza said her aunt and uncle accepted her for who she is and loved her no matter what but I still have this feeling in the back of my mind now, knowing all that I know, that I want to protect her.

She can see me slip into hockey mode because she smacks my shoulder and squints at me. "Relax. I'm fine, they're fine. Don't get all dark and brooding on me now." I frown a little before dramatically rolling my shoulders back, shaking them out. That's the best I can do because as much as I try to unclench my jaw, that thing might as well be wired together. Arabella must have been watching us from the window because the door to the house was opened before Liza even had a chance to reach out to open it herself. There's something written across Arabella's face that I can't distinguish. At first glance it looks like pity and I tense at that because I've never been one to accept anyone's pity. But it's not pity. I know pity all too well and can spot it even in the best of actors' faces when they're trying to hide it. There's something different about this look though.

Apparently I'm daydreaming again because Liza clears her throat and nudges me, bringing me back to reality and I realize we've moved inside the house and Arabella had her hand extended out to mine to shake. Hesitantly I accept her hand and as we shake hands the smile on her face grows and suddenly she yanks me forward into another suffocating hug. I don't know what it is with the Pennelli's but their hugs are death grips and every single one of them seems to possess this trait. My face must have been turning red from lack of blood flow because Arabella suddenly releases me from her grip and Liza pats me on the back as I cough a small bit.

The big guy who I mistaked for Liza's father is in the living room with two of Liza's young cousins. Glancing into the room I can see him throwing his arms around in the air and poorly trying to stay in tune with the song the three of them are competing to on Just Dance. Based on what little knowledge I have just realized I actually have on Liza's family, I assume the two kids he is playing with are Arabella's youngest, Isaiah, 6, and Meena, 9. For a brief minute when Liza had talked about her family, she mentioned a girl she had to share a bathroom with. I think she said her name was Elliana?

"Ryn, if you want to go ahead and make yourself comfortable, I need Liza's help with something really quickly in the kitchen." Arabella threw me a bright smile, and turned towards the kitchen and Liza gave my hand a squeeze and small nod before turning to follow her aunt.

Slipping out of my Doc Martens and leaving them by the door, I pad over in my socks to the mantle that holds trophies, photos, and any other kind of decorative mementos that make a house a home. I don't think the man and the two kids playing in the living room have noticed my presence and I don't necessarily want to alert them to it either. I'd rather stand and observe this strange environment from a distance. Of all the times I've been to Liza's home I've never taken the time to actually look at the things in it. I've mostly just gone straight up to her room or to the bathroom.

Absentmindedly I run my hand over the mantle ledge where the pictures sit and I stop when I come across an older looking photo that has to be of Liza. Judging from the innocent look in her eyes that is somehow different from the one she still has today, and the braces lining her teeth in the eye-catching smile she's giving the camera, Liza must be 14-15 in this picture. I can't help but wonder if this was taken before she came out. And before her parents cast her aside. My jaw clenches at that thought and I wish more than anything I truly *did* have the keys to the kingdom for terrible parents.

From where I'm standing in the house I can see into both the living room, the kitchen, and the dining room, with the stairs right next to me. When I look into the kitchen I can see drawings and report cards pinned by magnets up on the fridge. Most of the drawings are a little hard to make out due to the distance and due to the amateur art skills of Liza's cousins. But the one I can see the best is your typical little kid drawing with a house and family members outside standing under a physically incorrect model of the sun. Each person looked uncharacteristically happy and maybe even a little naive.

There's a person that's clearly cut and pasted onto the picture, added to it after it was originally drawn. I'm guessing that's Liza, and the picture was drawn before she came to live with her aunt and uncle, meaning it's a really old drawing since she came here to live with them four years ago. Moving on towards some of the photos on the wall I see Arabella and the man who yanked me from the car smiling, both ear to ear, Arabella wearing a white dress and the man in a form fitting tuxedo. It must be their wedding photo. In the back of the photo, through the blurriness caused by distance, I can make out two figures, and a little one at their feet holding what looks like a bouquet. Liza. And her parents. All three at Arabella's wedding, celebrating love, and celebrating two people loving each other. What a joke.

A high pitched shriek shoots through the house and immediately I tense and search for danger but quickly see the source of the shrieking. Liza's younger cousin Isaiah is being chased around and tickled by the grown man. Suddenly a memory, one I can't quite tell if it's a good one or bad one enters my brain.

"You may be fast but you can't outrun the tickle monster Elleri!!" His raucous laughter filled the hallways as I raced through them and started down the stairs. A memory so vivid it's like I'm there, watching it in slow motion with a bright filter over it making it look softer and happier than it was originally. Or maybe it was always that happy to begin with. Maybe I'm just trying to pretend it wasn't. Because maybe it's easier to pretend even the good times were riddled with his poison.

I don't have long to dwell on that possibly headache inducing revelation because apparently my daydreaming body is in Isaiah's way and he runs right into me.

"Oof." Even though my breath escapes me in a sound, my body was unmoving from the impact. Pros of being a hockey player, I can take a hit. Isaiah however bounces off of me and lands butt first on the floor. Heat spreads across my neck and cheeks as the kid sits there gaping up at me. He's watching me with a weird expression that makes me squirm but thankfully his sister pulls him up and away before he can stare into my soul any longer.

Suddenly that man who was so unapologetically loud and confident, the same man that pulled me from the car, seemed so unsure of himself as he made his way across the room to stand in front of me. After clearing his throat and fiddling with his hands a little he finally looks up at me to speak, "I– uh, I'm sorry, about earlier. I didn't realize that Liza hadn't told you yet, and even if she had I shouldn't have just been so affectionate without knowing if you were ok with that sort of thing. A– Anyways I'm Liza's uncle, Nakoa." He thrusts one arm forward for me to shake, a small gesture of him trying to right what he did earlier. Part of me wonders if his not being Liza's real father is a sore spot. It would explain why he looked so dejected after I referred to him as such. And once again that feeling that always follows me, the one that says I'm an asshole and makes things worse, is nagging at me. I shoved what may possibly be this man's biggest insecurity right back into his face. After the man, Nakoa, clears his throat again, I realize that I've just been standing there, no doubt, staring at him while he waits with his hand out, every second I don't take it becoming more and more awkward.

"Ryn." Finally Nakoa releases the breath he apparently has been holding and uses this opportunity to transition into introducing his kids and talking more about his family.

"The little boy that just ran into you over there is Isaiah, mine and Arabella's youngest, and then the girl is one of his big sisters, Meena." When he looks back at me he looks like his family's hung the moon and stars just for him. He grimaced a little though before continuing. "Our oldest, Elliana, she's at her friend's house right now. Not that she didn't want to meet you," he rushed to include that last part.

"It's ok Nakoa we can all be honest and acknowledge that Elliana is a bit.." Arabella trailed off, pursing her lips and looking up to the ceiling like she was searching for the right word to describe her eldest daughter, only having made the stop from the kitchen to the dining room in order to put the corn casserole she made out on the table. Although she hadn't quite made it there, instead being caught in Nakoa and I's conversation. "Hmm, eccentric?" She lifts a shoulder and raises her eyebrows and Nakoa chuckles with a small shake of his head.

I'd never met Elliana but Liza was convinced that the two of us put together might end up saving the world or destroying it. She said it while laughing but I still had taken it the wrong way and I got all defensive and mopey and ended up leaving her house early that night.

"Elliana has a 'take no prisoners' attitude. She can be a lot to people who haven't met her." Nakoa adds.

"But there's nothing wrong with being a lot. In

fact I think the world needs people who are willing to be unapologetically themselves and willing to push against the direction of the tide." Arabella has since abandoned the casserole on the table and is mindlessly twisting her wedding ring around her finger. A habit I'm guessing she's had for a while judging based on the way she easily twists it back and forth. All three of us stood there in an awkward silence. We all know that that comment was also aimed at me but no one's brave enough to admit it. As Arabella and Nakoa stare at each other they seem to have an entire conversation that felt like three minutes but in actuality was probably only fifteen seconds. Arabella then politely excuses herself back towards the kitchen and I awkwardly shuffle away from Nakoa and make up some mumbled excuse under my breath.

I slip down the hallway away from the family and all the noise and chaos in the living room and kitchen, taking this opportunity to check my phone to see if I have any texts from my mom or Daniel.

No dice. I don't know why but I have this uneasy feeling in my stomach that one or both of them will call or text needing me with something important at home.

While I don't have anything waiting from them, I do have a string of texts from Duke, Spitz, and then a separate chat where they've thrown me into their friend group chat.

Your Grace: [Link to kpdougal26 TikTok]

Your Grace: Is it just me or does this totally look like Spam?

Your Grace: Stupid autocorrect, Spitz not Spam.

Your Grace: Should we slip the announcer a note to change his name in Friday's game to Spam? Or is that too mean?

Your Grace: I'm gonna call him Spam and see what his reaction is

Saliva: DID YOU TELL DUKE TO CALL ME SPAM?!?

Saliva: He just texted me and told me you wanted to tell the announcer to call me Spam on Friday's game!!

Saliva: Not cool Ryn, not cool. *fake sniffs and over dramatic voice* I tHoUgHt We wErE fRiEnDs

Saliva: No but seriously please don't do that

Saliva: Update, Duke fessed up that it was his idea, I was gonna threaten to put itching powder in your helmet before the game but you scare the living shit out of me so I didn't even want to bring it up, but now that I know it's Duke do you want to help me?

Saliva: Where the hell does one even find itching powder?

Saliva: Like that can't just be something they sell at Walmart or Target

Saliva: Right?

Saliva: Ok I just ordered some from Amazon

Saliva: Thank you mom for Prime 2-Day shipping

Your Grace: Should I be worried that Spitz hasn't tex-

ted me back in 5 minutes??
You've been added to a new group chat
Unknown Number: *If youre gonna recite poetry to us you could at least give us enough of a head start to shoot ourselves before*

Ah the loving sarcasm of Natalie completely tired of Spitz's bullshit.

New Contact Created
Unknown Number: *oh c'mon nat, he doesn't do it that often*
Russian Spy: *You dont live with him I hit a squirrel the other day while driving and he made me pull over so he could conduct the beginnings of a squirrel shiva complete with Robert Frost poems.*
Russian Spy: *And then for the rest of the week he continued to conduct the shiva properly throughout the week He stole all my candles and when I pointed out that this squirrel did not meet any of the shiva connections that require one to hold a shiva he told me that it didnt matter and that he was mourning the squirrel because even if they werent related the squirrels family wouldnt know how to properly mourn and he wanted to honor the little squirrel since I had "so rudely ended his poor little life"*
Camouflage Man: *Amber I gtta agree w Nat on this 1.*
New Contact Created
Brown Tree Liquid: *stay out of this hunter, no one asked you*

Plane: Anybody else suddenly craving Wingstop

Clifford the Big Red Dog: *Jet my man I like how you think*

Clifford the Big Red Dog: *Anyonr who wants picked up let me know*

Clifford the Big Red Dog: *Anyone**

Unknown Number: *FIELD TRIP*

Your Grace: *Sloane what are you talking about you're working*

New Contact Created

Sloane: *I am but it's super slow here and I don't think the Boss Man would care too much if I closed up shop early.*

Unknown Number: *Does he even know you call him "Boss Man"? Not gonna lie I'm a little scared of that guy*

Camouflage Man: *thts bcuz ur a wuss Hannah*

New Contact Created

Hannah Banana: *Shut up Hunter no one was talking to you*

Clifford the Big Red Dog: *Ok so that's Sloane, Jet.....*

Russian Spy: *Im down*

Your Grace: *Wait Nat you're going?*

Russian Spy: *I mean yea I like wings*

Your Grace: *I'm in too I guess*

Camouflage Man: *aw Duke's a lttle btch bby*

Your Grace: *Stfu Hunter, I mean it*

Camouflage Man: *but y I'm hving so much fun*

Saliva: *I hate this group chat*

Brown Tree Liquid: *awww, we love you too spitz*

Just as I'm about to respond to any one of the many texts the idiots I call friends have sent me, a small higher pitched voice startles me and steals my attention away.

"Whatcha doing?" Meena's standing a few feet away from me and looking at me with big brown eyes filled with curiosity and a hint of suspicion.

"Oh uh–" Before I can even finish she cuts me off by speaking again.

"Why are your jeans ripped?" She tilts her head and stares at my holey jeans and suddenly I have the urge to cover my exposed skin under her tiny scrutinizing gaze. Once again before I even have the chance to answer she's plaguing me with another question. "Why are you tall like a man?" This causes me to smirk involuntarily even as I'm still stiff as a board. My entire life I've always been tall but no one's ever had the courage to point it out to me in such a blunt and demanding way.

I lean towards her just a little bit and look around conspiratorially. "I'm actually a giant taking on a human form, but there's only so much I'm able to shrink down," I whisper to her. While I've never been good at talking to children, even when I was one, I think that was among the list of right things I could've said because her eyes lit up as soon as I said it and now she's bouncing on her heels a little.

She opens her mouth to possibly start hammering me with more questions but is interrupted by an angel among us. Liza stumbles into the hall where Meena and I have been standing and just like Meena, Liza's eyes brighten when they land on mine and she holds my gaze for a second before she realizes that Meena is standing beside me looking between us with a knowing look a child her age should not be able to wield.

"There you guys are! Lunch is ready. We've been looking for you." She reaches out her hand to Meena and in return Meena bounces down the hall towards her and takes it. Then as she starts to turn around she looks back at me with so much light in her eyes and for a second I'm convinced there might even be a bit of glitter in them too. At this time Meena chooses to pull Liza down to her level and whispers something in her ear. Suddenly Liza's mouth falls open and then she's using her other hand to stifle her laughter as she leads Meena out of the room, who is grinning widely at me.

I'm not sure what she said, but she definitely was talking about me. And I'm weirdly a little terrified.

"Hey what'd she say!" I start briskly following after them and they start running towards the dining room giggling and laughing. "Guys!"

It's definitely more of a brunch considering the time but the food that Arabella prepared is anything but. The table is filled with all kinds of food and my mouth waters just looking at it. As I mentioned earlier there's a corn casserole, but also on the table are mini chicken pot pies, some type of flatbread with what looks like hummus, tomatoes, and some other ingredient I can't name. An herb of some type. I can tell that much from where I'm standing. There's a salad –or at least I think it's a salad– with rice, asparagus, peas, and some other things I can't distinguish. A loaf of freshly cut banana walnut bread is sitting next to the salad and it looks so fluffy and good my insides melt a little. And to top it all off with a main source of protein, is chicken laid out on a sheet pan with lemon and I think parsley. I'm sure there's a much fancier, much more descriptive title for the dish but I'm just going off of what I can see.

Nakoa's already sat at the table as well as Isaiah, Meena joining her brother and taking her seat beside him. Arabella must realize I'm standing awkwardly because as she starts bringing a pitcher of water to the table to add to the pitcher of lemonade, she motions for me to follow her, nodding her head towards a seat that places me between Liza and herself at one of the head ends of the table.

I've got my fork in hand about to dig into the chicken pot pie next to my plate when Liza takes the fork out of my hand and places her's in it instead. I look down at our intertwined hands puzzled and begin to open my mouth to complain that I'm hungry and that's my eating hand when Arabella takes the other one that was in a fist on the table. Before she could actually intertwine our hands together she first had to use both of hers to pry my fingers open while I still looked around glaringly trying to figure out what the fuck kind of cult shit was going on. Then Meena started speaking and *oh*.

They're praying.

I'd almost forgotten that Liza's family is Catholic and fairly devoted at that. They aren't like crazy dedicated and live, sleep, breathe the Catholic Church, but they do go to Sunday Mass, not every week, but pretty regularly. Other than that they don't really agree with a lot of the rules the Catholic Church preaches, like no sex before marriage, men are providers for their family, divorce means you go to hell, and my personal favorite, that gay people were sent from hell to tempt and bring the world into chaos.

Ok, let me correct that. At one point I'd had this conversation with Liza before, where I was showing my immense skepticism in the faith and Liza corrected me and told me that nowadays many people in the Catholic Church are accepting of gay people and of things that were typically seen as taboo because the newest Pope has declared it ok. Why Catholics need a man in white robes and a church mansion for a house to tell them it's ok to treat *everyone* with love and kindness is beyond me but to each their own.

As for me, I'm not a big fan or believer in whatever higher power you may think exists. I mean how could I be when they let the bad things that happened to me, and especially to my saint of a mother, happen and not only that but not do anything to stop it. And I don't want to hear crap about the higher power not being able to intervene or whatever else you wanna say, but the fact is my mom didn't deserve it, and even on my worse day if you wanna say that I maybe deserved a little of it, she never did. And yet here I am in Forthsworth, Minnesota, hating a lousy drunk excuse for a father.

I'm brought back to the table when Liza gently tugs her hand from mine, the prayer apparently over and everyone around me begins to dig into the food.

And just like that I'm not hungry anymore, a bitter

taste taking up residence in my mouth. Unfortunately for me and the ball of nerves clenching in my stomach, this is the first time I'm meeting Liza's parents –or aunt and uncle– and I want to make a good impression. So instead of gorging myself on the once delicious smelling food, I absentmindedly push my food around and force down some of the pot pie and pick apart a piece of bread that turns into a pile of crumbs appearing to be the remains of a slice of bread now in my stomach.

An hour later I'm standing at the sink in the kitchen washing plates and dishes while Liza sits on the countertop next to me drying them meticulously and stacking them in corresponding piles.

"I know that look." When I glance over at Liza she's stacking the dishes with such an intensity in her eyes I can't help but look away.

"I don't know what you mean." This earns me a sigh and suddenly Liza turns sharply to face me, her hand coming down roughly on the counter rattling the plates next to her hand.

"Cut the bullshit Elleri." First name, wow, I must really be in trouble. "You barely touched your food and to be honest you were kind of rude to people who really matter to me. I know you struggle with family matters and what happened with your dad but I asked you for one day." All I can do while she's berating me is stand there and stare, never breaking eye contact with her for one second. At this next part her voice softens and she starts to tentatively step towards me. "You've been doing so good lately." She reaches out and starts running her arms up and down mine. "Don't close up on me now."

And before I can stop myself I yank myself away and put distance between us. Instantly regretting my actions but unable to set aside my pride I stay away. "Liza, not all of my problems revolve around my father." But she knows that's a lie. My voice is venomous and rising slightly in volume and not of my own volition as I continue to ruin my own life, "Stop trying to fix me. I'm not your NHS project. You wanted me to come here today. Well guess what, I did. If you don't like what I had to give then that's on you because this is me. Take a good look. I'm a moody asshole and I lash out. You wanted this."

Suddenly I'm thrown into a memory I've long since buried and tried to erase. It's almost like I'm there.

"What do you want from me Katherine! You knew what you were signing on for when you married me! Flaws and all. You don't get to criticize me or judge me." As he shouts across the kitchen, slamming cabinets and kicking the counters. I'm hiding in the pantry, watching their fight unfold in front of my seven year old eyes, peaking through the slot between the barely cracked door. When he had come home my mom hissed at me to hide somewhere. I didn't understand why.

"Don't try to turn this around on me Jack. I didn't marry a DRUNK."

Crack.

Glass breaking and falling to the floor. Followed by a gasp. One I'm not sure if it came from me or my mother.

"Take a good, hard, long look, Kate." Slowly, menacingly, he starts closing the distance to my mom, bleeding on the floor from where the bottle he threw made contact with her temple. And then in a voice that haunts me to this day, "You wanted this."

Before anyone can say anything, I jerk towards the sink and violently hurl anything I might've eaten at lunch up and onto the plates that needed cleaning anyways.

"Oh my god Ryn!" Liza's hands fly up to her mouth and then quickly find their way to my hair, holding it up as I vomit into my girlfriend's kitchen sink.

And to make matters worse, Arabella and Nakoa came running into the kitchen when they inevitably heard my retching from the other room.

"Liza what's goin– Oh my god! You poor thing, are you not feeling well?" Arabella starts filling a glass of water from the brita and comes over to stand on my other side, absentmindedly rubbing her free hand up and down my back.

All of it is too much and I can't take their help.

"Everybody back off!" Arabella's hand raises from my back, and Liza's freeze and tense from where they were holding my hair. "Please." But even I know that please is a little too late. I shrug away from everyone, wiping my disgusting mouth on my sleeve. Keeping my head down I stomp down the hallway and when I make it to the door I shove my feet into my boots and start for the door as Liza shouts after me and starts making her way down the hallway to stop me.

"Ryn wait!"

"Liza," I swallow, "please, I'm fine, I just– I just need to be alone." That last word sounded dangerously close to a sob and I know I need to leave now before I lose it and then have the urge to walk in front of a car.

Thankfully she doesn't say anything or move to stop me. She just stands there and stares at me, her eyes darting back and forth between mine and I can feel her analyzing me. I quickly look away and take a deep swallow. And with one final quick look back at her stone cold expression, I yank open the door and fly down the steps and sidewalk, running out into the street.

11:45 A.M

Walking down random streets of Forthsworth, Minnesota is so not how I saw this day going.

"How exactly did this happen?" The doctor stitching up my mother's forehead looks skeptical as my dad holds her hand and soothes her every time she cringes from the pain.

"I was out getting groceries and when I was making a trip inside, my foot must've snagged a corner of the pavement wrong and I tripped. Since my hands were full with groceries I had nothing to break my fall. I turned my head as I hit the ground. My husband and daughter were coming out to help bring in what was left and they found me on the ground." God he was a good actor. At this moment he took the opportunity to give a small frown and reached up to stroke my mother's hair.

"That's when we left the groceries in the driveway and immediately came here." He so helpfully adds. Meanwhile I just sit on a chair towards the corner of the room. I'm not looking at anyone or anything.

I know I should've said something. Should've called them out on their lie. Part of me wishes I did but my mom has reassured me time and time again that our life would've gotten a whole lot worse if I had. I don't know how she can say that. Because it did get worse. For her especially.

They gave her a chance to tell them the truth. Some sort of hospital protocol. The doctor sent him out of the room and asked her again, told her it was a safe space and that they could help her, us, if we needed it. They looked her straight in the eyes and asked her point blank, *"Did he do this?"*. And she lied.

A car horn honks and suddenly I realize I'm standing still in the middle of a very busy street almost certainly flirting with death. "Fuck." I dive out of the way and scramble to my feet and continue to briskly walk through the streets of this city. I'm about to walk past another store when I recognize the green and orange glow from the neon sign. A 7-Eleven. My feet are carrying me in the doors with a mind of their own.

Even if it's hundreds of miles away from where I grew up, from where I used to call home, this gas station brings me a little peace of mind. When I was little my mom and I used to come to the 7-Eleven down the street from our house and get slushies almost every day after school. We started doing it when I started kin-dergarten. I cried so much that day. Both my mom and my dad dropped me off at school. I remember cling-ing to my dad's leg and begging him to take me with him to work. My mom got down on the ground and hunched to be eye level with me. She promised me that if I went into the school and I stayed for as long as I could, (it had to be longer than two hours), then after school she and I would go to the 7-Eleven on our way home from the school and get slushies. She even promised me that I could get the jumbo size.

Lord knows that was a sacrifice and selfish promise on her part. A five year old with that much sugar. She was signing herself up for hell. But she did it anyway. All so that I wouldn't be scared. Somehow, probably because she's a mother, she knew that after two hours, and really probably after the first forty-five minutes, I would be wrapped up in the activities of the day and would be surrounded by so many different kids with my energy, that I'd forget why I was scared in the first place. And she was right.

Suddenly I feel a tap on my shoulder and I'm thrown into fight or flight mode. I turn around and before I even know what's happening or register who's tried to get my attention I'm punching. I don't even know who but it felt right in the moment. When I come back to reality I realize I've just decked an old man.

Everything and everyone in the room comes to a screeching and deafening halt. The old man is on the floor moaning and holding his jaw, and there are random standerbys crouching down to attend to him. I look around and see a mom holding her child close to her while the kid buries her face in her mom's clothes. I see a couple of teenagers pull out their phones and start recording. The cashier is huddled by the phone with it up to her ear, her hand cupped around the mouth piece to shield what she's saying. A few guys who set down their beer and snacks are starting to slowly approach me.

My head is spinning and the thudding accompanying it is making matters worse. I'm shaking my head and my hands are slowly going up in the air. I know I should just let them sit me somewhere and let the police, who I assume the cashier has called, come deal with my mess. But instead I notice an aisle with no one in it and before I can stop myself, I run.

It's all happening in slow motion. I leap over the man on the floor and start barreling towards the door. It takes all of two seconds for the guys trying to corner me to start chasing after me. I, unlike them, have a relatively direct path to the exit. As I'm tearing down the aisle I'm knocking things off the shelves blocking anyone from easily following behind me. I don't even know why I'm doing it. Because I'm young, in shape, and terrified as hell I make it out the doors and am barreling across the street before the guys can get me. All I can hear are the muted sounds of nearby police sirens, shouting from pedestrians I've continuously bumped into and knocked aside. I'm dodging in and out of traffic and just narrowly avoid getting hit by a car. The honking and everything else is overwhelming. I don't know where or why I'm running but I keep running down the street. At this point I think I've run two blocks from the store and am about to start screaming from everything swirling in my mind, when I hear the shouting. A large booming voice yelling at me to stop moving. I freeze. I know it's not him. Realistically it couldn't be him.

"Elleri Ryn, stop crying!" My barbie slams into the wall and I jump. "Get your ass upstairs now. I said it was bedtime and I'm not arguing." His hands are digging into my tiny arm as he drags me up the stairs while I wail and cry.

"Ma'am freeze! Put your hands in the air and slowly turn towards me." Swallowing and with shaky hands my body listens. I don't know when I started crying but I can taste the salty tears that have stained my face. I stand there in the middle of the street, surrounded by those guys, three cops and their cars. On the sidewalks are nosy onlookers all with phones recording like I'm some sort of freak show. And I guess I am. Everything's blurry, but I can make out the shapes of two of the officer's coming closer. One with their gun trained on me and the other removing handcuffs from their belt. My hands are yanked out of the air and I can feel the cold steel from the cuffs find their way around my wrists.

Click, click.

Click.

I remember the morning after I first witnessed one of their big fights. We had gotten back from the hospital early in the morning. As in roughly 2:30 in the morning. I don't remember when I fell asleep, or really when we left the hospital. But I remember slipping in and out of sleep while he carried me inside the house and up to my room. What's ironic, and a feeling I so wish I could erase, I felt safe in his arms. With his strong arms cradling my small body, I felt like nothing could or would ever hurt me. Sometimes I spend so long trying to change how I felt in the memory. Like somehow I might be able to rewrite the scene and how it's stored in my mind.

My eighth birthday was about two months after

that. And for all those two months everything seemed normal. I didn't hear or see them fight anymore. Life seemed to be back to normal, like maybe that night had been a fluke.

Noises from the bustling police station where I'm sitting on a cold bench behind iron bars next to a round small man wearing baggy and dirt covered clothes fill my ears. Over in the corner, acting like she's so tough is an almost 30 year old wearing clothes so inappropriately sized for her age and chewing gum like an obnoxious 16 year old high school mean girl.

"Are you interested in buying a percentage of an energy supplement company? If you buy fifteen percent, all you have to do to double your profits is get five friends or family," The small, sour smelling man adds with a raise of his eyebrow, "Or someone you meet in a holding cell, eh eh." He starts jabbing me with his elbow like he's said something so clever. I don't think I've ever stared at someone with such a dead expression behind my eyes.

Just then an officer watching the cell interjects, "Aye! Lionel." She snaps in his direction to get his attention. "Stop it with the pyramid scheme, it's getting old." After unlocking the cell and taking him roughly by the arm, the officer escorts "Lionel" out of the cell and out of my view, but not before I hear a little snippet of their conversation. "You know the drill, one phone call, is it the same number as the last four times or are you gonna surprise me and try something new today?"

Four times? Guess Lionel's a regular around here.

Unlike Lionel, I have kept my mouth shut. I don't know much about the law but what I do know is that you aren't supposed to say anything without a lawyer. Or in my case you learn not to say anything because someone has a short fuse and who knows whether or not your scraped knee or the bug you found outside are enough to set it off.

"Elleri Bradford?" A commanding voice coming from somewhere to my right asks for me. I look up and see one of the police officers who was there for my arrest. "She's here."

6:17 P.M

After posting my bail and getting processed and told my court date I'm finally out of that dark and depressing hell hole.

The only thing lighting up the streets on the way home from Mia, my babysitter's house, is the occasional streetlight. It's way past my bedtime and I had fallen asleep at Mia's and was rudely woken up for the second time that night. Only this time it was to go back home to my own bed. My mom came rushing into my room and lifted me out of my bed. I didn't know what was going on. I was groggy and tired but she just kept whispering that everything was ok. That I was ok, that we were ok, that everything was ok. She said that word so much that night it started to lose its meaning. Now I was on my way back home, the streetlights and motion of the car that would normally lull me to sleep having no power over me whatsoever. My ten year old brain is awake and alert, listening to my parents' hushed voices as they argue in the front seats.

"Jack, I can't keep doing this." My mom sniffles and begs.

"I know honey." My dad reaches across the center console and puts his hand on my mom's cheek, stroking his thumb along her skin. "This is the last time. I'm getting clean. I know how this is hurting you, and hurting Elleri. And I'm sorry about the ticket. I'll work overtime to pay it off."

"How could you be so stupid?" She sighs before she continues, "Drinking and driving. You could've killed yourself. What then? You just leave Ellie and me? You leave her without a father?" My mom just barely glances over at him when she delivers that punch. Even back then I knew it hit. It was subtle but his entire posture changed, and he was quiet the rest of the way home.

Silence has never scared me. In fact silence has been my fortress of solitude for so many years now. But right now, my head is throbbing, and the silence is death gripping my throat while it plays through my memories. While it shows me the comparisons.

I have anger issues.

I punch and kick my way out and through things.

I use violence whenever I'm scared or angry or hurt or really any emotion I don't know how to deal with that's heavy.

I got arrested.

I'm his carbon copy.

"Even if you take her out of this house and you run half-way across the world she's still gonna end up just like her dear old dad!" He shouts at my mom and I, as we take very few belongings out the door with us, venom lacing his words. "You hear that Elleri? You are just like me. Always have been, always will be." My mom tries to shuffle me out the door, both of us grabbing what we can and shoving it into our bags. She's trying to talk over him but his voice has always carried through these walls. "Don't think you can run away from that. If I'm a screw up, so are you. If I'm a drunk, so are you. You can spend your whole life running but you'll never be fast enough to outrun that truth. You are exactly like me, a fucked up, miserable bastard who's only ever gonna hurt people in life." And with that last remark, he comes right up in my face, my eyes wide and my mouth slightly open in disbelief.

And for the first time he does what he never dared do before. He slaps me across the face. Hard. My mouth is open, my cheek stinging but no tears come to my eyes. None of this feels real. Apparently my reaction isn't good enough for him because he kicks me in my shin, hard, hard enough to send me to the ground. I can hear my mom yelling at him to stop but she's powerless to him. He yanks my head back by my hair and forces me to look up at him. And when I do he spits on me and punches me in the face. He shoves me to the ground and straightens back up. His finale ringing in my ears when he speaks, "And don't you dare EVER forget it." And with one last blow he kicks me again, this time in my stomach.

And how could I. I've become everything he said I would. Absent-mindedly I reach up and stroke the cheek he slapped just barely two years ago. I know I need to break the silence but I'm not entirely sure how. My tongue feels like it's made of lead and any sounds I make feel foreign and sluggish. I'm pretty sure I spend the next three minutes willing myself to speak before I actually do. "I'm sorry you had to pick me up." All she does is make a small sound, somewhere between a grunt and a murmur. "I– I didn't know who else to call." When I look at her she just looks tired.

"How about your parents?" I don't know why I called the only person who has ever actually intimidated me and astounded me at the same time. But to be honest, as much as I try not to think about Daniel being related to me now through marriage, and the family that comes with it, if anyone deserved to be called my grandmother it's her. "You going to tell me what happened or are we going to sit in silence till you decide to call your mother, hm?"

"Wait. I thought you'd already told her? And aren't you taking me home?" My head is pounding from the massive amount of chaos that has taken place today and what she's saying doesn't make sense.

"Why would I take you home? You called me because you clearly weren't ready to deal. I'm not going to rat you out and force you to do something you aren't ready to do. That's not my style. I really thought you would've known that by now." She mutters that last part as she flips the turn signal up and turns down the street, going the opposite direction of my house. After a beat of silence she continues. "I don't know what exactly happened this afternoon, and while I know you don't think anyone knows you, I know you well enough to know that you probably don't want to talk about any of this."

"I don't–"

"Bup-bup-bup. I wasn't finished." She cuts me off, waving her finger in the air between us. "I also know that this has something to do with your father." My eyebrows knit together and she just laughs. "I was never talking about the game." After she says that I sit there trying to figure out what the hell she's talking about. What game she's referring to and how the hell it has anything to do with my father as well as how the hell she knows anything about him.

"You don't know what you're talking about." My voice is low and quiet, almost nonexistent when I speak.

"That's bullshit and you know it." Her accent comes out a little thicker than normal then. But still I don't answer her and continue to stare straight ahead trying to lose myself in the way the road moves. "Ok. You wanna play this game? Fine, I'll bite. Your father, Jack Knox, is ruling your life without even being in it." My jaw clenches and I can feel my body heating up from anger at hearing his name.

"Your father, Jack Knox, was abusive. Not only physically, but emotionally, and mentally. And not only to your mother, but to you too." My knee starts nervously bouncing as she continues to torture me in this prison on wheels. "Jack Knox, understandably, did a number on you. This man who was supposed to love you and support you unconditionally and never let anything or anyone hurt you, took it upon himself to be that very thing. All of that alone is unfair and cruel. And you have every right to be as upset about it as you want to be. And you have every right to deal with it in the ways that you choose to deal with it. But you have to deal with it in ways that are healthy, and you have to deal with it, period." She looks over at me, eyes wide and eyebrows raised when she finishes.

"Now you don't have to talk to me, but you need to talk to someone. Your mom mentioned that you've been skipping your appointments with that doctor lady you're supposed to be seeing. What's up with that?"

Fuck. I knew Dr. Shaw would let my mom know I wasn't going to the appointments but when she didn't say anything to me the first time I missed, I thought she would drop it and not press me on it.

Because I'm a landmine that might blow up. I let my anger and times that I've lashed out recently act as a barrier between me and her. Inadvertently, I let her think she has to walk on eggshells around me or else I'll explode.

Just like he did.

And suddenly I feel sick all over again.

"Pull over."

"What? I'm not letting you out of this car no matter how angry or how much you want to walk awa–"

"I said pull over." My answer comes out more urgently this time and I think she senses something is wrong because she does. The car is barely stopped before I fling the door open and dry heave onto the pavement. The only thing coming up is a little bit of stomach acid, seeing as how I've already emptied my stomach once today and haven't eaten since. Maria Torres is a saint of a woman because she doesn't say anything, just unbuckles her seatbelt, gets out of the car and comes around to my side where I'm bent over out of the car and crouches beside me, pulling my hair back and out of my face in case anything does come up. She uses her other hand to rub soothing circles around my back and starts humming a tune I don't recognize.

About eight minutes later we're back on the road again and my tongue starts making words and breaking the silence between us before I realize what it's doing. "What were you humming?"

I can tell she hadn't been fully present in the car with me because her response was quiet and delayed, "Hm?" Her eyebrows knit together as she registers what I asked her just now. "Oh, it was a song my mother used to sing or hum to me whenever I was feeling any emotion other than joy. If I was sad, angry, or feeling ill. Anything. It's Colombian." She pauses as she considers her next thought. "The translation doesn't even carry half its beauty in English."

For the first time when I look at her I don't see the strong and independent woman who commands a wild household without saying a single word. Instead I see a broken woman. A child reminiscing on a life long left behind.

"Do you miss it?" My words are quiet and soft as they leave my mouth. I stay staring at her, waiting for her answer.

"Hm? Do I miss what?" Her tone matches mine, almost like she's still not fully in the conversation.

"Colombia. The life you lived there."

Because she doesn't have the radio on, the car is silent after I ask and I begin to rethink whether or not it was a good idea to ask her this. I'm perfectly fine letting the conversation die awkwardly but to my surprise she answers me. "Of course I miss it." There's a certain melancholy to her voice now. "It was and will always be my home and a part of who I am. Something like that doesn't just go away." She pauses again before continuing, as if she's thinking really hard and carefully about what she's going to say, and once again for the first time I find myself wondering whether or not she still struggles speaking English. "It's a beautiful country. Of course it has its problems, but no one and no place in this world is free of that."

"Do you ever feel out of place?" I begin to chew on

my lip. Honesty tends to make me fidgety. "Like maybe you're just standing still in the middle of a crowded room while everyone moves around you. Almost like they're moving at a normal speed but everytime you try to reach out and get someone's attention you're moving in slow motion." I glance quickly at her out of the side of my eye to gauge her expression. I see her grimace and her skin tightens around her eyes and I assume her eyebrows are pinched. Swallowing, I go back to chewing.

And then out of the corner of my eye I can see a slow grin spread across her face. "Yea, something like that."

"I had a panic attack." Silence. "Well, I– I think I had a panic attack." I swallow back the excessive amount of saliva building in my mouth, "It started when I was at Liza's. I kept having flashbacks of him. Of being a little girl." I'm not looking at her but I can feel her eyes on me for a moment before she turns back to the road. "Some of them were good, but they turned sour pretty quickly. Like they always do." The entire car is shaking from my leg bouncing up and down but she doesn't tell me to stop. "I did what I always do and closed myself off and became quiet and reserved and Liza called me out on it. So in true Ryn fashion, I lashed out." I sit there for a few seconds, trying to organize my thoughts and prepare myself for the words I'm about to say out loud.

"What I said is what set the panic attack off." Deep breaths Ryn, deep breaths. "As soon as the words left my mouth I had a flashback that I think I tried so hard to forget. My mom and dad were having a fight. It was the first one I saw between them. I used the same exact words he did in his reasoning as to why he was being terrible. He tried to turn *his* issues and mistakes on her and I said *the same damn thing.*" My voice breaks at the very end of the sentence. I can feel and then taste the tears that started slowly falling down my face. I quickly wipe them away because I don't want her to see me cry, which is honestly a stupid thought considering she just saw me vomit on the side of the road.

"Oh mijita." She sighs and I hate the tone of her voice.

"Don't." I sniff so hard the pressure makes my head spin. "Please." It comes out much more desperate than I'd like it to. "Don't pity me."

"I'm not pitying you. There's a difference between pitying someone and genuinely caring about the way they feel. And right now it's clear that you feel like a piece of shit." My head whips towards her, my mouth slightly agape and eyes wide in shock.

She laughs when she sees my face. "What? You never heard a swear word before?"

I try to fix my expression before I answer. "I started vomiting. Almost like my stomach was trying to expel the bad thoughts in my brain through my stomach." I can taste the bitter stomach acid on my tongue as I remember spilling my guts into Liza's sink and then trying again just a few minutes ago. "After I was done I just couldn't stand there while they all looked at me.

So I ran. Liza tried to follow me but I asked her not to. Practically begged her not to." My stomach is turning as I remember the look on Liza's face as I closed myself off and walked out the door. There was something in her expression that changed. I could see the walls going up behind her eyes. I could see their focus change from deep into mine, to something far off in the distance.

"I hurt her." The tears in my eyes build so much they blur my vision. There's a pain in my chest that feels like I might be having a heart attack. But if I am, what the hell, it'd just simultaneously be my karma and my savior in all of this.

Maria is silent for a long time before she speaks again, long enough that when she does it's as we're pulling into the long driveway of her home. She puts the car in park and sighs deeply before turning her entire upper body to face me. "You did a bad thing, mijita. That doesn't make you a bad person."

And with that she shuts the car off, unbuckles her seat belt, and gets out of the car to go inside. And I just sit here looking at the empty space where she was sitting and finally break down sobbing.

6:24 PM

"I was starting to think you were never coming inside." When I walk into the kitchen of the massive house, Maria is standing at the island stirring a spoon around in a mug. The metal of the spoon clinks against the ceramic.

I nod towards her referencing the drink. "Coffee?" She makes a clicking noise with her tongue before responding.

"It's tea. You don't make someone coffee to comfort them." After she takes the spoon out of the mug she walks over to the table where I've sat down and places the mug down in front of me.

I raise my eyebrows and look back and forth between the mug and her. She just rolls her eyes and repeats.

"It's tea," then adds, "drink it."

Reluctantly I pick up the cup and sip the hot liquid. I've never been a tea person and I'm still not but to be honest she scares me enough to make me drink it even if I don't want to. And I really don't want to.

"Are you ready to talk about it more?" I audibly groan when she asks because I thought that I'd done enough sharing for tonight. Or maybe even for the whole weekend. God, she might be worse than Dr. Shaw. I just glare at her over the edge of the mug of tea that I didn't realize I was still sipping

She calls my bluff and crosses her arms and her mouth sets in a small frown. I feel like a puppy who did something bad and is being reprimanded, my tail between my legs.

So I spilled. I told her everything that happened leading up to when I puked in the car on the way home.

And then I told her some more. Like how everyday I feel like a piece of me slips away and is replaced by him. About my job at the greenhouse and how I've kept it a secret from mom and Daniel. About the self hate, and the nightmares where I wake up drenched in sweat, about all of the guys I've ever beat up, about my first girlfriend and how it ended, about my fear of disappointing my mother. I tell her about how sometimes I just wish that one day I would actually pick on someone stronger than me, someone who would fight back and hurt me as much as I hurt everyone in my life around me.

I don't know how long I sat there, speaking more then, than I have ever spoken in my entire life. But when I finally finished it was dark outside.

Somehow when she speaks next her lips don't move and the sound comes from somewhere behind me.

"Ellie?"

Mom?

"What the hell? You said you didn't call her?" My eyes are wide as I push away from the table and stand up.

"I didn't call her."

"She didn't call me."

"Then how the hell is she here?"

"Ellie, please just sit back down." My mom's eyes are pleading with me. Something unmoving in her expression. I don't sit down though. Instead I move and stand, leaning against the wall, crossing my arms defensively.

"How'd you know where I was?"

"I texted her." Of course they both collectively decide to be smart asses. I scoff and roll my eyes. Reading my mind, Maria oh so helpfully points out, "Hey you asked if I'd called her, and I didn't. And I said I wouldn't call her so I didn't lie about that either."

"Ellie, baby. Why didn't you call me?" Silence fills the room. I stand there staring at the floor.

"I'll give you two some space." Maria gets up and I eye my mom as she moves to sit down where Maria was and I move to stand in front of the table.

There's a heavy blanket of something I can't identify hanging in the air and it's choking me. A thick fog that's see-through but undeniably holds all the secrets I've been hiding for the past six months. If I'm being honest with myself it's the secrets I've been hiding for the past two years. But like a thick fog that eventually turns into a cloud, these secrets are about to inevitably come pouring down around me.

And they do.

"I work at a greenhouse." Slowly.

My mom looks so surprised by the admission that she actually looks like she's fighting back a grin. Her eyes are narrowed and the corners of her mouth are pinched to keep from letting the grin break free. She opens and closes her mouth a few times like the Venus Flytrap that I take care of at work. A little ironic isn't it?

"Every night after practice I trek across town to this greenhouse owned by the sweetest little Ukrainian woman. She doesn't know about my past or the way I am outside of the greenhouse. She only knows me as the girl I am in the shop. And that girl is sweet, helpful, slow to anger. Nothing like the mess I actually am."

"Ell–,"

"Don't interrupt me, please. I'm trying to be completely honest and if you tell me things like 'that's not true' or 'you are sweet' it'll only–," I take a deep breath in as I continue trying to be something I rarely am in my life. Honest. "It'll only invalidate what I'm feeling. And I know you don't mean to do that but telling me things I don't believe and not letting me finish what I'm trying to say isn't going to make me believe them anymore." Her frown deepens and there's a hurt look behind her eyes.

"I create things there. I foster all different types of plants from when they are just seeds in gestation. What I do there matters. Instead of destroying things or breaking them, I'm the reason these plants thrive and live."

"How long have you been working there?"

"Around four and a half months."

"Are you making money there?"

"Yea I do. About a month in Mrs. Kahn made me the assistant manager, which isn't much of a title considering the only people who work there are her and me. The woman pays me more than she should, and I should know considering I do the bookkeeping."

Her face takes on a comical sort of look as she cuts in, "You do the bookkeeping? You, who currently has a D- in stats and analysis, do the bookkeeping?" She can barely get the rest of the sentence out without giggling. I glare at her as my mouth sets into a tight line.

"I'm sorry, I'm sorry," She really isn't because she's still laughing. After clearing her throat and pulling herself together she continues, "Go on, please, I want you to." Reaching across the table, stretching a bit as she does, she puts her hand over mine and squeezes and gives me a small smile.

"I've been putting the money in various places. I started a savings account at that bank on East Plank Street–"

"The one that smells like mold and looks like a run-down gas station?"

"Yea that one, ok it was the only one that would take my money and give me an account without needing any signatures or help from an adult."

"That's probably not the best way to ensure the safety of your money," she quickly rushes to finish her sentence when she sees the annoyance in my eyes and mouth. "But that's not important, anyway carry on."

"That's mostly it involving the greenhouse. There's a limited number of people who know I work there and those people are you, Duke, and Li–" I cut myself off because saying her name brings me back to her kitchen and her front door when I basically shoved her out of my life.

I don't think I've ever had a headache as bad as the one I have now.

"Mom I fucked up." My gaze is fixed on a smudge on a glass plate framed on the wall across the kitchen, my voice barely above a whisper.

"Oh honey." Small sobs start to wrack my body as she gets out of her chair and comes to kneel in front of me, grabbing my face to look at me. She wipes my tears with her thumbs and then pulls me into her body.

Even though I have five inches and probably twenty pounds of muscle on her she still is able to somehow bring all of her to encase me. Must be a mom thing.

"I yelled at her. Accused her of treating me like a charity case. Someone that was broken that she could fix for her own ego. I even used some of the same words that he did." My mom just sits and listens, slightly rocking her body and stroking my hair like she did when I had anxiety attacks when I was little. "Why did he never come after us?" I know this is all a hard subject for her. She endured so much more than she ever let on and to this day I'm sure I don't even know the half of it. I can hear her heart thudding with my head on her chest but it's steady, and not fast. After breathing in I can feel the flow of air that she lets out, sighing into the mostly empty room.

"To be honest I don't know." She waits a beat, collecting her thoughts, before continuing, "For a while Daniel and I thought for sure that he would come after us. That maybe he would try and get some sort of custody of you even though you were so old." I snort when she calls me old and she pulls away slightly to look at me. "What?" A small smirk forms on her face as her forehead and eyes crease.

"If you think I'm old then what are you?" She rolls

her eyes but chuckles.

"I meant," The syllables are drawn out in that second word as she continues in her story. "That you were old in terms of custody over a child. Just a few years till you turn 18 and become an adult, that sort of thing."

"Now it's under a month."

She cringes and squeezes me tighter, "Nooo, don't remind me." Her voice comes out muffled as she squishes her cheek to the top of my head. She snuffles and releases her death grip on me a little. "Anyway, after a few months of being away from him I stopped worrying as much. But those first two weeks, when you and I were trying to figure out where to stay or go, I think I got less sleep those nights than I did throughout your entire newborn to toddler years. I was so worried that he would come after us or track us down and hurt you or worse." Her voice cracks a little as she tries to continue. "I slept a little easier when Daniel came into our lives."

I know that Daniel saved my mom, but hearing her say it, and feeling the pain in her voice as she talks about the past really reminds me of that.

My voice is thick and wavering when I ask my next question. It's one that is often on my mind and sometimes I don't think I want to know the answer. "Do you ever regret marrying him?"

As she jolts away from me to look me in the eyes a shiver goes down my spine and goosebumps form all over my face and body. "No." Her eyes are pleading with mine and she grabs my face and forces me to look at her, ducking her head so that her face is in line with my gaze pointed at the ground. "Not once have I ever regretted marrying him." She tilts her head and purses her lips with sympathetic eyes, "Marrying him gave me the best gift in the world." She's choked up, answering me, "It gave me you."

"That's probably the cheesiest thing you've ever said to me." I chuckle through snot and swipe at my eyes.

"Well it's true. I don't regret him, because I love you." And with that she stands up and offers me her hand to get up off the dining room floor of Maria's house. We sit back down at the dining room table, where we have much bigger things to discuss.

I don't remember falling asleep. I remember sitting on the couch in Maria's living room with the tv playing reruns of "How I Met Your Mother." But I wasn't watching it. I was just sitting staring off into space. My mom and Maria were in the other room discussing my arrest and what would happen next. I'll be given a trial date of sorts, is what my mom said. Maria offered to pay for a lawyer, to which my mom appreciated but said wasn't necessary.

I had several missed calls and texts from Duke and company but I didn't return any of them. I even had a few from Coach. And while Duke and the others' messages and voicemails were sweet and concerned, he was not so kind. Out of all the messages I got last night none were from Liza. And after just checking again now there's still none. I don't know what I expected. I told her not to chase after me. And she has self respect so she's gonna listen.

Kicking off the blanket someone covered me with at some point during the night, I pull myself up off the couch and start to wander lazily towards the kitchen in search of food. My mind might be hazy but my stomach knows exactly what it wants as it growls to tell me to eat.

"Would you look who's awake?" Maria takes a long sip from her coffee as she looks me up and down from her dining room table. "Want some?"

I know my response isn't intelligible because all I'm doing is grumbling. My hand hurts, my head is pounding and my eyes are swollen from crying so much last night. I'm not 100% certain that I didn't fall asleep crying. I shuffle my feet as I make my way to the sink. The cold water hits my mouth as I hold my head under the water to rinse out the rancid taste that's all over my tongue and teeth. Not only did I not brush my teeth last night, but I also didn't brush them after throwing up several times throughout the day.

My mom strides into the room with a smaller woman following behind her. She looks tired, the woman. The skin around her eyes is pinched and there are several strands of gray hair pulled back in her bun. She's a little plump and round, the kind that comes with aging. Staring at her now, there's a kind of familiarity about her, one I can't place.

"Maria, Ryn," My mom looks at me pointedly before continuing, "This is Olivia Cooper. She is a lawyer and has been kind enough to fly in from Florida to help you," She looks back at me, "With this," She pauses, extending the syllable of her last word while she tries to find the right one to continue, "predicament." Predicament, she means my arrest. I kind of forgot about that. Or maybe not so much forgot but had pushed it to the very back of my mind where it felt forgotten.

There's not a whole lot currently on my mind. I feel numb. Like every thought that tries to come to the forefront of my mind having to do with anything in the past 24 hours or anything that could lead to the events of the past 24 hours, meets an electric fence that shocks any thought that gets too close to consciousness.

"Hi Ryn, it's nice to finally meet you in person, however, I can't say that I would've liked them to be under these circumstances, but here we are." The plump woman walks towards the island and places her briefcase on the counter in front of her. Meanwhile I'm trying to place why I know her, and why she evidently knows me. I give a small nod of recognition to what she said and continue to lean against the counter, arms crossed in front of me.

10:15 A.M

Somehow I've ended up in a room alone with this woman who apparently knows me but I don't know her. My mom trusts her. Before she left the room with Maria the two of them were whispering back and forth to each other and looking at documents in her brief-case. I watched them, my eyes darting back and forth between the two.

"Ok Ryn, let's address the elephant in the room shall we."

"I don't see an elephant." My tone is dry as I cut her off before she can keep talking. But instead of getting angry or annoyed with me, she laughs. Like actually laughs. My face twists into an expression one can only describe as utter confusion, or at least that's how it feels.

After gathering herself from laughing way longer than she should've at my smart-ass response she apologizes, "Oh goodness, I'm sorry, sorry. It's just your mother was so serious over the phone and then even a few minutes ago when she brought me in. It's refreshing."

"I'm glad you think so," I grumble under my breath. "Everyone's been acting like I'm going to jail for the rest of my life." They've been looking at me like I'm him.

"Well I don't think you are." She starts to reach across the table to put her hand over one of mine, the two of which are currently placed on the table in front of me while I pick at the skin around my nails, but she stops herself and pulls her arm back. Clearing her throat she reaches into her briefcase and starts pulling out files and a yellow page notepad. "I talked to the police station and got information on the arrests and the charges. The man you punched, Mr Jasper, is pressing assault charges. If for whatever reason he decides to drop those, the DA could still decide to, and either way you're facing a charge for resisting arrest."

"Wait, but I didn't resist arrest. I put my hands up, I stopped, I got in the car without thrashing around."

Taking a deep breath she addresses my rambling, "Yes," she draws out the last of that word, "But you ran. They had to chase you down the street with the siren and corner you with the cop cars. You stopped because you had to. Otherwise you and I both know that you would've run until you'd gotten away from all of it. But I don't blame you. And I don't think a judge or jury will. But that's only if you cooperate." She clenches her jaw and shakes her head a little before adding, "And tell them the truth, about *why* you ran. So why did you?"

I've mostly spent the last few days going through the motions of my previous life. School, practice, work, sleep, repeat. My friends were extremely understanding about the entire situation even with the little bit of explanation I gave them. "*I've been seeing a therapist the past few months for my anger issues. They all revolve around my father and what he did to me. I keep having panic attacks and that's what happened at the 7-Eleven.*" I don't know why they all keep forgiving me for the things that I do or why they're not terrified.

Now I'm currently splayed out on Duke's couch in his basement while he and Spitz play a very heated game of tennis on Switch Sports. Meanwhile I'm stalking Liza's social media. I've currently scrolled all the way to July

9th of 2019. One could say I'm spiraling.

Monday was dull and painful. I kept seeing her in the hall and wanted to just reach out and hold her and tell her how sorry I was. But I didn't. She never even looked at me every time we passed each other. For the first time in months I ate lunch alone. I couldn't eat at our spot and I didn't want to sit in the massive cafeteria without her. So instead I ate lunch on the bathroom floor of the first floor girl's bathroom in the Dockner building. It might've been the most depressing lunch period I've ever had. I sat there by myself picking at my food while Julia made out with her girlfriend in one of the stalls turned comfortable cubby.

I honestly don't know when or how they were able to remove the toilet in that stall but they put in a padded bench, added fairy lights, put posters on the wall, and overall just made it a cozy little nook. I would've preferred to eat my lunch in there rather than on the floor, but as Julia drunkenly slurred, "You snoozeth, you looseth."

I've spent a lot of time at home. And not only at home but not hiding up in my room or in the attic with all my plants. In fact on Monday night I actually sat, smushed on the couch between Daniel and my mom watching Jeopardy. The two are very competitive and at one point I actually thought my mom was prepared to cut Daniel for not using his faux buzzer or more accurately his "That Was Easy" button.

The doorbell rings and Spitz runs upstairs to get the

pizza we ordered fifteen minutes ago. The couch shifts underneath me as Duke plops himself down next to me on the very small amount of space left on the couch from me taking the majority of it up.

"She's gonna come around." He nudges my arm which is slung over the edge of the couch with my cheek pressed down on the cushion. "I don't know what the two of you are fighting over but you'll work through it."

"Yeah well that's where you're wrong. We aren't fighting, we didn't even have a fight. I think that's part of the problem." I sit up and push myself off the couch and wander over to the dart board that's up on his wall and grab the darts that are sticking in the board, he follows me and I hand him three. We stand there and throw the darts at the board a few times. When I walk over to the board to pull them out and give him his, I stop, hand up to the board, holding a dart in place. "I snapped at her."

Duke doesn't actually respond, when I turn around and face him he just has an eyebrow raised and his head tilted. "I snapped at her and said horrible things that I would take back in a heartbeat." My voice breaks a little on the word horrible. "But she didn't fight." The dart I throw makes a small thunk sound when it makes contact with the board, gaining me thirteen points. "She didn't tell me to go to hell, she didn't try to fight me on what I said, to push back. She just stopped. She gave up." Thunk. "She didn't fight for me, for us."

Duke just looks down and shakes his head before throwing his darts.

"What?" I squint at him and cross my arms defensively. Duke isn't one to hold his tongue when it comes to advice so I know whatever he's gonna say he thinks will upset me. "No, say what you're gonna say, you never hold back so don't start now."

He chuckles a little and takes a deep breath. Thunk. "Well, if I'm being honest, and please, feel free to use the punching wall after this, it has one hole, might as well give it more and dedicate it to blunt force for the rest of time." The punching wall is the name we have given the wall I accidentally punched a hole in during a heated game of Hangman. But in my defense, I had guessed the letter "w" earlier in the game and Spitz drew an arm and said no, so obviously I'd be mad when he revealed the word to be worcestershire. For a word that is very clearly hard to spell you would think the idiot would remember the one letter in the word that isn't repeated throughout it. I'm getting sidetracked and angry just thinking about it.

"But, you messed up here. I don't blame Liza for not wanting to talk to you. And if anything, I think you're the one who needs to fight this time." Thunk.

"What are you talking about, 'this time'." Stomping over to the mini fridge Duke bought for down here, I grab a bottle of cherry pepsi and a diet root beer for him.

Taking it from me he continues, "Look Ryn, most of your relationship, and your friendship with Liza has consisted of you doing something out of anger or stupidity, granted most of the time it was never directed towards her, but she always fixed your mess and brought you back to reality." I don't even have to ask him what he means because one look at me and he elaborates. "Everytime you got angry, you shut down and you pushed her and everyone else away. Yet every single time she wouldn't leave you alone, she pushed you to let her in. She fought for you when you weren't willing to fight for yourself.

I only grumble in response and chuck a dart angrily at the dart board.

"I'm not saying this to piss you off, you know that right?" He's turned fully to face me now but I'm only looking at the board. If I look at him I might cry and that's the last thing I want to do in front of the guys. Saving me from this conversation after I give a small hum of recognition to Duke, Spitz comes bounding down the stairs like a child.

"Pizza's here!"

Today is game day and I'm lucky. I'm lucky because yesterday I had a hearing with the principal, the athletic director, Coach, a member of the MSHSL (Minnesota State High School League), and my mom and Daniel. This meeting was to decide my fate regarding the hockey team. More specifically it would decide whether or not I would be allowed to remain on the team considering my "recent transgressions."

Coach was *really* pissed when he first heard the news. It also probably didn't help that he heard it from the news about a girl who went psycho on a poor old man and not from me. They had blurred my picture in any videos, but he still was able to piece together they were talking about me. I swear to god I saw steam coming out of his ears when I finally got the beat down in person. He made me play goalie while everyone practiced their power shots. Basically he just had all the guys fire pucks at me all at the same time while I flailed and tried to stop them but instead mostly got hit everywhere by tens of tiny little puck bullets.

I was pulled out of Stats and Analysis, which I am very much not complaining about. I wasn't paying attention during the class anyways. I was sketching out a new plant display idea I had for the greenhouse on the back of the test I was supposed to be doing. I didn't realize Daniel would be in the meeting. I knew it was happening though because Coach made sure I wasn't going to miss it. In fact he told me if I did miss it he would "shove your hockey stick so far up your ass," it got pretty graphic after that. Well I think it did, I started spacing.

When I got to the meeting I stopped and scanned the room taking in all the people who were there. And seeing as how I recognized five out of the six people in the room, I figured that the tall blonde man in the navy blue suit was the representative from the MSHSL. He looked very serious. I wasn't nervous before but suddenly I realized everything that was riding on this meeting. Somewhere along the way I've started to come around to the team and I don't know who I would be without them. I probably would've lost myself a long time ago and maybe that's a bad thing. Not being able to separate myself and cope on my own, using the team as a crutch to avoid facing my problems head on. But it's one of the things that saved me from drowning. The team and Liza.

And that's what I told the man, and everyone in that room that day. Because Olivia told me I needed to tell the truth. So I'm giving that a try.

"Look sir, I don't know your name, I know you said it at the beginning of the meeting but if I'm completely honest I tuned out everything up until a certain point, not wanting to hear what you guys were saying about me and what happened the other day. But I do want to say this." I interrupted halfway through the meeting and addressed the man from the MSHSL head on. "I was recruited for this team for one reason and one reason only. Coach Maddox decided to take a chance on a girl with blatant anger issues." I grimace and continue, "He told me he believed that hockey would be a good outlet for me to work through my problems. But it came with stipulations. Those being that I had to see a therapist to also help me work through my problems and the biggest, joining his team. I agreed."

I looked down at my hands and swallowed, trying to let the barriers I constantly have up in my mind fall down, "I don't know why I agreed, I think there was just this, this *voice* that told me to accept his offer. So I started seeing my therapist, Dr. Shaw, who is truly a wonderful woman for putting up with me and I have been a terrible patient for avoiding her and not giving her the respect she deserves by not showing up to my appointments. Which I promise I will be starting to go back to starting next week. I can put that in writing if you'd like." My mom gave me that mom look that said that if I didn't keep that promise I wasn't going to live to see eighteen.

"I know that I have...issues," Coach Maddox covered his face with his hand and slid down into his chair with that comment. I couldn't tell if he was trying not to laugh or groan. "But I would be lying to myself and everyone in this room if I said that this team didn't save me. I don't even want to begin to imagine where I would be if I wasn't a part of it. For the first time in my life I have friends. Friends who, surprisingly, like me for me. In fact I'm sure that if you looked out the window of the door right now you would see two heads looking through the glass trying to listen in on what's happening." The man's eyes flicked up to the door behind me and squinted with his lips parted when he looked back down at me, probably questioning how I'd known Duke and Spitz were out there. What I told him was, "They're my team, they've got my back." But how I really knew was I could hear Spitz' breathing after inevitably running from wherever his class was to make it here in time. I also got more confirmation when I could hear their scrambling after they were caught and Duke whisper-screaming "GO! GO! GO!"

"This isn't me trying to feed you some sob story so you'll let me continue to be on the team. I under-stand, probably for the first time in my life, that my actions have consequences." I thought about Liza in that moment, and how I still hadn't heard from her. "But I'm also trying to stop lying, not only to the people around me, but to myself. I want to do better. And I sincerely hope you will give me the opportunity to do that. Thank you." Everyone was silent in the conference room when I finished. I swear you could've heard the heartbeats of everyone if you'd wanted to. I quickly added for good measure, "And sorry for interrupting you, I'm not good at talking. Or reading social cues."

Thankfully for me the man, who told me after my speech that his name was Mr. Patrick, which honestly doesn't feel like a fitting name for him but I wasn't going to risk offending him if my speech had worked. If it hadn't then maybe.

Hey, I'm trying to tell the truth more, not stop being a smart-ass, that was happening long before the anger issues and panic attacks, and it'll be happening for a long time after.

After my speech and after Patrick reintroduced himself, I was sent back to class so the "adults" could talk about what would happen. Unsurprisingly I ran into Duke and Spitz in the hallway trying to look inconspicuous by the water fountain. It most certainly did not work. Spitz had his leg up against the wall and leaned against it, arms crossed, and Duke was staring very intently at a poster hung on the wall next to the fountain. The poster was for free feminine products in the counseling center.

"Hey Duke if this is your first period I've got some great tips. And don't be scared when you bleed a lot, it's perfectly normal." I used a falsetto tone that made me sound motherly and put my hands and his shoulders and squeezed. Spitz started chuckling and I had to come for him next. "What are you laughing at? You look like John Travolta's younger nerdier brother in 'Grease' who stole his jacket and is trying to be like him." That made Duke laugh and Spitz removed himself from the wall sheepishly.

"How'd it go?" Duke was the first one to ask about it as we walked down the hall towards our classes.

"Well I'll find out tonight when I show up to practice and Coach sends me away or tells me to get my ass dressed for drills." None of us know how to react in the situation. We're all uncomfortable and worried about my fate as their teammate. It's nice to know I'm not alone. There were so many times when I was younger that I would get called to the principal's office, and no one ever asked me what had happened, or if I was ok. No one cared. I'd always walk out of that office and back to class alone. But yesterday I had two friends skip their classes to be involved in my business, in my mistake. I'm starting to think that they really would go down with the ship.

And by some miracle I got cleared to play. It's game day baby.

7:05 P.M

It seems like some sort of cruel irony that my first game back after getting arrested and having my entire place on the team reevaluated is against the very same team with the douchebag I beat to a pulp.

And because the fight was filmed by several tens of people, the stands are packed fuller than they usually are for a high school hockey game. But they aren't here to see a game. They're here to see me. And I know that makes it sound like my ego is astronomical, but I don't mean it in a positive way. The people in the stands tonight, the ones who don't usually come to these games, are here to see me fuck up.

I'd like to say that's not gonna happen but I don't have that much confidence in myself. Thankfully other people do. Cliff skates up to me and pats me on the back, except it's less of a pat and more of a shove that pushes me forward on the ice since I wasn't prepared to actually go anywhere. I've got my hair down today. A girl is gonna kick that jack weasel's ass. But not literally. Hopefully.

For some reason, Daniel has picked today for his entire family to come and watch me play. They're sitting right beside our team's penalty box. I don't know if they just wanted to be towards the floor and in the center or if they purposefully sat by a box that I will potentially spend a lot of time in tonight. No matter what the reason I am still offended. Even the aunt who never shows up to anything has made an appearance and is sitting up in the stands looking bright and bubbly with vibrant red hair.

I spent most of my afternoon today doing drills out on the ice. I don't know why I'm so nervous for tonight. I had to run the Zamboni three times because the guy who usually runs it got mad at me for messing up the ice so much that he tossed me the keys and stormed out of the arena. At one point I considered lying down on the ice and making snow angels because there was so much buildup. But I just spotted the reason for my nerves. Liza.

I wasn't sure if she would show up. I know she's friends with Duke. She's always been a bigger person than me, not literally, but in the ways that actually matter.

She's here with her friends from the cheer team. I really only know of a few of them. Even though she's on the team, Liza has never been close to her teammates. Always much rather being with me or with people like Duke and Natalie. When I first met her, and even for a while afterwards, I thought she was this popular girl who was always out with friends and fit in anywhere and enjoyed it. And she does fit in everywhere. But she doesn't really like to go out with just anyone.

I've been standing still on the ice for too long because all of a sudden Jet comes sliding to a stop next to me and claps his hand on my shoulder, startling me out of the haze I'd drifted into.

"You gonna be ok tonight Bradford?" Jet lowers his head a little to be eye level with me, and his eyes flit back and forth between mine, like he's looking for something behind them.

"Yea." My eyes don't come into focus, instead I just push my helmet back on to my head, and before putting my mouth guard back in, add "Let's go."

7:30 P.M

Before I know it we're all in our positions on the ice. I'm in the center, facing off. Out of the corner of my eye I can see the jackass whose face is lucky to be where it's at.

A ref blows his whistle and I slap the puck away from the guy across from me and pass it over to Spitz, who thanks to Duke and I putting in overtime hours to help him work on his game, is starting tonight for the third game in a row.

I'm calling plays and the only sound I can hear is the way the blades from my skates slice up the ice. Next thing I know I'm getting slammed into the boards when I don't even have the puck and am nowhere near it. The guy skates off and the number on his jersey makes me clench my jaw so hard my vision goes black for a second. It's bad enough a penalty wasn't called.

Don't do anything stupid. Digging my heels into the ground I push off on the ice and take off after him. Gliding by, I cut in front of him really quickly to make him lose balance. It's a more legal, nicer way to keep someone from getting to the puck before you. I yell to him over the noise as I pass. "What the fuck's your problem."

For the next two minutes I didn't get close enough to him, and him me. But when we were facing off again, he took that opportunity to run up behind me as soon as the whistle blew and speared me right in the lower back. Growling slightly and turning around, he just stands there looking at me. Waiting. Suddenly he's up in my face, I haven't moved a muscle. And he's yelling at me. Trying to start a fight.

"Daddy's little girl thinks she's so tough but she can't even finish fights that she starts." *Don't.* He pushes me just as the refs come over and try to get in between. They're pulling him away and Jet slides up next to me, keeping his distance but close enough to reach out and grab me if necessary. I turn towards Jet and nod my thanks and move a little towards him. "C'mon you stupid bitch!" He's yelling now, and the entire stadium has gone quiet. "Show me how tough you are." *Don't.* His teammates are trying to get him to stop. He's already going to be thrown out of the game for cussing at the refs and trying to take a swing at me as he was being dragged away. Thankfully he's almost made it to the door. I haven't looked back at him. And I know I shouldn't.

"I looked you up...Knox." Slowly I turn back towards him. Every muscle in my body is tight and jumping at the seams. It's taking every ounce of self control I have to not charge him. Breathing in deep, I close my eyes to try and collect myself, gritting my teeth so hard I might just break them. "If you look hard enough you can find anything on the internet. Just cause you and your mom run away from home and change your last names doesn't change that you will always be–" His sentence got cut short when a pair of knuckles connected with his cheekbone. Knocked him out cold too. I hear gasps and whispers and I look down at my hands because I don't remember punching him. My gloves are still on and I'm still a good distance away. My head snaps up to see who did what I really, *really* wanted to do to this guy and slowly a cheshire grin spreads across my face until it's a full on smile.

Duke is standing next to the guy shaking his hand out and opening and closing it with a grimace on his face. "Holy *crap* that really hurt." I start laughing, slightly uncontrollably but I can't help it. Duke, the golden child, team captain, all-righteous pacifist that he is, punched a guy. For me.

Throwing my hands up in the air and shouting, "My man!" I skate up to him, as the other guy is fully off the ice now and is being tended to, and dap him up. I don't have to thank him. He gives a slight nod of his head because he knows what I want to say and knows I don't want to have to say it.

Even though what Duke did for me really solidified that he is one of my best friends in the world, it also meant that he got ejected for fighting (the entire stadium booed, even the other team's fans). And because we lost our best goalie, it also meant losing the game. But that didn't really matter right now. Because right now Duke, Spitz, Jet, Cliff, Hunter, Amber, Hannah, Natalie, and I were crammed into a half circle booth at Gino's gorging ourselves on several different types of pizza.

"Alright, alright." I slide out of the booth, holding my drink in my hand, unused fork in the other and say, "I would like to propose a toast to Duke." Cliff bellows out his name at the mention while Hunter woofs.

Natalie smacks Hunter in the chest and shushes him. "Even though we lost the game, I think we can all agree that tonight was totally worth it," I take a deep breath for dramatics before continuing, "Because we all got to witness Duke Ballinger punch out his first victim." Everyone starts clapping and cheering and Duke bows his head and blushes as Natalie shoves her shoulder into his.

After about an hour we were the only group in Gino's. It's a miracle the man didn't throw us out on our asses. For once in my life I was being a normal teenager. Staying out too late with friends, being rowdy and loud and annoying older generations. It feels good.

It was a nice night outside considering it was early March in Minnesota. I rode my skateboard home from the pizza place turning down a ride in the crammed car that everyone piled into on the ride over. The season was almost over. We have our first playoff game next week, but I don't really think any of us are too invested in the outcome. Jet and Cliff already committed to Minnesota State, Spitz will be starting his senior year next year which means he'll have a whole other season to try and go far in the playoffs. Duke's still deciding between Forthsworth State and University of Minnesota, but he's already promised that he would drive back to Forthsworth to be an assistant coach for the team next year. Hunter says he's gonna go on some long road trip around the country. On a motorcycle. That he doesn't know how to ride.

We're all very much looking forward to that disaster. Basically we're all cool however the season ends. I myself haven't heard back from anywhere I've applied to. Maybe I'll just take a gap year and work at the greenhouse in the meantime. Plus with this whole trial coming up, if a college did send an acceptance letter, they were definitely alerted to the whole debacle and they are probably breaking into a post office as we speak to steal the letter back so I never see it. In other words, I don't think college is for me, or that I'm for college. Mrs. Geller really wants me to look at those pamphlets she gave me.

After struggling to unlock the front door, (I decided not to climb up to the attic), I'm greeted by Daniel who is still up and sitting on the couch. He has the tv on but he's not watching it. He's sitting, laid back against the couch, with his leg crossed over his other in that wide dude stance that allows them not to crush their balls. In his hands is his book of crosswords. The man is obsessed with crosswords. He believes that by doing them regularly, his brain will remain "sharp as a tack."

Throwing my jacket on the table I walk back towards the living room. When I sit down at the other end of the couch, the weight of it caves underneath me. Crossing my arms I sink further into the couch. Daniel clears his throat, making it clear that I've interrupted his flow. I can feel his curiosity burning a hole in me. Looking over at him I nod to the crossword he's set down on the coffee table. "Got another one?"

He raises an eyebrow and points to the book and then reaches over to the side table on his end. Opening up the drawer he reaches in and pulls out another book, and hands it to me along with a pen he pulls out of the breast pocket of his button up. And with that, we both sat there, absently watching reruns of *Seinfeld* while working on crosswords, occasionally leaning over to show the other a word or completed puzzle, but never saying anything more than a "hmph."

I have spent the last eight minutes sitting in the waiting room of this dingy psychiatrist office. I have missed exactly five appointments. Which means that I have missed five appointments of being on the receiving end of knowing eyes. Five missed appointments where I'm on the receiving end of cryptic messages. And five missed appointments where anger and disappointment have built up in Dr. Shaw, all leading to this moment when she steps out of her office and into the waiting room and calls my name.

When I stand up, swallowing, I can't help but put my head down in shame. Just before I do, I see Dr. Shaw bring her hands in front of her and fold her hands together. Wordlessly, I follow her back into her office, passing the secretary and the closed doors of some of the other psychiatrists who also work there.

"I can practically hear your thoughts. You can calm down." Reaching for her office door handle she throws a glance at me.

"You're not mad?" I can literally feel the deer in the headlights look on my face. How is it that all of the adults in my life manage to make me feel like I'm a child who stole the last cookie and then lied about it.

"Oh no I'm mad." Her answer came fast and without any hesitation. "But I know that in your mind, you think you did it for good reasons. It doesn't make me less mad. You disrespected my time." Sitting down in her chair as I take my seat, she looks at me pointedly as she continues, "Don't do it again."

"Yes Dr. Shaw."

"So why'd you do it?" She brings her notebook into her lap and pulls a pen out of the holder on her desk.

"Do what?" I'm already picking at the skin around my nails.

"Don't you think it's a bad sign that you don't immediately know what I'm referring to?" Her accusatory look is burning holes into my eyes as she looks at me waiting for an answer.

"I've learned early on that I shouldn't answer questions like that." When people ask they typically have a specific thing in mind. If you answer that question and give any other answer than what they already had in mind, you put yourself in more trouble than before. So it's best to play dumb.

"Ok fine, I'll bite. Why'd you start skipping our appointments?" She throws the notebook on her desk and leans forward, resting her arms on her knees, hands still folded.

"I don't know." I lean back against the leather loveseat against the wall. "I guess with the first appointment, when my mom told me I would have to take the bus or skateboard, I was already well on my way to not coming. When I got on the bus to come I got so distracted and lost in my thoughts that I ended up riding it all the way back to my original stop. By then I decided I'd had enough time psychoanalyzing my own thoughts that I didn't necessarily need therapy that day. And I guess, once I did it one time, the other times became a little easier. I just kept finding excuses for why I didn't need to come."

"That was a lot of words at one time."

I chuckle under my breath and look off in the distance. "Yea, well I'm trying something different."

"Different is good." There's an awkward silence that fills the air. Although maybe it's not as awkward as I'm interpreting it to be. I can hear the clock hands as they tick every second making their way around the circle. "I heard about the arrest."

My lips pull into a tight line and I can't look at her.

"I'm guessing you had a flashback of your father."

She doesn't even say it accusingly, just a quiet confirmation of something she already knows.

"One of the worst ones I've had since we left."

"Have you seen the guy you hit? Since you hit him and were arrested?" She leans back in her chair and rocks a little as the back bounces.

"No." Suddenly I'm defensive. "Why would I do that?" I'm not being mean or aggressive, per say, but there is a clear wall my words are building.

"I think it would be good for you. Give you a chance to confront the problem. Not to mention apologizing." Olivia mentioned something about that. She sighs as she looks at me glaring at her. "Look, meeting with this guy, and talking to him, I think it will give you a chance to reconcile what you did. And to accept it. At some point you have to stop running Ryn. I keep trying to get you to learn that your problems will follow you no matter where or how far you run–."

"I know." I shout, cutting her off. "Fuck," I breathe out. "I *know* that I need to stop running." My voice is wobbly and tears are threatening to spill out of my eyes. "But I *can't*. Because if I do, if I stop running for just a second, I'm worried that whatever little bit of strength I have left will fall away. I already feel like the shell of who I used to be. I don't know if I can handle being a shell of a shell." I don't even know how she hears that last sentence because my voice is so low and quiet that I'm not sure I said it.

She doesn't respond, not right away at least. Instead

she leans back in her chair again and folds her arms across her chest, having put down the pen and notepad she always scribbles things in. I think we sat there in silence for 10 minutes before she finally spoke.

"Do you think you're a bad person?" Her knee is crossed over her leg and she's looking at me so casually, so indifferent to what my answer may be.

"W– what?"

"When you take a second, to actually look at yourself, and think about who you are, the choices you've made, do you think you're a bad person?" Her eyebrow is raised and suddenly this feels like a test. I know she isn't, but it looks a little bit like she's amused by all of this and that just pisses me off.

"I don't think I'm a good one." I grumble and pick at the skin around my nails.

"And that's because you –what? Have anger issues? Suppressed trauma that was dealt to you for most of your childhood that you still need to work through? Because you make mistakes? Because you're human?" By this time she's theatrically waving one of her arms about gesturing to all these examples she's so helpfully listing.

"No." My tone is sharp when I cut in and I have to take a deep breath not to lose it when I continue, my voice still low and gravelly. "Because I hurt people." I've been biting my tongue so hard to try and keep from crying that now I can taste the familiar tang of iron that's in my blood.

"But that's not on purpose."

"It doesn't matter. Good people don't *hurt* other people."

"Ok. So in your eyes, what *do* good people do?" Her arms are resting on the armrests of her chair, weakly gesturing to the open floor of her office for me to elaborate.

"God! I don't know. Ok? Good people care about other people's feelings. They don't-don't walk around beating people up. They help others and they *try*."

"And you don't?"

"My trying is different. My *trying*, is just trying to survive."

"Can I read you some of the observations I've made throughout our sessions?" She asks.

"Do I really have a choice?" Groaning in response I throw my head back against the wall.

"You always have a choice."

I can't help but scoff at that because this entire thing, me even going to therapy in the first place is because I was *required* to. No choice.

"I'll take your silence as an invitation to continue." She starts flipping through her notepad looking for god knows what. Finally the sound of pages flipping stops so she must've found what she was looking for.

"Observation #6: Ryn pulled down a classmate's pants at lunch in front of half the school, classmate had been making unwanted sexual advances towards another classmate, it was after she noticed these advances that Ryn did what she did." I don't really see where she's going with this.

She starts flipping through the pages again looking for another thing to read to me. "Observation #13: Ryn beats up guy who says terrible things about her mother and is misogynistic. Ryn had not been violent towards other people since the first and only time she punched a kid in elementary school." Ok so at this point I'm just guessing she's pointing out the many accumulating low points in my life that seem to be happening more and more now. That's a real pick me up.

"Observation #26: Ryn continues to hang out with Duke, Spitz, and some other members of the team; she's made friends." Well that one isn't bad. "Observation #4: Ryn found a job working at a greenhouse," She stops to look up at me with a smirk. "Yes, I know about the greenhouse." I can't even answer her, my mouth just barely hanging open from the admission.

"She has taken on a lot of responsibility there, helping the older woman who owns the place with anything and everything. Observation #17: Ryn has bonded with family on Daniel's side, forming a quick connection with her step-grandmother, her mom has told me about the way she interacts with her step-cousins, gentle and attentive, with an ease about her she hasn't seen in a long time. Even if she thinks she's not good with them, she still pays attention." I didn't realize my mom had really been paying attention to me the few times I ran around the backyard of Maria's house with

Daniel's nieces and nephews.

"Observation #15: Got a call from Ryn's school today, they say her grades are improving, not by much but enough to know she hasn't given up. Also wanted to note that she pinned a guy to his locker and made him give the burger he had stolen from a freshman back to him, after he had, she released him and shoved him on his way before going about her own business again." I hardly even remember that. To be fair though I've also stolen from the freshman.

"Ok." I cut her off before she can continue, at this point all of this is becoming wildly annoying and I really don't see its significance if there even is any. "What the hell is the point of all of this? That you take a lot of really creepy notes about me? Or that you know way more about my life than I've actually told you?" I can tell she's getting fed up with me by the way her jaw clenches and her expression becomes stony.

"The *point* Ryn," She puts emphasis on the second word. "Is that you may think you are this big, bad monster. Someone who walks around with a bully persona. But I bet you don't even see the pattern in your own behavior." I roll my eyes and shake my head as I look away. I'm about three seconds from getting up and walking out that door if she doesn't get to the point. It's like she's trying to goad me into yelling at her, into blowing up. Maybe that's the point she's trying to make. "Ryn, you're rarely violent towards other people." A beat passes. "And, aside from the little boy you hit when you were little and the man you accidentally punched *once* because you were startled, the other guy kind of deserved it. And I'm not saying I condone violence, ever. But what you did, so many other people would've also done.

"And that doesn't mean that they are bad people. It just means that sometimes, we let our anger get the best of us. Everyone does. And it doesn't help when someone is purposefully trying to push our buttons." She's talking to me like a child. "I'd also like to point out that you only beat up guys, and you only trip or pants guys. Guys that do shitty things to other people." A smirk grows on my face as she cusses but she just rolls her eyes and continues.

"The way I see it, all of the times that you lash out, and I don't mean the times you have an attitude because that's just a defense mechanism you use with everyone and I don't think it's the main source of your problems. But when you lash out, you do it to protect someone." All I do is stare her down, willing her to elaborate further and she does. "As a little girl, you were never able to protect your mom, or yourself. But if we're both being honest you've never been too concerned with your own safety, only hers. I think that need, to protect her from anything that could hurt her, only grew and started to extend to others.

"You would rather beat yourself down to crumbs and broken pieces, if it meant that other people were safe– and happy." At this she leans forward with her arms on her knees, ducking her head to meet my eyes, close enough so that she could reach out and grab my hand but far enough to let me know she knows I wouldn't want that. "To me? That doesn't seem like a bad person. Just a confused one."

"How can you be so sure?" My voice is quiet and I hate the way it cracks, the way I seem to need this validation. I didn't think I cared what Dr. Shaw thought, part of me still doesn't. But I can't explain why I need her to answer my question like I need to breathe. Like if she doesn't answer, my organs will stop functioning and I will shut down.

"Well, to start with, if you were a bad person, you wouldn't've come back." She raises her eyebrows and shrugs her shoulders at me. All I can do is breathe out and slightly nod. She's right though. I didn't have to come back. Everyone knew I had been missing my appointments. That wasn't news to anyone. Yet no one was pushing me to go back. I was the one who made the decision to step foot back in this office. That might be the first thing she's ever said to me that causes a small, albeit confused, smile to appear on my face.

Today's session is going long. Dr. Shaw went out to tell her secretary that since she didn't have an appointment scheduled right after mine, that she would be using that time to continue with me since it seems I'm "making real progress" and we're "on the edge of a breakthrough."

"My attitude hurts people." I know she was only half listening because her head slowly started to turn towards me, her eyes taking a minute to follow as she was sending an email to a colleague before we continued. When she finally is turned fully towards me, she tilts her head to the side and a crease forms between her eyes as she looks at me questioningly.

"What's that?"

"My attitude hurts people." It's easier saying it a second time.

"Is this because of what happened between you and Liza?" I don't have to nod or respond because she already knows the answer, once again asking rhetorical questions. "Tell me what happened between you two."

"She invited me over to meet her family. I don't know why but– the events of that day triggered a lot of flashbacks for me." I continue to fidget with my hands, not actually seeing anything because my eyes have glazed over. "It was the first time I really took the chance to look around at all the photos and mementos in the house. One of the memories was happy. But I think those are the ones that hurt the most."

Tears are flowing freely down my face, but my voice is strong and I'm still staring into the void, like I'm detached from it all, even if it is triggering tears. "I *hate* that my childhood is so defined by him. I wish I didn't feel him behind me everywhere I go. There are times where I think I see him in a store but it was just some man with brown hair, or when I'm skateboarding home, I'm always so paranoid." Dr. Shaw throws me a sympathetic look and for once that doesn't make me angry.

By now I've spent enough time with the woman to know that the last thing she will ever do is pity me. It's just not something she believes in, pitying people when life happens to them. She sympathizes with them but she doesn't pity. "It was bothering me so much that I ended up looking him up a couple days ago. I didn't tell anyone because I didn't want anyone to know. He's in jail. In case you were wondering. Got arrested about four months ago for drunk driving." Her breathing hitches slightly as she listens to me talk, probably not wanting to interrupt this rare moment of honesty on my part.

"He had been coming home from his shift, apparently drinking on the job, and just a few hours later he ended up back at work, just not the way he usually was." Silently Dr. Shaw pushes the box of tissues on the small square coffee table towards me. The tears that are still falling don't bother me though, occasionally one slips past my lips and I can taste the salt in them. "I don't have to worry about him getting out though. He killed two people in the accident. So on top of two life sentences, and the years he gets for drinking while on duty, he'll be there till the day he dies."

"Shouldn't that bring some sort of peace?"

"That he killed people?" I can feel the disgust on my face at her question and she sighs and pinches the bridge of her nose.

"That he can't *hurt* you anymore." Well that's rich.

"Except that isn't true. He's hundreds of miles away and he's still hurting me every second because I let him!" A small smile spreads across her face as she looks at me and takes in what I just said and for the first time I'm actually considering that she might be a sadist.

"Say that again." Her voice is calm and encouraging and I don't like it because that look and that tone means she thinks I'm on to something.

"Even though he's hundreds of miles away he's still hurting me?"

"Not that part." And then it clicks what I had yelled out in frustration a minute prior.

"Because I let him." And once again I realize that I'm my own worst enemy. I have had every opportunity to grow and move on from this experience but I haven't. Because I haven't allowed myself to let him go. The groan that escapes my lips as I angrily scrub my hands across my face and sink lower into my chair fills the small office space. "Fuck."

And then I'm forced to peek through my fingers because she laughs. She actually *laughs*. I have no idea what's going on and all I can do is stare confused.

Finally after what seems like ten minutes, she gets a hold of herself and lightly shakes her head, waving her hand in front of her like she's trying to clear the air.

"I'm sorry, I'm sorry. It's just so funny to watch you be mad at having a breakthrough. I mean seriously, only you would be frustrated." She giggles more to herself and scribbles something on her notepad.

"So what now. I'm healed?" She chokes on a laugh.

"Absolutely not." Why in God's name is she smiling while saying that. "Nobody is ever 'healed'. We're always going to be going through things that will change us or cause us some sort of trauma. But being human means being able to work through those moments.

"There's going to be moments in your life where this doesn't bother you at all, but there will be times when suddenly it hits you out of nowhere and it hurts just as much as it did when this all first happened. It sucks. But I'm not going to lie to you, you know I don't do that. The reason you're in therapy, and the reason a lot of people are, is so that you can learn how to manage these feelings when they come up. Manage them productively that is." Her eyes widen a little as she emphasizes that last part.

"What? Are you saying that punching random old guys in 7-Eleven's or skipping an entire day of school hiding out on a billboard isn't healthy coping?" She rolls her eyes at my smart-ass response.

"No it's not, but thanks for telling me you skipped school." She smirks at me as I realize I told on myself.

7:45 P.M

Spring seems to be coming a little earlier than usual in Minnesota. Everyone who's native to the area keeps going on about it and how this time last year they were still getting an inch or two of snow. It's nothing like Florida spring weather, or even Florida winter weather, but it's nice. The threads from my ripped jeans blowing back around my leg as I skateboard over to the greenhouse. My birthday is next Thursday, the 28th. My mom and Daniel have suddenly stopped talking every time I enter a room so I know they're planning something.

It doesn't matter how many times I tell them I don't want to do anything special, or how many times I grumble under my breath whenever they bring up my birthday, they still insist on doing something for me.

I honestly should've expected this though knowing them. I can't expect them not to care, it is a big birthday. The big eighteen. A legal adult. Which is actually kind of the problem I'm having right now. Because I'm about to turn eighteen the district attorney is pushing to try me as an adult.

I think that's why my mom and Daniel have been pushing so hard to make this such a special party. All the planning will keep their minds off of my trial. If I do go to jail it's not like we'll be able to celebrate anyways since the trial is right before my birthday.

Spitz says that the good news about me going to jail is that I won't ever be anyone's bitch. He fully believes that I'll be running the place because "everyone's scared of you." He and Duke also said that they would come visit me and talk to me through the little phone on the wall.

When I walk into the greenhouse I'm greeted by the beautiful smell of water mixed with the earthy tones that waft through the air. I have an excess amount of strawberries that I'm gonna bring home for Daniel to make something with. I haven't been giving them to Liza, so the supply has piled up.

Recently, I've been trying to convince Mrs. Kahn to purchase the small area of land next to the greenhouse to create an open outside garden that people can walk through, and visit during the warmer months, and maybe add a pavilion where we can put plants people can buy underneath during warmer seasons as well.

I've promised her that I would do all of the work building the pavilion (with the help of the guys who do not know they've been volunteered to help but like Spitz said, I'm scary), and I would get the garden ready. Her only concern is that in the winter we would have the space there with a dead garden and empty pavilion. So now all I have to do is come up with a way to make sure the dead stuff from the garden gets removed on time so it's never sitting around making the garden look ugly, and find something to fill the space during the winter.

To be honest I'm thinking of decorating the garden in accordance with the holidays and selling Christmas trees in late fall all the way to the actual holiday. However, that plan is also partially flawed because after Christmas the pavilion will be empty again and the garden will essentially just be an ever-revolving door of decorations that we will have to store somewhere. I'm gonna have to go back to the drawing board.

"How was practice today?" After the whole debacle I'd gotten myself into, I knew Mrs. Kahn needed to know at least a little bit about me so I came clean about hockey.

The place is actually a little busy today. Because we're getting into spring weather, the perfect time to start planting, people are going to be coming in a lot more. Mrs. Kahn is carrying a plant that's far too large for her over to the register to ring up for a customer. I take it from her and continue to walk behind her towards the counter.

"It was good. For some reason morale was up even though we lost the last game and it was a little hectic. First playoff game is Thursday. Until then Coach is gonna be putting us through any drills he can possibly think of to make sure we're as ready as we can be." Throwing my apron over my head I take the strings in the middle and tie them around my back.

She finishes up with the customer and turns towards me, one hand on her hip. "Did you get me my ticket for the game?" Coming clean came with a lot more support from the woman than I was ever prepared for.

"Yes, yes, I did." Reaching into my back pocket I hand her one of the tickets I was given for family and friends.

She smiles and pats me on the arm as she takes the ticket and moves around me to go back out onto the floor. Which leaves me to wander to the back to tend to my plants in the nursery, the ones that aren't ready to be put out on the floor yet. We don't put the baby plants out where we have customers. I've taken on the responsibility to take care of them for the most part. It will never cease to amaze me how this woman kept the place running for so long on her own.

If I ever voiced that to her though? She'd chase me around the greenhouse spritzing me with a spray bottle while yelling Ukrainian obscenities at me. And while two weeks ago, I might have felt like I deserved it, right now I'm trying to be a person who doesn't. I'm more than just a little grateful that she didn't fire me when she found out about the arrest. I was fully prepared for her to fire me and tell me to never come back. After all, I'd hidden so much from her. For months I let her believe I was this normal high schooler. When in actuality I was one wrong wire cut from blowing up all over everyone and everything around me.

Fuck. I'm supposed to be trying not to think like that. But Dr. Shaw says that it'll take time to rewire the parts of my brain that have been molded from almost a lifetime of mental and emotional abuse. *"It won't happen overnight."*

It might be a bad idea to sit across the street in the shadows on my bike and stare at Liza's house while I try and figure out what I'm going to say to her. I took the bike out of the garage for the first time tonight to get some time on it. It's finally nice enough outside to ride. However, sitting here, I don't know how I'm going to get the courage to park the bike and walk up to the door and knock. I know sitting here makes it look like I'm a stalker, but I'm not, I swear I'm not.

I just want to apologize for how I treated her. She didn't, *doesn't* deserve any of this. I've already chickened out three times tonight and drove off only to find myself back under this maple tree in her neighbor's front yard.

Slapping my cheeks a few times and shaking out my arms I put the brake down and turn the bike off. I'm doing this, no chickening out this time, Elleri Ryn Bradford does not chicken out. Ok I do sometimes. That's evident from avoiding therapy for five appointments. And not wanting to hear the disappointment from Dr. Shaw.

Maybe that's why I haven't actually knocked on the door. Liza's the best thing that's ever happened to me. What I used to think was a burden, her constant barrage of questions and pestering that I once thought of as an annoyance, grew on me. She, in all her sunshiney goodness, kept attaching herself to my side. She saw a goodness in me that I wish, *want* to see in myself. If I knock on that door and find out that she no longer sees that goodness in me, I don't know if anyone else will ever see that much goodness in me.

I never even got to tell her I love her.

"She's not here ya know." I look up from my handle bars to see Nakoa standing across the street next to the trash can at the end of their driveway, arms folded across his chest. The fight or flight response in me really wants to immediately start my motorcycle and race away as fast as I possibly can from the questioning and firm gaze coming from Liza's uncle. He takes my silence as permission to continue, "I'm surprised you didn't realize that, seeing that her car isn't here." He points to the empty spot in front of the house where her car usually sits. And for what feels like the millionth time in my life I feel like an idiot.

"Oh, yea." I look down at my lap and mumble a quiet "sorry" before taking off back towards my house.

Except I don't go home. Instead I'm on my way to do something stupid. And definitely won't win Liza back.

I shaved about an hour off of my drive by speeding way faster than I should've been considering I have an open arrest and adding a ticket to that would be the last thing I need right now. Well actually the last thing I need right now is to be pulled over and then being accused of trying to run once they ran my name through the system. Then instead of spending a night in jail, I'd be spending the entirety of the time before my trial there.

But I didn't have a choice. This trip needed to happen tonight or else I would chicken out. But maybe that would be the better outcome, walking away before I can make this thing between Liza and I much worse than it already is.

But instead I'm sitting in front of what I believe is

Liza's childhood home. She'd described it to me once, back then I'd just assumed it was the house she lived in before she moved to Forthsworth with her parents. Only now I know it's the home she was evicted from by the people who were supposed to be there for her unconditionally.

She never said the address in her story. Obviously. That's not something you normally do when telling someone a story involving a place. *Oh yea it was this beautiful house with a big tree in the backyard that I tried climbing. That good ole' house at 412 Hudson Lane.* Nobody speaks like that. Not even writers.

So instead I'm going off what little information she gave in her description of the house. She said it was a relatively big house, with a bay window on the left end of the house. Parts of it were brick and others were periwinkle colored paneling. Her description of the house honestly felt like something out of a fairytale complete with ivy moss growing up the sides of certain walls. Too bad it couldn't stay that way for Liza.

I swing my leg over my bike and stand up, taking my helmet off and placing it on the back of the bike. I already look menacing enough, between my height and build, the leather jack I'm wearing and the permanent scowl that lives on my face. The only person who's been able to get it to slip for a second is the very person I'm trying to do right by. She may be too good and too kind to stand up for herself, but I'm not. So if my inability to mind my business gives Liza something she deserves, someone telling her parents off for their terrible treatment of their own daughter, then it's worth all the trouble I've ever gotten into.

As I walked up the path to the front door I caught a glimpse of the mailbox and the white cursive letters that spell Pennelli and I think I have the right place. Once I get onto the covered porch I can't help but run my hand over the mossy stones that surround the wide oak double doors. It really is a beautiful house. Taking a deep breath I rap my knuckles on the door, trying to be loud enough to be heard at this time of the night but also not so loud I seem threatening. It takes about five minutes but finally a woman about an inch or two shorter than Liza opens the door, pulling her robe tighter around her body. Her eyes are darker than Liza's. But her hair, a dark brown in tight coils that frame her face, screams her name.

"Can I help you?" She looks me up and down and tries her best to plaster on a sweet smile but I can see the way it slightly falters with the tight pull of her lips as she forces the smile.

"Are you Liza Pennelli's mother?" And now I know for sure that I have the right house because her entire body tenses and she looks a little nervous.

"Why?"

I run my hand over my jaw and laugh a little. "Her girlfriend's asking." I'm sure her blood runs cold now. Her eyes have doubled in size and her mouth is hanging slightly open as she stares at me.

Suddenly Mrs. Pennelli is trying to frantically shove the door closed but I'm faster than her want to get as far away from the homosexual standing on her porch. I shove my foot in the door and slam my hand on it to start pushing it back open, already making my way inside the house.

"Can I come in?" The eyebrow raise and smirk on my face feels like it might be borderline evil. She stutters as she stumbles backwards, fear evident in her eyes. I can tell she's trying to call out for her husband. "Go ahead, he needs to hear this too." I nod towards the stairs that I'm sure lead up to the master bedroom. Finally she finds her voice.

"Marco." She yells behind her, her eyes never leaving mine, like if she takes them off I'll lunge at her. She sounds desperate. I give a tight lipped smile as a thanks for summoning her husband. The man, excuse me Marco, comes bounding down the stairs, running so fast he almost trips and comes tumbling down the rest of the way. When he spots me, both of his eyebrows raise and he looks puzzled between the two of us and slightly concerned. Marco's eyes run up and down his wife to check for any injuries or any signs of distress and he seems to find some because immediately his attention snaps back to me but he looks angry this time. Good thing I'm angry too.

"Can I help you?" He moves to stand next to his wife, placing his hand on the small of her back in an effort to comfort her. His tone is warning, like I better leave or offer up a good explanation as to why I'm causing the commotion that I am. In my opinion, my explanation is the best one in the world, but I know they probably won't see it that way. At his question I move further inside the house and walk over to the mantle in their living room. Sitting on top of it is a picture of the two of them. But it's clearly been cropped.

"This is a beautiful picture." I ignore his question and press on with my own agenda. But first I want to watch them squirm. I can see Marco start to reach for his phone, probably to call the police. "Don't even bother Marco, I don't plan to be here for too long and I have no intention to hurt you." And then I realize that may not entirely be true, so I add in the name of honesty, "Well, physically." When they look at me with skepticism mixed with fear in their eyes all I do is shrug before turning my attention back to the picture. I've now lifted it off the mantle and begun to walk aimlessly around the room with it.

"Kind of a big house for just the two of you isn't it?" I pose the question as I tilt my head innocently to the side. I can see Mrs. Pennelli as she swallows down the anxiety coursing through her. It makes me falter for a second. The mask I'm wearing, slipping because at this moment she looks too much like Liza. Too much like the last time I saw her with fear in her eyes. Except it wasn't fear *of* me when she looked. Instead it was for me. Standing here now though with Mrs. Pennelli looking at me like this is enough to snap me out of anything stupid I was planning on doing. She's not even here and Liza's still saving me.

I hope I can save her too.

Taking in a deep breath I walk back to the mantle and set the picture down gently. I run my fingers over the edge of the metal frame, pausing to collect myself before turning back towards Liza's parents.

"I'm sorry." I can't entirely explain the sudden sheepishness that takes over me but I scratch the back of my neck and motion towards the couch, a silent question if I can sit. To my surprise a certain kindness takes over Mrs. Pennelli's face and she nods slightly before schooling her features. Neither parent makes a move to sit down opposite me, instead opting to stand where they have been, just watching me. "I guess I should introduce myself properly." The words are quiet as they come out of my mouth. "My name is Ryn Bradford, I–I'm your daughter's girlfriend." I don't owe them any explanation but the curious looks on their face must be the reason I keep babbling. "Or at least I was? I honestly don't know anymore. We haven't talked in a few weeks. It was my fault, it always is. When I came out here it was to defend her honor, to yell at you guys for turning your backs on your own flesh and blood." Marco's shoulders tense as I continue talking but Mrs. Pennelli just continues to look at me. Her expression is blank.

"I know what that's like. I have....complicated feelings about my father. He drinks himself under the table day and night." I didn't know I was crying until a teardrop landed on my hand in my lap. "That was a choice he made. To put himself in that position instead of getting actual help."

Marco is seething. I'm not really sure what's keeping him from kicking me out of the house. Maybe it's his wife, who at some point during my lecture has moved further in front of her husband, not quite holding him back but standing in his way nonetheless.

"You were great parents to Liza before she came out. Normally I'm not very good at believing in people, seeing the best in them, but Liza is. And I'm really trying to hope some of that has rubbed off on me. I think you have the potential to be good parents again. Or at least to start to mend the damage that you've caused.

I don't know if she'll want you in her life again, hell I don't even know if she'll want me back in it. What I do know is how strong she is, how smart and kind she is.

"She's gonna be valedictorian you know. Out of 864 students she's the smartest. And she's gotten into so many good colleges and has so many opportunities to change the world for the better. And I know she can do it. The question is do you guys want to be a part of her life when she does?"

I sit there, awkwardly staring at the coffee table, leaving them with that information and then get up to leave. I set down an envelope on the coffee table and tap it once before leaving it, not entirely sure if I should. Before I left, I gave them each one last glance in the eyes, Mrs. Pennelli met my gaze but Marco's still staring straight ahead where I sat on his couch with his jaw clenched and eyes filled with rage.

If I slept hunched over on my bike in front of the school like some loser instead of going back home after visiting Liza's parents, that's between me and my bike. Well, and Reuben whose bitch-ass woke me up with a small shove to my bike and snapped a picture of my angry morning glare when I looked up at him.

"Why do you insist on tormenting me Reuben?" I groan as I drag myself from my bike and start walking towards the building. Instead of going our separate ways Reuben continues to follow along, even increasing his stride in order to keep up with my longer ones.

"I don't know why I suddenly feel the urge to be brutally honest with you but," and because he's Reuben, he takes a deep breath and pauses for dramatic effect and I roll my eyes on impulse. "I don't really have a good explanation." His voice is oddly soft and when I look at him, eyebrow quirked, all he's doing is staring straight ahead and looking like a child whose parents are trying to explain the birds and the bees to him. In looking at him I see a bruise on his knuckles and once again find myself rolling my eyes.

"So among being a pain in my ass and a thorn in literally everyone's side, you're also a hypocrite?" That seems to get his attention back because his head snaps so fast to look at me I'm surprised I didn't hear a loud crack.

"What the fuck is that supposed to mean?" All I do is nod towards his hand and his eyes track the movement till he seems to realize what I'm talking about. Something in the atmosphere between us changes and I know that because the sudden urge to stand in traffic when I've made things uncomfortable becomes prevalent. Just as quickly as the feeling comes, Reuben begins speaking again. "It's nothing, did boxing for my workout this weekend and forgot to wrap my knuckles, that's all." I almost drop it but then–

"I was pushing Ellie around in one of those shopping cart cars and got too close to the wall and slammed into it."

I look at Reuben again. Like really look at Reuben, maybe for the first time ever. He's small. That's something I've always known. Looking at his frame though, there's no muscle on him, no definition to his otherwise semi-wide frame. And his eyes are sunken. He's got dark circles that would rival me on nights where my strongest demons strangle my every thought and occupy every crevice of my brain.

"Hey." I stop in my tracks and reach out and put my hand on his shoulder to stop him from moving. To the untrained eye, and even to me on a day when I'm not particularly paying attention, his slight, slight, flinch when my hand lands on his shoulder would go unnoticed. But apparently accepting your own trauma opens your eyes to others'. "You weren't boxing were you?"

You could hear a hairpin drop from two miles away from the silence that falls. He doesn't have to say anything because right now, looking at him, I can see something my mom tried to hide for so many years. "Look, uh–." I pull my hand back slowly and rub the back of my head, suddenly not sure where to start or what to say. But then I think about how my mom didn't have anyone. How she had no family to turn to, both her parents dying at some point during her childhood, and she had no friends because he isolated her from them. How she didn't have anyone to confide in until Daniel.

"I'm not gonna make you say anything, and I'm not gonna make you talk about it. But for whatever it's worth, you're not alone." I have to swallow down a lump forming in my throat threatening to make my voice break. "And no matter what, whoever is doing this to you is telling you, and whatever the voice in your head that you hear when they're gone says, you don't deserve this. Even on your worst day." I might have been able to keep my composure but Reuben's eyes are shining with unshed tears. Before I even know what I'm saying I follow it up, "I know you and I have never been buddy-buddy, but if you ever just want to hate the world a little bit without anyone trying to make you feel better, I'll join the shitshow. And if you need a way to release the anger you're feeling, keep doing what you're doing, I can take it." I shrug at that last part and smirk a little before continuing walking towards the building. While Reuben may not know the answer to why he torments me, I think I finally do.

I wish I could say that the game tonight was super eventful. Don't get me wrong it definitely was good and intense but for the most part, it was a hockey game. Oh yea, and we won. Which means we play again Saturday. I don't really care about that at all right now though. The locker room celebration was insane. Coach celebrated with us for a little bit and rolled his eyes at Hunter after he had dumped the water cooler on him. Jet brought a few bottles of sparkling cider and we sprayed it all over the place like it was New Year's Eve. It was childish and a little cringey but at that moment we were all on cloud nine.

It amazes me every time when the families of players hang around in the lobby waiting for their player to come out of the locker room. I'm fully aware of how long we all take to get showered and out of our uniforms and obviously tonight was no different. But by the time Duke, Spitz, and I strolled out of the locker room, laughing and shouting over each other about stupid shit that happened during the game, every person I had given a ticket to for tonight was standing around waiting for me. Duke and Spitz noticed at the same time I did and politely waved goodbye and gave nods to my friends and family.

A few times tonight I saw Mrs. Kahn up in the stands with my parents. The excitement was clear on her face even from down on the ice. She was decked out in my school's colors and merch and had little handheld pom poms they hand out to little kids to wave. She had blue and white paint swiped underneath her eyes and if I had to guess where she got the face paint, it would be from the 39-year-old man whose entire face is half white, half blue with a matching faux mohawk to match. My mom at least just has her hair in pigtails strung with ribbon while sporting a school shirt and foam finger. It might be a little sad that that is tame compared to Daniel and apparently Mrs. Kahn. Yet it doesn't surprise me. I can't help the smile that spreads across my face as I walk up to hug my mom. And to Daniel's surprise I hug him next and am almost ripped from his arms as Mrs. Kahn excitedly hugs me, practically jumping up and down while she squeezes me in her death grip. I step back and readjust the strap of my bag over my shoulder when I hear someone clearing their throat and all but shoving Daniel to the side.

Of course the only person to throw Daniel around like that is Maria, who must've been hidden behind her son while everyone was waiting for me. As she emerges she yanks me down by my shoulders and I swear my back cracked at least five times. Once I'm hunched over to her height she plants a big, slightly wet, kiss on my cheek and punctuates it with a large "mwah". She pats it afterwards like she needs to make sure the love she put into it got into my skin. Straightening back into my full height I feel my spine crack like a glow stick with each click. That might hurt worse tomorrow than any hit I took on the ice tonight. My mom lays her hand on my arm and tells me Daniel's father is pulling the car around and they all start heading that way, but my feet are glued to the ground as I spot Liza across the stadium lobby with some friends. Her curls are falling over her shoulders with the front pieces pulled back. Even from here I can see the sparkle in her eyes.

My mom hesitates when she notices me not moving and follows my gaze, probably seeing what's got me frozen like a deer in the headlights. Moving back into my space she leans over to whisper in my ear, "Go talk to her." I don't look away from her, almost like I can't. I've always been a little bit lost. I know that I still am, probably always will be. But not with her.

I can't say that I've fallen in love with her. I am

in love with her, but falling is the opposite of what's happened. The ground beneath my feet feels a little less like it's gonna cave in everytime she smiles at me. She makes me feel like I'm standing on solid ground more than I ever have in my entire life.

And that terrifies me.

Because I know that it won't always be solid. Hell, right now it isn't. Yet I'm still standing and I think that has a little something to do with her. But I'm terrified that whenever this broken ground comes up or starts to shake, and she's involved with me... I'm gonna let her slip through the cracks, and she deserves so much more than that.

She deserves so much more than the angry, pissed off at the world, blunt, girl who has nothing in her life figured out. Who has only just recently figured out she *deserves* a life, and a good one at that. And I don't know if I can give Liza that.

"Whatever you're mulling over in your head, put your dignity aside, because that's what you need to go tell her." My mom cuts into my shame spiral and I shake my head slightly. Not yet. I can't talk to her yet.

"I will, soon. I promise. I know you guys, Liza, and everyone around me, think that I am worth all of the stress and heartache I cause." She gives me this look and I know she wants to interrupt me. "Don't. What I'm trying to say is that I don't want to try and convince her to let me back in when I don't think I'm worth the trouble myself. As cheesy as it sounds, I need to learn to see for myself what you guys see if I ever want to be deserving of her. Or else I'm just gonna blow it again." Suddenly the look on my mom's face is something I've seen a decent amount recently but to a magnified extent. It's a mix of a lot of things but I can't tell if it's good or bad. "What? What is that face?" Her face is now one I've seen often, exasperation.

"Ellie what is wrong with my face?" She puts her hands on her hips and juts her chin out at me.

"You've been doing this weird thing with your face recently. At first I thought I was seeing things but now I'm starting to get worried. Is it a stroke? Are these the signs of a stroke? Here, smile. Let me see if it's lop-sided." I motion to her face and she swats my hands away and scoffs.

"Elleri Ryn I am not having a stroke." She whis-per-shouts and her forehead vein twitches. I shrink in on myself a little, turning sheepish. She takes a breath and the anger leaves her face and she scraps a hand over it. "My *face* recently has been *proud*, you idiot."

"Wha– that is so rude. I can't believe you would call your own flesh and blood an idi– wait. Did– did you say you were proud of me?"

"Oh Ellie." She reaches out to palm my cheek. "Every day that you stand up, and dust yourself off with your head up high, is a day that fills me so full of pride." My upper lip quivers and I look up at the ceiling willing the tears in my eyes to go away. I don't want to cry. " When are you going to realize that crying isn't a weakness? It's a sign of your strength." My eyes whip back down to hers and a few tears escape my eyes as I search hers for some sign that she's just telling me what she thinks I need to hear. She's not. And I think I believe her. I really believe her. I drop my bag at her feet.

And I run.

But I'm not running away. Not this time.

I'm honestly really lucky I haven't gotten hit by a car.

After tearing out of the rink lobby I frantically searched the parking lot for any sign of that silver Cadillac. I had almost given up hope when I noticed it at the front of a very long line of cars waiting to turn out onto the main roadway away from the rink. So I took off again.

Now I'm weaving through the parking lot while people try to navigate out of it and try not to hit the crazy 6'o hockey player running through it like her life depends on it. A red Honda almost hits me and my hand slams onto the hood as I bounce off and keep running. At this pace I'm gonna beat my fastest PACER sprint.

I finally make it to the line of cars and I am flying by

each one, a blue Ford Focus, a white Pacifica, a black Mercedes Benz. I'm two cars away from her before she pulls out onto the main road. Stopping almost in my tracks I start panting. Feeling defeated, I'm just about to turn around when a voice somewhere, deep inside me says "*You always did quit.*" I'm tired, and my body is starting to hurt from all the hits I took tonight, but that voice is enough to get my feet moving again, slowly and with a growl I start jogging, and then running.

"*Elleri why can't you remember to pick up your fucking toys when I tell you to.*" Faster.

"*You're pathetic. I don't know why I thought I could train your mother out of you.*" Faster.

"*If you don't shut up with that nonsense right now I swear to god I'm gonna break your teeth.*" Faster. Faster.

"*It's days like this I'm glad you're gay because it means I'll eventually get a second chance for the daughter I always wanted.*" Faster. Faster. Faster.

My legs are pumping so hard by this point and I'm trying to keep up with cars going 35 miles an hour. Tears are flying across my face and the tracks are gonna freeze like war markings and maybe they are.

Maybe there is a god above because there's a stop-light. I can see her car again and I tell myself just a little further.

"*One day you're gonna wake up and realize you turned out to be just like me. Then what are you gonna do? Anger and violence is who we are, Elleri.*" Just. A. Little. Further.

Smack.

I probably look deranged right about now. Hands on the hood of the car, hair falling out of place, eyes wild with tears shining in them. Either way I made it to the car and I'm looking her directly in the eyes. Her brown eyes look like saucers or maybe more accurately a deer in the headlights. Which is kind of ironic considering all things.

She throws the car in park and climbs out of it, visibly confused and maybe a little irritated. "Ryn??" She runs her hands over the curls that are barely restrained and I can't help but smile a little. "What the hell are you doing? Did you want me to hit you?" She all but shouts.

"Just stop for a second, let me talk, I just ran like two and a half miles in less than fifteen minutes. And that's after playing a hockey game. Clearly I have something to say." She looks me up and down, seeing me swaying back and forth with my hands on my head like a runner does after a marathon. She calms down a bit eyeing my flustered appearance and pauses to let me catch my breath.

"What are you doing here Ryn?" I swallow and wring my hands out in front of me. It's now or never.

"I came to apologize." She raises her eyebrow at me and crosses her arms and the irritation is back on her face, plain as day.

"That's it?" God she's not making this easy. I grunt and look at her in the eyes before continuing.

"Being angry is exhausting. I don't like it." Her stance falters just the slightest and if I wasn't watching her so carefully I wouldn't have noticed. "And if I'm being honest being angry makes me angry and it's a vicious circle that drives me insane sometimes. And I don't know much about anything. I don't know who I am or where I'm going. But what I do know is that being angry is not a part of who I am. I used to think it was something that coursed through my blood with every heartbeat. I know now that it's not. Not if I don't want it to be and I don't." I've stepped closer to her now.

"There is no excuse for how I treated you the other day. I've thought about it about a million different times wondering if I'd been able to keep that hairpin trigger in check where we'd be at today. I can't know that though and even if I could I think I needed you to stay away." She shakes her head a little, confused.

"Everyone in my life is so willing and so ready to tell me that I'm worth something. That I'm more than my father. I needed to see it for myself. I know that I'm the furthest person from perfect that you'll find within a 100 mile radius but that doesn't mean I'm gonna stop trying. I can't ever stop trying because I can't lose you. I can exist without you. I'm not trying to tell you that I need you to be with me because I can't live without you. I'm trying to tell you I don't want to live without you." She gasped and I put myself completely in her space.

"I have never understood myself *more* than when I'm with you or around you. Liza you have infected me with your joy and it's melting the ice in my veins and I don't want it to stop, please don't let it stop." I almost don't get the last word out before she's closed the space between us. Her hands fly up to my face and cup my cheeks and instantly I wrap my arms around her waist like I've done it a thousand times. One of her hands moves to my hair and she grips it like it's her life line and I tilt her head back and she opens her mouth a little, deepening the kiss. Between the honking and shouting from people angry at us holding up traffic I hear someone wolf whistle.

We break away and I continue, "I don't know what the future holds for either of us but I want to be there, as your girlfriend, and whatever else you want me to be." She gives me another small peck and then leans back but doesn't leave my embrace. Instead she tucks a strand of my hair behind my ear and I can't help but grin like the Cheshire Cat.

"I want that too." I lean my head forward until my forehead leans against hers and just breathe her in knowing that I don't have to worry because I know that I'm gonna work hard for this. "Hey, does this mean we're going to prom together?" That causes a laugh to break out of me and suddenly all of the tension I was holding onto earlier slips away with each sound that escapes my mouth, Liza laughing right alongside me.

Liza and I stumble into her house, hands all over each other and she's practically climbing me. Her movements are more aggressive then I thought they'd be and that turns me on more than I already am.

The car ride back to her house was chaotic. Liza drove like a maniac through traffic and I wasn't sure why until she finally stopped in front of her house and practically climbed over the center console to get to me.

On the way there I had called my mom and Daniel to let them know I was alright and who I was with. Naturally they made me put Liza on the phone as proof I wasn't lying. To be honest I think they missed her as much as I did, just not the same way.

The house is empty once we finally get into the door,

Liza struggling with the keys because of how frantic she was. Her family isn't home. She mentioned briefly about them going out for a late dinner and movie. I was only half listening.

Now my hands are all over her body and I'm pushing her back towards the stairs. She's got her hands in my hair and moans a little when I push my tongue into her mouth. The kiss is a little sloppy but it's perfect because it's us. Because it's Liza.

I may have only just gotten her back but that's all the more reason for us to be like this. All the words and feelings we didn't, couldn't, say to each other these past few weeks are being poured into every kiss, every touch.

I'm leading her back towards the stairs and she almost trips when her foot hits the bottom step. But since I'm all over her, never letting there be a moment we aren't touching, I steady her before she does.

We had to break the kiss to make it up the stairs. We both giggled and laughed as we raced up them. Something breaks open in my chest at that moment. Letting myself laugh so openly and hearing Liza right beside me. I would've taken the steps three at a time if she wasn't in front of me. Her hand never left mine on the way up, our fingers intertwined, Liza squeezing just slightly.

Once we're both on even ground she smashes her mouth back into mine, both of us slipping out of our shoes as we make small steps further into the upstairs hall. The kiss isn't rushed though. It's deep and it's like she's pouring every ounce of love that she feels into it and that makes me melt a little. Her hands are sliding up and down my body and I hoist her up, one hand under her ass and the other at the back of her neck. As soon as she's off the ground she wraps her legs around me and starts kissing down my jawline and eventually my neck. I'd stay here forever against the wall with her if she didn't whisper *"bed"* in my ear.

A chill runs down my spine and I take off running towards her room as she throws her head back laughing and tightening her grip around my neck. I lay her down on her bed and she pulls me down on top of her, kissing me slow and deep as she does. Her hand snakes up underneath my shirt and she gasps as she runs her fingers along the rigid lines on my stomach which makes me chuckle. What I whisper in her ear makes her shiver underneath me and I've regained a confidence I haven't had in a long time. Suddenly she's pulling at my shirt trying to get it off so I straddle her and sit up, letting her pull it off of me. I'm left sitting in my black joggers and dark green sports bra, panting. Liza's lying below me looking at me like I've never seen her look before.

"I know I'm not completely naked, but the way you see me, truly see me makes me feel exposed." Leaning in, kissing along her jaw I tug her hair and her head tilts back granting more access to her neck. I can feel her heart beating as I suck right under her jaw.

Her pupils are blown and she licks her lips and all

I want to do is chase her tongue as it goes back in her mouth. She gasps again as she answers, "You don't get to say such sweet things while doing– ah, *that*." I nip at the skin behind her ear while she talks.

"I love seeing you like this. I love that I'm making you like this."

Next thing I know she's pushing into me and practically whines "*Want you.*" If I wasn't already so in love with her that would've sealed the deal. It's her turn for the shirt to come off but I don't yank it off like she did mine. Instead I slip my fingers under the hem of her shirt and ghost my fingers along the top of her jeans before slowly moving them up her sides, goosebumps appearing right after my fingers leave each spot they just touched. Finally I bring them back down and grab the hem of her shirt. I lift it up just enough to duck my head underneath and start leaving light kisses up towards her lavender lace bra, nibbling on the skin of her stomach occasionally. Once again I pull a whine out of her, this one desperate and needy.

"Ryn *please*." That's what does it. Her small begging makes me stop teasing her and I pull the shirt all the way off and chuck it to my right, never taking my eyes off of her. Now it's my turn to drink her in.

"You sure this is what you want? That *I'm* what you want?" I only just started feeling like I'm worthy of something good but I guess not all of me is ready to believe it. There's a small bit of doubt creeping into my voice but she palms my cheek and responds so seriously.

"It's the only thing I want." I lean down and give her a gentle, slow kiss, much different then the ones we were sharing coming into the house. "Now stop messing around." The twinkle in her brown eyes looks like a fire right now and I can't help myself.

The fire in her eyes intensifies as I move back down and scoot her forward on the bed. "Yes ma'am." At the point of no return, I wink and the button on her jeans comes undone.

6:34 A.M

The groan that escapes my mouth as I try and bury myself deeper under the covers and away from that god awful noise makes the lump next to me giggle. And then I remember that the lump is not a lump and is actually Liza. Whose bed I'm in on a Friday morning after not coming home. Fuck. I can already hear the lecture now.

"Baby please for the love of god turn that awful thing off." I sound like a little kid as I put the pillow over my head trying to drown out the sound of her alarm clock.

"Stop complaining, we have to get up." She kisses me on the shoulder and slides out of the bed. "We're gonna be late and somebody is gonna be wearing the same clothes as yesterday." She looks my blanketed figure up and down and adds, "Because you sure as hell aren't fitting in any of my clothes." I huff at her and pull my head out from under the covers.

"How do you look so put together after just waking up? Are you a Disney princess?" This makes her blush and I feel smug.

"Shut up," She grumbles. Her face grows serious and she looks down at her hands that she's playing with and turns away from me. I sit up slightly, my elbow propping me up as I look at her. "Are we ever gonna talk about that day? About what happened?" I sit up fully after that and sigh. I knew this was gonna come. But I can't run from it. I won't run from it.

"Let's talk about it at lunch. Ok?" She whips around, eyes wide and she looks surprised. Surprised that she hadn't had to beg me to let her in. That makes me feel bad so I remind her of what I told her last night. "I meant every word last night. I'm not going anywhere and I'm gonna work every day to get better, to be better."

She climbs back into the bed and snuggles into my chest, my arms wrapping around her. We stay like that for a while before she looks up at me and asks, very seriously, "Are you taking a shower before we leave?"

I scoff and ask, "Are you saying I smell Pennelli?"

"Hey it's nothing against you but you did play a hockey game last night and *then* run super far, super fast through traffic. So yea, you smell a little." I hit her with the pillow and push out of the bed, sauntering towards the shower as I grumble under my breath.

"Since when is it ok to tell your girlfriend she smells?" And just like that Liza is cackling again as I walk down the hall. Her laughter becomes muffled the farther I get away.

I'm not even at my locker five minutes before the two bozos I call my best friends come sauntering over like the cats that caught the canary. I slam my locker closed and give them a deadpan look, arms crossed. The shit-eating grin that takes up most of Spitz's face is nauseating and I growl a little looking at him. The growl does nothing to stop him from bouncing on his heels while Duke, who has a similar expression, nudges me in the shoulder with his fist before speaking.

"Sooooo. How come you're wearing the same clothes as yesterday?" I was an idiot to think they'd let that slide.

"Shut up," I grumble in response.

"Somebody's doing the walk of shame." Spitz sings-songs and draws out the *"shame"* part. I roll my eyes and pick my bag up from the ground.

"Like you even know what that is." I punch Spitz in the arm and he stumbles back, Duke instinctively uses both arms to catch him and starts to move around him to follow me as I turn and start to walk off.

"No but seriously," Duke jogs a little to catch up to me. Spitz almost falling having slowed him down. "Can we assume that something last night happened with Liza? I mean that's like the only option. So what happened? At the game you guys weren't even together and now you show up to school looking exhausted and wearing the clothes you left the game in? What gives Bradford?"

I reach behind me and pull Spitz forward by the shirt, he was behind Duke and I, trying to catch up, and I shove Duke into the small corner that leads to an emergency exit. The area is empty and away from nosey assholes who stick themselves into everyone's business. Duke laughs as Spitz straightens out his shirt, trying to make it look unwrinkled and not like a fist was just in it. "Ok, yes. I was with Liza last night." I can't help the coy smile that plays on my lips. "And yes, I am in the same clothes as last night. They probably smell a little too considering I ran like two miles or something in less than fifteen minutes." Both of them wrinkle their noses at that like they are noticing some smell coming off of me and I smack them both on the sides of their heads. "I showered this morning you jackasses." Duke full on laughs at that and Spitz just rubs the back of his neck, looking sheepish.

"Wait, why did you run so far after the game?" Spitz looks utterly confused and this is one of those times I'm immensely worried about how he's going to survive in the world.

"She was clearly running after Liza, Toby." Duke face-palms and continues, "So what happened when you caught up to her?"

It's my turn to look sheepish now. If I hadn't been through so much with these two I probably wouldn't even consider telling them but they've been with me in my darkest moments and still stand in abandoned sections of the hallway with me gossiping like a bunch of teenage girls. I am a teenage girl. I don't know what their excuses are.

"I told her what she means to me. And for once in my life I was truly vulnerable with someone who wasn't my mother. I told her I love her." Spitz gasps like the dramatic bitch he is and Duke just smiles like a proud dad.

"You told her you love her," Spitz practically shouts and it slightly echoes throughout the hall. Quickly I slap my hand over his mouth.

"Would you *please* use your inside voice. I don't need the whole fucking floor to know I confessed my love to my girlfriend last night. Reuben'll never let me hear the end of it." I grumble the last part under my breath. But now that Spitz brought up the question and I think back to everything I did say last night, I'm not so sure I did. Spitz gets a look in his eyes and I've seen it before. "Do NOT lick my hand." I give him my best death glare and his eyes widen and he partially shrinks in on himself. I take my hand away, still glaring because I know he was thinking about it.

"I can't believe you told her. Congrats Bradford." He goes to dap me up and I just go through the motions, not very there as I realize I didn't actually say the words *I love you.*

"Ok, but I may not have actually said that in those exact words." Now Duke just looks dead exhausted with me. If I wasn't having my own internal crisis right now his face would be comical. He even pinches the bridge of his nose.

"Did you, or did you not say 'I. Love. You.' Ryn?" Duke makes sure to punctuate each word and when I slightly shake my head he groans and Spitz's mouth drops open like he can't believe what he's hearing.

"How the *fuck* did I not say I love you?!" I whisper-shout at them. My eyes are bulging and I'm sure I look insane. The bell goes off signaling ten minutes to get to first period and I start to move out of the hallway before Duke tugs on my sleeve a little and I growl and glare at the contact. He laughs and throws his hands up but keeps walking besides me.

"Even if you didn't say the actual words it looks like you got your message across." He motions to my clothes at this and once again I'm rolling my eyes at him. "Hey," He smacks my arm and turns serious,

"This just means you get to orchestrate how you want to tell her. Make it the perfect moment. And not something desperate where you think it's your one shot to get it right. You got the girl Bradford. Now you just gotta tell her how you feel." He gives me a soft smile and it helps calm my nerves just the slightest bit. But in Spitz fashion he ruins the moment when he finally snaps out of the fog he was standing back in the hallway in, and runs to catch up to us.

As he does he yells, "Wait so did you or did you not get laid last night?" Duke bursts out laughing so hard he doubles over and I just start grumbling under my breath, feeling my face heat up so hot I'm sure it matches a tomato. Of course Spitz wasn't quiet, so everyone in the hallway heard him and are now throwing glances our way. I could kill him right now.

9:37 A.M

"I gave these to you four months ago." Mrs. Geller slaps down a bunch of pamphlets and flyers with information about jobs and careers that have nothing to do with college on her desk in front of me. All things she wanted me to follow up on. I told her I would. I lied.

Judging by the look she's giving me now as she stands over her desk glaring at me with her arms crossed, I'm guessing she knows I haven't looked at them at all.

"You're not leaving this office until we go through each and every one of these and you actually talk about them." She sits back down, exhausted with me already and I can tell this is gonna be a long visit. To be honest I could tell that from the moment I got the slip calling me to her office.

So I spent the next hour in Mrs. Geller's office reading through pamphlets about being an electrician, a plumber, a police officer (absolutely not), construction worker, a firefighter. My brain was starting to go numb after the fifth pamphlet. I was ready to just say I would be a plumber to get her to stop shoving jobs down my throat.

"Please, Mrs. Geller, if I promise, and I really mean promise this time, to take these and seriously look them over and give them consideration, can you *leave me alone.*" I look at her, my eyes pleading and she seems to take pity on me for just a second but she turns around and reaches behind her and grabs more pamphlets and slams them down on the desk in front of me. I groan and slam my head on top of the pamphlets and feel like crying a little. This is torture. She knows I hacked her computer. She has to.

I shouldn't be this nervous. I really shouldn't. I made the reservation for 7:20 at Liza's favorite restaurant. Ok, Spitz made the reservation. I tried calling and got in a fight with the hostess who wouldn't guarantee me a table towards the back of the restaurant where Liza likes to sit. So instead we called back 15 minutes later, this time Spitz was speaking, Duke holding me back from grabbing the phone when she folded right away.

But now I'm standing in Liza's living room, with Arabella just 15 feet away in the kitchen, occasionally poking her head in and sizing me up, waiting for Liza to come down from her room so we can leave. It's only a 35 minute drive, 40 if there's heavy traffic, across town to the place and it's only 6:14. There's still plenty of time for us to get there so there's no reason for me to be nervous.

Except this is my grand gesture. Or I guess my second grand gesture since I didn't do the first one fucking right. I'm wearing my nice leather tonight. Nothing's ripped or beaten about it, it's polished and shiny and fits nice in all the right places. My black skinny jeans go nice with the cream colored henley I've got on underneath the jacket. It's one of the few light-colored shirts I own and I figured tonight was the night to wear it. Arabella made me take off my lace-up hiker boots at the door when I came in so I'm standing in navy blue socks with my hands shoved in my pockets, occasionally pulling out my hand to bite at my nails.

All of a sudden the soft thudding of heels on carpet starts coming down the stairs and I slide a little on the floor as I rush over to where Liza is making her way down the staircase in the most beautiful dress I'd ever seen. Or maybe it seems that way because it's on her. The dress is this lilac-lacey, floral and leaf pattern off-the-shoulder strapless dress. She's got her hair pulled back just so that it's out of her face but not so much that the curls are restricted.

"Wow." I utter, breathless. She giggles as she continues walking down the stairs, shaking her head slightly, trying to hide the blush rising on her cheeks.

"You really have a way with words don't you." I huff and roll my eyes at her. Once she gets to the bottom of the stairs I make my way over to her and give her a kiss on the cheek. She looks me up and down, nothing like the interrogating look her aunt's been giving me from the kitchen every few minutes, and runs her hands up and down my sides underneath my leather jacket. "This is a nice shirt." She practically purrs.

"We need to get to the restaurant. I don't want to be late. Our reservation is at 7:20." I take her hands in mine and motion towards the door.

"Is that why you told me to get ready so early? So we would have 30 minutes to sit and wait around in the parking lot once we got there?" I can't tell if she's trying to tease me or if she's insinuating something but either way I'm embarrassed.

"Shut up." I mutter under my breath. She just takes my hand and starts walking towards the door, dragging me with her and calling to her aunt in the process letting her know she'll be back later.

Ok so maybe I didn't have to really worry about us making our reservation. We've been sitting in the parking lot of the restaurant for the last 12 minutes waiting to go in and we still have about another 13 before we should even consider getting out of the car.

We've killed time in.....various ways. But you can only make out for so long before it goes further so now we're sitting in the back seat of Liza's car –we decided not to take my motorcycle– just cuddling and talking about the day.

"I think you'd look really sexy as a construction worker. But like only if you wore a specific construction type outfit. Not all of those outfits work." A deep laugh escapes my chest and she nestles in further against me.

"Do any of those outfits happen to have me in a cutoff vest that showcases my muscles?" I peer down at her as I play with her curls.

She smirks slightly as she responds, "Only slightly."

I take a deep breath as I continue, "Anyways I don't really think I'm going to be researching any of the jobs much further." She whips her head to get a better look at me, looking between my eyes.

"How come?" She's looking at me so seriously and it makes me feel vulnerable when I haven't even started speaking.

I take a deep breath and just run my fingers through her hair for a few seconds trying to take down the walls that are always up no matter how much progress I make. "Because I've spent so much time in my life trying to deal with the trauma that my father gave me, that I'm not really sure who I am outside of it. And I don't really know where to start. I mean I found hockey because I was angry." I look outside and I can see some of the snow melting into the grass making a muddy concoction of slush. Something in between two types of beautiful. "And I was angry because of my father. The only thing that I really know that I like are plants but I don't want to make a career out of that. That's my safe space and I don't want to bring any possible stress into that." Liza turns fully in my arms once I'm done talking and looks at me with those big brown puppy eyes, eyes that used to drive me crazy when we first met.

"You are so unbelievably mature. And I am so glad that I know you. For all of the pain that you believe that you cause– not that you actually cause that pain," she adds quickly. "You offer so much more good." It would be impossible not to kiss her after that.

"I love you." Her eyes widen slightly and she looks at me shocked. "I meant to tell you the night of the game and I planned on doing it again tonight at dinner but I couldn't not say it now. I love you."

She pulls back a little, her mouth open slightly and just blinks at me. I don't like the silence that falls throughout the car after I said I love her because now she's just looking at me. Not saying anything. If I wasn't too busy having my own panic attack over the fact that she's *just looking at me* then I'd be worried she was having a stroke and that's why she hasn't said anything. I think the silence might be worse than her just ripping off the bandaid and telling me she doesn't love me. Because that's what this has to be, right?

"I love you too." But then she says it. "I've never been in love before. And I didn't wanna say it if I didn't mean it. And I also know we just got back to being us which is why I paused for a second. Not because I had to think about how I felt about you, because I know how I feel. But because I needed to realize that you know what this feeling is. And I can see in your eyes that you do. Feel it in your touch, in the way you hold my face as you kiss me. It's overwhelming, makes it hard to breathe, love. You've made me feel safe from the moment I met you in the cafeteria." She laughs a little under her breath and I pull her impossibly closer.

"Even if those circumstances were a little out of the ordinary." That causes me to laugh too. I rest my forehead against hers and brush my nose against the tip of hers and feel her shaky exhale as she releases all the tension she must've been holding. That fear of being so vulnerable with someone, not something easy to do, even for someone like Liza.

"And I would do anything to make you feel that same way. And I know you would continue to do anything to keep me feeling this way. That's love. I think I was in love with you when I had you meet my family." She pauses here, like she's treading in rough waters, unsure how to proceed. Or if we'll keep our heads above water if she does. "I realized something after you left my house. You were right. I had been trying to fix you. I think some part of me was so obsessed with helping you that along the way I stopped seeing what you actually needed from me, which was to just hold your hand and love you while you hurt." She palms my cheek and runs her thumb under my eye as a tear escapes as she finishes her sentence and she adds, "I'm sorry that I lost sight of what matters." A few tears escape her eyes and her lip quivers slightly.

We've been through so much. But we're still standing.

I finally did something right.

Once again we won our game. If Spitz hanging half-way out the bus with Cliff holding his legs in so he doesn't fall out while Duke fusses over them like a worried mother isn't one indication of that victory then I don't know what is.

Liza spent the night over at my house after our dinner and for the first time in my life I had what felt like a normal family interaction. Daniel cooked dinner for him and my mom and afterwards we all sat around the table playing board and card games and I laughed a lot.

Unlike everyone else in the house, I had to get up early this morning because I had to report to the school by 7:30. Our bus was leaving by 8. Liza showed up to the arena with my mom and Daniel in tow and this time she sat with them. Before our bus left Natalie got pictures and a few quotes about how we were feeling about our second playoff game for her article for the school paper. Duke was all smiles.

She'll have a good article to write about too. I was fouled three times and spent a grand total of 15 minutes game time in the penalty box myself. If that wasn't enough we went into overtime. I'd be celebrating with the rest of the team right about now if I wasn't dreading the consequences of my own actions breathing down my neck in the coming days.

Tomorrow I confront my problems. Or die trying.

I've circled the block of the little gray house the man I hit lives at, about five times now. I thought it was better to make long elaborate laps than just sit and potentially get arrested for stalking.

I haven't worked up the courage to park my bike and actually go up to the man's door and ring the bell and start the process to try and make peace for what I did to him all those weeks ago. Like I do most things, I've put it off till the last possible minute. My hearing is tomorrow. It's now or never if I have any hope of him dropping the assault charges.

Olivia has no idea I'm doing this and probably would lose her mind if she did. I know it's probably not my brightest idea to track down the man I assaulted and try and convince him to drop the charges for so many reasons including the fact it could make the situation worse, but I have to try something. I can't just walk into that hearing tomorrow and hope for the best.

After coming around the block for what I think is now my 7th time in total I park the bike across the street from his house. He lives across the street from a park. It's beautiful right now. Peaceful. There are no little kids and the snow that's melting is making the grass look more alive than it probably has all winter. I wonder why he lives here. Maybe he has grandkids that come and visit him. Or maybe he's lived in the same house since his kids were little and this was the park they played on when they were kids. I peer at the park trying to get a better look. It doesn't look that old. The paint job looks relatively new but I guess that doesn't mean anything. You can use anything to cover up ugly parts of yourself you don't like, that doesn't mean they aren't there or were never there. I know that better than anyone.

I look back and forth between the house and the park. Each on either side of me. I groan and swing my leg over the bike and walk over towards the park. Sitting down on the swing, I fell a lot further to the seat then I thought I would. My long legs drag across the ground as I swing lazily back and forth without any real effort, barely moving.

I let myself get lost in the simple sounds around me. The few birds who have come back or stayed through the winter, the creaking of the metal of the chains on the swing and the small whistle of the wind as it blows at my hair.

Suddenly I hear a new noise. It sounds like laughter.

The laughter is coming from me. Childlike and free. Except it's different from the laughter of my childhood. It's lighter. I'm giggling.

Pushing my feet back and off the ground I start swinging fully and the giggling turns into full-on laughter. This is happiness.

"You know this is usually where I go to get away from the world." I'm startled from my childlike state of happiness when a man's voice speaks from behind me. I put my feet down trying to drag myself to a stop and I flail about chaotically as I come careening to a stop.

When I turn my head and look to the voice, I see the man who I came to visit and who I, very childishly, am avoiding.

"Oh, uh, I'm so sorry. I meant to go see you about— uh, I actually don't know how much time I've spent avoiding you. Not that I'm trying to avoid you. Shit. I'm sorry." He looks me up and down and offers me a slightly sympathetic smile.

"May I sit?" He gestures to the swing at the other

end of the set. I nod and he sits down, another seat in between us. He starts to sway back and forth slightly before speaking again, but he doesn't look at me, he just stares out into the distance into the park as he does.

"Your name is..." He trails off, clearly unsure of what exactly my first name is and not wanting to get it wrong and offend me. I don't know his name either. I've just been calling him an old man which isn't exactly pleasant.

"Ryn. My name is Ryn." He gives a curt nod and we resume our silence. This time I'm the first one to break it. "You said this is usually where you come to get away from the world. How long have you been coming here?" He looks around and digs his feet into the rocks beneath us and twists a little bit in his seat, the motion making him seem so much younger than he actually is. If I had to guess an age I would say early to mid 70s. His hair is mostly white with a few gray ones thrown in the mix and his skin has taken on that leathery look that it does when you start to reach a certain age.

"I lived in that house," he gestures back behind us where his house is, "For 42 years. I raised my kids in that house. I actually watched this park get built from that house." He reaches out and runs one of his hands down one of the poles that holds the swing-set together and looks at it with a faraway look in his eyes. One I'm all too familiar with.

"I'm from Florida." I start. This catches his attention and he turns and looks at me. I'm staring out into the park, a distant look on my face.

"They got any nice parks down there?"

"They had parks." I take a deep breath before continuing because I desperately want to keep my composure throughout all of this. "I don't have a lot of happy memories from down there."

"I'm sorry to hear that." Silence falls over us again. Neither one of us knows quite what to say to the other one. "What are you doing here Ryn?" He finally asks.

"I did– *do*, want to talk to you. About what happened." I begin. "I guess I want to start by saying that I don't want to make excuses for myself. I shouldn't have hit you. The amount of times that I sit wishing I could go back and redo that day probably won't ever end because I fucked up– please forgive my language– but I fucked up royally that day in so many ways from start to finish, not just with what I did to you." He's looking at me fully now. He's turned his body sideways in his seat so he's facing me and his expression looks interested at the very least.

"I was meeting my girlfriend's family. And she is wonderful. Beyond wonderful. Someone I'm still sometimes learning I'm deserving of." I pause again and look down at my shoes. "Seeing her interact with her family that day, specifically her uncle with her younger cousins, caused me to have some PTSD flashbacks." This causes him to shift in his seat. Confusion etches on his face as I continue talking, "I've been in therapy for a few months now. I didn't get that childhood. I mean I guess I did. At times, I did. But those memories are tainted now."

My voice shakes a little as I continue. "My father hit my mother. Sometimes in front of me. And he yelled at me. Threatened me. We only left him about two years ago and moved here last summer." My lip is quivering and tears are filling in my eyes but I really, really don't want to cry. "The worst part is I look just like him. And that day, at my girlfriend's house I said something to her, something that he would say to my mom all the time and I started spiraling because I felt like my worst nightmare was coming true so I just left the house and started walking. And I walked into a 7-Eleven because it was familiar but for all the wrong reasons and I didn't realize it would trigger me more."

"You were just trying to help me and for that I am so, so sorry." I turn to look at him when I say that. "I don't want you to think I'm here to pressure you in any way, I mean I'd be lying if I didn't say I was hoping you would drop the charges, but I just really wanted to explain myself more than anything. And to say I'm sorry." I quickly added.

There's an understanding behind his eyes. A kindness to them. He looks like he wants to reach out and touch me, to comfort me but he's afraid. Because the last time he did that he got punched. And that makes me want to sob harder.

Instead I make the first leap. The first gesture of kindness. Of healing. I slowly reach out my hand across the space between us and after a moment, after he looks at my palm face up in the open space between us he reaches out in the space between us and takes my hand and squeezes it.

After a while we let go and we continue to just sit there in silence for what seems like forever. Once he finally decided to get up and go back inside his house, he said that it was nice meeting me and thanked me for coming to see him. He then told me he would see me tomorrow.

My meeting with the judge is bright and early today. Well kind of. It's bright and early for me and I haven't stopped chewing my nails since we got to the courthouse.

Yesterday, after I met with Harold, whose name I learned before I left, I met up with my mom and Olivia at a department store so they could dress me for today's meeting. I don't really have any fancy clothes and apparently jeans were deemed not appropriate attire for a court meeting no matter if they were free of holes or not.

So now I'm sitting here in a stuffy burgundy pant-suit, (they thought black combined with my constant brooding felt like I was going to my own funeral so they wanted color and I refused the mustard colored one Olivia held up and smiled around.) My mom couldn't convince me to go without any rings or bracelets and that made the vein in Olivia's forehead pop as she tried to stress to me that the goal was to make me look as less threatening as possible. Honestly it all went in one ear and out the other.

My mom made me shove my feet into these slightly pointed-toe brown dress shoes and right now the tapping of the heel on the terrazzo floor is all I can hear throughout the empty hallway. What started as a nice, well-put together bun is now slightly falling apart and some of the pieces are falling down around my face but just as I start to stand up to go to the bathroom to pull the pieces back into the large nest on my head, the judge's secretary or something comes out and calls us back into the conference room where Harold and his lawyer are already in there waiting for us. Liza came over for breakfast this morning before leaving for school and tried to convince me everything would be ok. Duke and Spitz want to know as soon as I'm out and what the verdict is.

I had to convince them not to come to the courthouse that day because the last thing I or the justice system needed was two idiots wandering around causing mayhem while they waited for me. The rest of the group just sent their well wishes to me through text, like normal friends.

"Ms. Cooper, Mrs. Torres, Miss Bradford, please

take a seat." The judge, a man who looks to be in his late 40s, early 50s gestures to the left side of the conference room table, meaning we have to cross the room and cross in front of both the judge, Harold and his lawyer, and the assistant district attorney.

I lean over to Olivia as we're walking and whisper, because I can't help myself, "Where's the typing lady, the one who writes down everything I say, including the stupid shit?"

Olivia rolls her eyes as she pulls out her chair and sets her briefcase down on the table and whispers back. "You mean like this question?" She then sighs and continues, "They don't have a whole lot of those anymore, they just record the audio and then have someone type it at a slower playback speed later." Huh. That's actually kind of cool. It's like a true crime podcast.

After taking my seat I can't help but squirm a little, twisting back and forth in the swivel chair. It was a bad idea for them to place these chairs in such a serious setting if they wanted me to act serious sitting in them.

"Let's get started shall we." The judge continues. "Earlier this morning, Mr. Jasper and his lawyer came to see the assistant district attorney and wanted to discuss the charges they brought up against you." I tense a little at this and my mom puts her hand on my knee. "As I'm sure you are aware, you are currently facing assault in the fourth degree and obstructing the legal process. Both are misdemeanors, the punishment for the assault charge being up to one year in prison and a fine of up to $3000. The punishment for obstructing the legal process is also up to one year in prison and/or up to $3000 in fines." I gulp. I knew it was bad but possibly two years in prison? Two years of my life gone down the drain because of some stupid mistake I made when I was having a panic attack?

That's two years where any reconciliation I've made with Liza goes down the drain. Two years where my friends move on and start their new adult lives without me in it. Two years where my mom and Daniel have to come visit me behind glass and talk to me through a phone on the wall. Two years where the world moves on without me while I'm stuck standing still. And if that thought doesn't make me want to crawl out of my skin.

If I make it out of this, I vow to never let anything he did influence my life negatively again. This might be my second chance, to make my legacy something more than him. To really put in the work to be something better. For the people around me, and most importantly for myself.

9:47 A.M

The room is spinning around me. It's hard to tell what exactly is being said between Olivia and the judge right now because all the sound in the room's been sucked out and now everything is muffled and there's a slight ringing. My mom is using a tissue offered to her by Mr. Jasper to dab at her eyes.

"Mr. Jasper has decided to drop the charges." Olivia is standing up now and reaches across the table to shake Harold's lawyer's hand and then his, and she nudges me to follow suit. Clumsily I stand up from my seat and extend my hand to the man who looks a little less than pleased that his client decided against going through with turning my world sideways. Which is kind of a douchebag thing to want if you think about it because

he gets paid for his time here either way. But I shake his hand, a tight, unyielding grip, anyways and then I look at Harold and a small smile takes over my face. I reach out my hand to him a lot slower than I did his lawyer just now and he reaches out with both hands. One hand takes mine and the other comes around the other side and he squeezes and pats the back of my hand.

"Take care of yourself Ryn." He says it so sincerely that I start to tear up a little and all I can do is give a quick, curt nod before sitting back down in my seat and stare at my shoes while he and his lawyer leave.

"Miss Bradford, I'm sure you're aware that we still need to discuss the other charges brought up against you." I look up and nod slightly.

"Good, then let's begin."

11:02 A.M

"Ok I believe I've heard enough." The judge finishes after Olivia and the ADA, who seem not to
like each other very much, lay out their arguments.
Both are really good at their jobs because whenever the other was speaking I was fully convinced
I was either going to go to jail and deserved to or
I was completely innocent and it was all a misun-
derstanding. And that's honestly saying more about
Olivia's skills as a lawyer than anything because we
all know how I feel about my involvement in this.
"Based on the collective statements from Miss Bradford and Ms. Cooper, as well as the written statement from one Dr. Shaw and a Mr. Maddox, I see
no reason for this case to go to trial." For the first

time since Harold left the room I breathe a breath of relief.

"As for the charges, Miss Bradford I am requiring you to pay a $300 fine on top of completing 50 hours of community service." I almost laugh from how happy I am at the words that just came out of his mouth. "I'm also requiring you to go to a mandated anger management class once every two weeks for the next six months." What. I nearly choke. I'm not even 18 (I'll be 18 in literally three days so I mean close enough but still.) I'm not even 18 and I'm gonna be in anger management? The thought makes me want to snap a pencil and...ok I might see why he's making me go to anger management. If the grip my mom has on my leg is any indication of how funny she thinks this is then the marks later are gonna make her cackle when she thinks about it.

After the judge tells us we can go, Olivia gets the information from the ADA for my case manager, which is the person I'll be reporting to about attending anger management meetings and actually performing community service. Basically someone who makes sure the flight risk doesn't take flight. I thought that was supposed to be my mother but I guess they wanted someone in the legal system.

Walking out of the courthouse I stop on the steps and let the light hit me in my suit. Behind me I hear the click of a camera and a small snicker. Whipping my head around I see my mother standing just outside the doors of the courthouse with her phone in her hands typing on the screen. I cross my arms and the material of the suit pinches slightly around my biceps.

"Who are you sending that to?" I ask her, eyes squinted and my mouth in a frown.

She just laughs to herself before casually responding, "Liza." My jaw drops open and my hands drop to my side and all I do is sputter. "Close your mouth honey, you're gonna catch flies." She pats my cheek as she walks past me and unlocks the car in the parking lot.

"I– I just have so many questions." I hop down a few more steps to catch up to her and pull my hair down and run my hand through my hair to shake it out. "Do you do this often? Take random photos of me to send to Liza? Why did you take one just now?" In my rant another thought hits me and I stop dead in my tracks and almost screech. Well screech as much as I can screech.

"Do YoU sEnD tHeM tO OtHeR pEoPle?" When I tell you the nerve of this woman as she just cackles. Like I'm the funniest fucking person she's met in her life. I love her but I've never wanted to run us both into traffic more than I do right now in my life. I'm not going to obviously but it would end my suffering and let me exact my revenge all in one go. Getting to the car, I slide into the passenger seat, grumbling the whole time.

My mom puts the car into drive once we're both settled in and as we're driving down the street she glances over at me and says, "Why don't we celebrate?" And a thought settles over me. One that feels like home and nothing like it did a month ago.

"7-Eleven?"

Today has been one of the most chaotic days of my life. It's only the semifinals, god forbid what happens to this school if we make it to the championship.

The entire school was decked out in streamers and balloons. Our student council made posters about us beating the other school. All of which were extremely cheesy and very on brand for something an overly peppy high school club may create.

Everyone on the team wore their jerseys throughout the day and that garnered a lot of attention– for me it was unwanted, for Hunter it was very wanted, and for everyone else they liked the attention but they didn't let it get to them. For old times sake Liza and I ate in the stairwell of the Dockner building, away from everything. We invited Duke and Spitz and they came about halfway through lunch. It was nice. I needed to be away from the world to process and they supported me even though they didn't have to.

The craziest part of the day was probably the pep rally. Most of the festivities didn't even seem centered around us. The entire event just seemed like an excuse for the school to miss class (or for some, leave school entirely) and engage in stupid games like smashing whipped cream in the teachers' faces. Granted we did get to smash one in Coach Maddox's face which probably made the school laugh more at us then at him because we spent so long arguing over who got to do it.

I'm pretty sure at one point he was convinced it wasn't gonna happen because he was standing away from us with his arms crossed and a smug look on his face. I ended up stealing the tin out of the air from Jet who was holding it hostage from Spitz, who couldn't reach that high, and calmly walked over to Coach while he was laughing and didn't see me and pushed it in his face. The team was a little bummed but I think in the end we all knew it needed to be done.

The team stood in the center of the gym while the stands of students and faculty yelled and cheered the fight song for us. I stood there awkwardly with my hands folded in front of me waiting for it to be over, while Duke pumped his hand along with the rhythm next to me. Natalie had been taking pictures throughout the entire thing and I think Duke had snuck off to talk to her at one point.

Another rally game was musical chairs which got pretty intense for high school. Cliff literally threatened to snap the chair in half *around* Hunter if he didn't admit he cheated, which he very stubbornly wasn't doing. He did, by the way, cheat. Some random kid got a bloody nose during this balloon pop game where you literally use another person to pop balloons. Cliff and Spitz teamed up together, Cliff was popping them on Spitz. And it was a recipe for disaster. Cliff jumped on Spitz once and the entire gym went silent. I swear you could hear the air fizzle out of him and I know it wasn't the balloon because it was distinctly Spitzbarth. Yes, that's his full last name.

Now I'm sitting on a bus full of a bunch of guys who have become family as we ride towards a game that could very well be our last for the season, and for many of us the last of our high school careers. And isn't that a sad thought. Tomorrow I start community service and I've talked with Mrs. Kahn and we've decided to cut back on my hours at the greenhouse for the time being so that I can work to get them done before the school year ends. I still don't entirely know what I want to do. I know it's somewhere in those pamphlets that Mrs. Geller gave me, and I know I need to figure it out fast. I won't be leaving the greenhouse entirely, I have a shift there on Saturday after my community service hours, but it's hard to spend all my time there now that I have a life I want to pursue outside of what I was being made to do.

"You look lost in thought." Duke sidles up next to me on the bus, gripping the seat in front of us and nudges me with his shoulder.

I give him a small smile and pull the airpod out of my ear closest to him. "Did my mom invite you to my birthday party?" He looks taken aback by this. Like this was the last thing he expected me to say right now. He also looks like he wants to figure out how to run away from this conversation without being rude.

"What birthday party? I–uh," He scratches at the back of his neck, "I don't know about any birthday party."

"You're the worst liar on the planet Duke Ballinger." I roll my eyes at him. "It's ok. I already knew she was throwing a party. She's not very subtle and neither are any of the other people in my life either so it's not like it was gonna stay a secret for very long." He sighs a little and runs a hand through his dirty blonde hair. He really is a golden retriever if I've ever met one. "Just don't let her do anything too crazy. I know I'm turning 18, but I swear to god I will ditch the party if it's too overwhelming." He doesn't laugh at that because he knows I'm serious. Just nods and puts his hand on my shoulder for a beat before getting back up and going back to his own seat.

4:22 P.M, Wednesday

Walking into the station was a perfect storm. People were rushing around me and I just felt like I was in the way. Somewhere above my head an alarm was going off and a voice was repeating the same numbers over and over. I kept bumping into people as they ran to the trucks to get where they needed to be. By the time the alarm stopped ringing and the chaos had stopped I was standing in an empty room, with no direction and unsure what to do with myself. That last part seems to be happening a lot recently.

I'm completing a majority of my community service hours, or at least these first couple, at the fire station closest to my house. I was supposed to come in today and help out and learn what they wanted me to do with my time while I was here and get started after school but I don't think anyone's here.

"Can I help you?" I stand corrected. Again, that seems to be happening a lot lately.

"Uh yea, I'm looking for," I pause to look at my hand. I wrote the name of the captain down on my palm before I left my house because I knew I'd forget before I got here. "Captain Diaz?" It comes out more like a question, because I'm not really sure what I'm doing here other than the mandated work I'm required to be doing.

The person chuckles to themself and then answers, "You just missed em'. He'll be back in a bit. Can I possibly help you with something in the meantime?" The man looks to be in his late 30s-early 40s and he seems sincere.

Instead of taking him up on his offer though I can't help but rudely blurt out, "Why did they leave you behind?" He makes an amused face, like I'm something funny and that pisses me off just a little bit and I can't help but glare at him and he laughs then shrugs.

"It's nothing personal. Somebody's gotta be man behind at the station so that if a person, much like yourself, comes in, somebody's here to talk to them and help them if they need it. Today, I'm that person." He finishes. "So how can I help you?" I tell him my name and apparently the station's been briefed that I was coming in case something like this happened because he's aware of who I am and what they want me to do around here.

Firefighter Isaac Hoopeston, whose name I learned once he started showing me around the station and telling me where everything I would need was, gave me a small tour of the place. I'm gonna be doing a lot of answering phones and cleaning things.

"Do you have any questions?" Hoopeston asks me as we're walking down the stairs from the loft and heading back towards the lobby where he's gonna set me up with a list of prompts of basic things to say to people who call in asking for things as well as training videos for me to watch so that I know basic information on how to help people. Anything that I can't help people with or that seems like a big emergency outside of where they can bring old fire extinguishers or things along those lines, I'm supposed to put them on hold and call for Hoopeston or for someone else if other people are back at the station.

It all seems pretty straight forward. The other firefighters have started pulling back into the station and I can hear them all ribbing with each other and joking around having a good time. The camaraderie in the air is something similar to the kind I have with the team and it's nice, seeing it exist in a place outside of my high school.

I think I could get used to this.

"No, I don't think I do."

8:34 P.M

The station has stayed consistently busy since I arrived a couple hours ago. I've mostly managed to stay out of the way and out of sight, the way I like it, but Hoopeston knows I'm here and will come into the lobby where I'm sat at the main desk taking calls and check up on me from time to time which I guess is nice.

I haven't had a lot of calls to take so I don't feel very helpful like I do when I'm at the greenhouse. I just feel out of place. Something I've felt a lot of recently.

Instead, I just sit and observe.

There's only one female firefighter. But she's tough. She doesn't take any shit from the other firefighters and she holds her own when doing tasks around the house. They don't treat her any differently than the guys. She's simply a firefighter.

They have a hierarchy here. Different levels of people in charge, both spoken and unspoken levels of power. Similarly to that of the team. Duke is the captain, that's a spoken level of power, we all know it and respect it. And then there's me. Someone who the team puts too much faith in. I don't know when they started looking to me for guidance and leadership but I'd be lying if I said I didn't start noticing it recently. That probably has something to do with why I've felt so out of place recently. I don't know who I am or who I'm supposed to be.

I don't have time to dwell on that thought because the phone rings and I'm pulled away from the image of my teammates surrounding me, looking at me with so much hope and belief, and I grab the phone and answer, "Station 245, Ryn speaking. How can I help you?"

10:32 A.M, Thursday

This morning I woke up tired and sore from practice for the final game tomorrow after my community service hours, to Daniel and my mother singing happy birthday to me with a stack of chocolate chip pancakes with eighteen candles stuck throughout the top pancake. After breakfast, while I was getting ready for school my mom stuck her head into my room to give me a gift she'd bought for me.

"Hey sweetie. She raps her knuckles on my open door and leans against the frame with her hands behind her back clearly hiding something. "Can I come in?"

I look up at her from my spot on my bed where I was texting the group chat and give her a small nod, slightly analyzing her mischievous smile.

"I got you something." She walks into the room then, and sits down on the bed beside me. She hands me the small package and bumps my knee with hers. "Go on, open it."

Tearing through the paper she wrapped it in and setting it down on my other side, I'm left holding a book. Turning it over in my hand I see that she's gotten me a first edition of The Great Gatsby.

"Oh my god." Tears immediately spring to my eyes and I wipe at them, trying to get them to go away so they don't fall onto the book. "How much did this cost?" I look at her incredulously. I know it must have cost her a fortune because I've seen how much they go for online. They average $4,000 depending on where you get them from.

"You deserve it. You've been through so much these past three years and you're still fighting. Plus I never got you a car when you turned sixteen and this is less than that. Consider it an early graduation gift as well as a birthday gift. But that doesn't mean you get to stop trying to graduate." That makes us both laugh and she brings her forehead to rest against mine. "You are my pride and joy, and every day you walk out that door you make me prouder than I ever could be." She kisses my forehead, "Happy birthday Elleri Ryn."

When I got to school today I was greeted at my locker by five smiling doofs. Cliff, Jet, Hunter, Spitz, and Duke had taken it upon themselves to decorate my locker for my birthday and were all proudly standing in front of their work waiting for me to see it.

I think I rolled my eyes so hard that they physically went into the back of my head and stuck there for a second or two. Now I'm sitting in third period and running my fingers over the pages in my new book. I'm already halfway through the book and I know I should be paying attention to my classes but I can't help it. The book may be old but to me it's shiny and new and it solidifies how much my mother has my back and cares about me. Even though we have Daniel now, we've really only needed each other. And as long as we have that, we're alright.

Our house was too small for the party my mom was going to throw for me so she had to throw it at Maria's house. She had Liza "stall" me while she, Daniel, and Maria got everything set up and everyone showed up to the party. Liza's version of stalling me included going rock-climbing after we got out of school. She looked adorable in her helmet and harness, both of which drowned her out.

Liza finally got a text from who I'm assuming was my mother around 6:40 telling her we could come to the house. She giggled at her phone and if I hadn't already known about the party I definitely would've by then.

The drive up to the house was almost too calm. Like

they had tried to convince even the wild animals to be calm once I had gotten onto the property. Pulling into the gravel driveway (where there were one too many cars for Maria's house,) Liza throws the car in park.

"You know I'm just realizing I've never actually met your grandmother."

"Well I can tell you this is going to be the most chaotic event to do it at. I'm not gonna have a moment of peace. Daniel has– like, a million siblings– all of which I'm sure my mother's invited."

Liza interrupts me. "Woah, woah, woah. What are you going on about? What event?" She tries to play dumb and I give her a pointed look and she throws her hands up in surrender. "Ok fine. There's an event." I lean over and give her a kiss on the cheek and get out of the car. My beat-up Doc Martens dig into the gravel as I make my way over to Liza's side of the car and open the door for her. "Well, aren't you sweet?" Liza blushes slightly as she takes my hand and stands up from the driver's side. After rock-climbing, she changed into a floral skirt that's longer in the back than it is in the front. The dusty punch color compliments her tan skin and she looks like an angel.

"You ready?"

"I love that you're asking me that. It is your party after all." She squeezes my hand and we begin walking up the path towards the big front door.

I knock on the door and Maria opens it up.

"Hi dear! Come in! Come in!" Maria steps aside and

lets us in and gives me a hug. "You must be the famous Liza." Liza blushes more furiously this time. "I've heard so much about you!" She pulls Liza into a crushing hug and then waves us into the house further. Once we take a few steps into the house more, Maria makes a big show of telling me happy birthday and I'm guessing that was their key word because after she does this everyone else jumps out and yells "surprise."

Throughout the room are some of my closest friends and family. Which up until this moment I didn't realize I had so many of. It actually makes me start to tear up. As I look around the room I see my friends. I see Duke and Natalie, Sloane and Spitz, Cliff, Jet, Hunter, Amber, and Hannah.

I see my mom and Daniel standing towards the middle of the whole assembly, both looking so happy. Next to them and scattered around the room is Daniel's family. All of which have come from their busy lives to celebrate me. There's that belief again.

It's all too much. I have to get away. I look around and see an opening between people and bolt through it and make my way through the kitchen and out the back door. The grass is squishy under my feet from the rain we got this morning as I make my way to the gazebo in the backyard. I stand there for a few minutes trying to get my breathing under control before I hear a throat clear from behind me.

"Hey." The voice comes from behind me and he seems unsure of himself. "You ok?" Daniel enters the gazebo and stands on the opposite side from me with his hands shoved in his pockets.

I shove at my eyes with the back of my hand wiping the few tears that escaped my eyes.

"You know your mom and I didn't mean to upset you. We just wanted to throw you a party as amazing as you are. She thought that maybe just a small thing with just your friends would be enough but I wanted to invite my family too because I want you to know they're your family t–oof." He's cut off as I make my way across the gazebo in two strides engulfing him in a crushing hug, burying my face in his chest and crying. He tenses for a second before relaxing and hugging me back just as tight.

We stay like that for a minute before I pull back and stand next to him. Both of us just looking out at the yard.

"Not that I'm complaining, but what was that about?"

I sniffle a little and bite my lip trying to hold onto my composure. "I just– thank you." I spare a glance at him and see he's looking at me with such seriousness. "I know I haven't always been the easiest step-daughter. And you've had to put up with a lot. But you've never stopped trying to include me. You've never stopped trying to include me in your life and in your family and I just– I wanted to say thank you for that." He clears his throat a little and looks up, probably trying to fight back tears, Daniel's a crier.

He throws his arm around me and pulls me into his side and says, "Anytime kiddo, anytime."

The rest of the party went off without any prob-lems. Everyone mingled amongst themselves as music filled the first floor of Maria's home. My friends and I all played Just Dance with Daniel's nieces and nephews, my step-cousins. Hunter sur-prisingly killed it at "Rasputin."

What was also surprising was Spitz being actually pretty good at the game, not just hitting the moves when he was supposed to but actually looking good while doing it. It was weird. Someone so gangly and awkward shouldn't be so good at dancing. It's unnat-ural. What wasn't surprising was Duke's inability to dance. It was an atrocity to say the least. He stepped on his own foot at one point, which I didn't know was humanly possible. We had to make him stop for fear he would injure himself and be unable to play in tomorrow night's championship game.

The kids loved it though and we all had a lot of fun and that's all that mattered. Liza and I did the *Dirty Dancing* lift (outside of the game) and then Jet and Cliff tried to also do the *Dirty Dancing* lift and it almost ended with a broken coffee table and a furious Maria. But that's what happens when 200 lb defenders try lifting each other in the air spontaneously with no practice or prior ability. The only reason Liza and I were successful was because she's so small compared to me.

Daniel made me a red velvet 4 layer square cake with vanilla icing. It was the tallest cake I'd ever seen and the whole thing got eaten before the night was over. I thought he'd gone overboard but apparently he knew very much what he was doing accounting for all the little kids who were then going to be hopped up on sugar just to have a sugar crash an hour or so later.

Now it's almost 11 pm and I'm padding around the house in my pjs getting ready for bed when I catch my reflection in the shine of the steel fridge once I close it after getting water and it stops me dead in my tracks.

I look like him.

I have his sharp green eyes. His messy brown hair. Sharp jawline, long nose. All of it. I shake my head to clear my thoughts and the reflection changes slightly and I'm looking at myself again but I still see him. My hands shake as I raise the glass of water to my lips and I have to try really hard not to drop the glass and wake my mom and Daniel.

Why does he still have so much control over me even thousands of miles away from me? Why does he still stand in my shadow when I've tried so hard to let that part go, when I thought that I did let it go?

Something's gotta give.

I stand there in the dark. The only sound in the room is my breathing as I pull out my phone and the click sounds as it unlocks. I scroll aimlessly for a few moments before my fingers start typing, having a mind of their own. And suddenly they're hovering over the bright screen. An impulsive decision– the most I've ever made in my life– at the end of my fingertips, and they connect with the screen.

I don't have a lot of time. I need this to be quick. As quick as an impromptu flight to and from Florida can be. I only stood around for five seconds taking in what I'd done before I took off up the stairs to my room and threw on clothes. I didn't need to pack anything since I'm going for one day and doing one thing. I'm traveling light. This could easily be the stupidest thing I've ever done in my entire life but I think I need to do it. For my own sanity.

I've got directions for the state jail once I've touched down in Florida. I guess once I'm there I'll take an Uber? That'll be a fun car ride. *Hey, can you take me to see my dad that I haven't seen in three years so I can tell him all the ways he screwed me over and maybe stop seeing him everytime I look at myself. Thanks.*

The one thing I do know is I better be back in time for the championship game or else it's my head on a stick. It's already gonna be my head on a stick if my mom asks Liza about my lie that I left early to have breakfast with her. I slipped out the way I used to sneak in and out of the house through the attic and drainpipe. I took one last look at the house before I ran down the block and called an Uber to take me to the airport.

The car ride doesn't feel as long as it should and I can't tell if that's a good thing or a bad thing. The faster I get on the plane and get to Florida the faster I can get home. And the faster I can keep myself from backing out. But at the same time the faster I get on the plane the sooner I have to face why I'm doing this.

We pull into the airport drop-off and the Uber driver lets me out of the car. My hair is flying past my face as I rush into the airport and scan the electronic monitors that hang from the ceilings telling me where the hell I'm supposed to haul ass to. The lines at security took forever and they seemed especially suspicious of me because I didn't have anything. The TSA agent giving me a pat down got a little too handsy. It took everything in me not to deck him. Finally making it through security and sprinting towards my gate I hear the words coming through the overhead speaker.

"Now boarding flight 376 to Jacksonville International Airport." That's my flight. No turning back now.

6:54 A.M (7:54 A.M Florida)

The plane just landed in Jacksonville after almost five hours and a connecting flight in Charlotte, North Carolina. I got lucky though and this flight only cost $78. My flight back is a little more pricey though. It's cutting it close getting back for the game and that's a little nerve wracking but I'm in Florida now so I have no option because I have to get home.

Shit. I'm in Florida now. I haven't been in Florida in eight months. I'm glad I'm in a time crunch because I welcome the excuse to not be able to roam the small streets of Micanopy. I don't need the unwelcome memories that come with the town. My phone pings with a text from my mom right as my Uber pulls up outside the airport. While I may have gotten lucky where flights were concerned, I'm gonna be taking a 58 minute uber ride, and that's gonna be about $100. I'm really draining my savings account recently, what with all my criminal endeavors and all.

Arriving at the jail was more intimidating than I thought it would be. The jail itself isn't scary. It's just this large gray building with a fenced in yard. There's a guard tower there too and I guess that should scare me but it doesn't.

"You sure this is the place you want to be at?" My Uber driver glances at me through the rearview mirror as he throws the car in park in front of the gates, him not being able to drive any further up to the jail. There's an eerie vibe around the place but once again that's not what scares me.

"Yea. Thanks." I pay the man and get out of the car, making my way over to the guards manning the entrance to the gate surrounding the prison and walk up to the one in the booth. "Hi, uh, my name is Ryn Bradford. I'm here to see Jack Knox."

The man in the booth looks me up and down and types my name into the brick-like, very ancient looking computer he's sitting at. "Did you fill out a visitor's application?" A what? I'm sorry he said a what? I swear to god if I came all this way and spent all this money just to be told now that I can't get in to see the son of a bitch.

I grit my teeth together trying to keep my composure. The last thing I need is to get worked up and get arrested in Florida and have to explain to my mom why she has to fly back down here and get her daughter out of a prison that her abusive ex-husband is also in. "No."

"Without a visitor's application I can't let you in"

"Are you kidding me? I flew all the way here from Minnesota on the redeye just to see him. I turned 18 yesterday and every single day he haunts me and I flew here to resolve some of that pain that he's left me with. I'm so tired of hating a man who was supposed to love me unconditionally and protect me all the time so please for the love of god just let me see him." The man just looks at me, blinks, then swallows and looks back at his computer.

"What did you say your name was?" He asks me.

"Elleri Ryn Bradford." I grit my teeth slightly and roll my eyes and add, "Or Elleri Ryn Knox." His face changes slightly and a buzz goes off at the gate and it slides open.

"Looks like you were put on a pre-approved list of people to visit the inmate." Oh. I don't know how that makes me feel. He put me on a list of people to come see him?

"Arms up." The guard instructs. I raise my arms as he pats me down and makes sure I'm not bringing any contraband into the prison. I already passed through the metal detectors and was deemed good on that front. I did have to take off my leather jacket and leave it with the guards at the entrance to the prison. "She's good." He announces to another guard.

The guard that patted me down takes me through a doorway to a hallway and we begin walking towards the visiting area. He goes through a list of things I'm not supposed to do. Hugging is one of them and I hold back a snort because that's the last thing I'm gonna be doing. The image itself is comical. To be honest though if I stop to think about it I can't really remember the last time I hugged him.

What am I even doing here? I know I wanted to tell him to go screw himself and that I hate him but what good is that gonna do? And shouldn't I have really planned this kind of stuff out before I took a fucking plane across the country in the middle of the damn night just to get here and not know what to say?

We get to the visiting area and he lets me sit down at a table and then just leaves me in the room by myself. Sitting here in the silence of the room, I can hear my heartbeat thudding in my ears. The next three minutes go by and all I do is sit and bounce my leg up and down while tapping my fingers on the metal table in front of me.

All of the sudden the door to the room swings open and the man who I've only seen in my memories is standing before me.

My dad.

Tick. Tock. Tick. Tock. The only noise in the room is the clock on the wall as it counts the seconds of the agony I've brought upon myself as I sit across from the man who looks so much like me. His green eyes are staring back at me and it feels like I'm looking at myself. A fact that makes me a little nauseous. Not for the first time I find myself wondering how my mom is able to put up with so much from me when I look so much like him. *Tick. Tock. Tick. Tock.*

He's lost weight. He's taller than I am at 6'3, so not by much. A new scar sits on his face. It runs down his lower cheek to his jaw. Part of me wonders how he got it. The other part of me wonders if it still hurts, wants it to still hurt for all the times he hurt my mother. His tan jumpsuit washes out his skin. We aren't pale people but no one would ever call us tan either. As I look at him I realize he almost looks nervous. Something I don't think I've ever seen him look like before. *Tick. Tock. Tick. Tock.*

I'm alarmed when he breaks the silence. "You really do look just like me." His voice is jagged around the edges. There's demons behind his eyes just like there are mine. The bags under his haunt him in a way mine don't quite.

"That's what you wanted wasn't it." A double edged sword. He swallows and his eyes flit to the side. The man who once seemed so large to me looks so small in handcuffs, like a dog with his tail tucked between his legs.

"What are you doing here Elleri?"

"It's Ryn and you know that." I cut him off. He looks slightly surprised but just nods his head, an apology.

"Why are you here Ryn?" His slight southern accent comes through when he's speaking softly.

I avoid his question and instead ask him one of my own. "Do you remember the day I came out to you?" He looks shocked by my question but I ignore him and keep talking, "I was just 13 years old." An emotion I don't recognize on him comes across his face. "You were so *kind*." I close my eyes on the last word as tears fill my eyes and my lip twitches. I shake my head and bite my lip, "You told me you loved me and then you told me this story about gay penguins who adopted an abandoned egg." I chuckle a little self-deprecatingly at that, it's hard not to.

"Where are you going with this?" He asks, maybe a little nervously.

"Don't interrupt me." I snap at him. This is my time to talk, not his.

"I'm sorry. I just– I do remember that day, of course I remember that day." He mumbles this next part, more to himself and less to me. "It's one of the few days of your childhood that I was actually sober."

"What?"

He looks up at me then, his eyebrows furrowing, "What? You can't possibly not know that I was a drunk and spent most of my time raising you drinking myself under the table." He states.

"No, I know you were drunk." I pause and take a deep breath, pressing my lips together and scrunching my nose. "I also know that you were mean and cruel and selfish. You hurt the people who loved you and who you were supposed to love. A father doesn't do that." My voice breaks a little as I continue. "My father wasn't supposed to do that." He swallows and clears his throat and just nods his head a little. I press on.

"I have spent so much of my life this past year being so angry. Angry at you and at the world and just life in general and the worst part is, it didn't even start this last year. I've been angry at you my whole life. It just turned to rage this year because everytime I look at myself I see you. I see you and I hear the stupid and selfish words you said to me when we left. You couldn't just let me leave, you had to drag me down with you." I'm crying now and as I look at him, I see a tear escape his eyes too. Good.

"I hated myself and I hated you too and I almost wrecked everything good in my life because I was so consumed by my anger at you and my fear of you, yes my *fear* of you, that I got myself arrested. That's right I ended up in the same damn place you are now. Except what I did wasn't nearly as bad as what you did, thank god. But that doesn't matter because at the end of the day I still get scared by my own reflection. So that's why I'm here *Dad*, to show you who I've become. I am a broken mess of a person fighting to keep her head above the water who just recently started believing she's worth fighting for, but still doesn't believe she's worth the love and belief others have in her, and you're the one who broke me." Once I'm done he looks stunned. Neither one of us says anything for the next several minutes. I know because I just sit and watch the clock hands tick by.

"Hated." That's all he says.

"What?" It comes out more as a breath, slightly exasperated.

"You said hated. Past tense. Do you still feel that way?" He stares at me.

"You didn't win." Once again I don't answer his question. After all, I'm not here for him.

"What do you mean?" He asks. His face is scrunched

and he looks confused.

"I have friends." I start. "A pretty good group too. Two that are literally my best friends in the whole world that I would do anything for and who would do anything for me, something I never understood until now. I have a family I've gained through Daniel, mom's new husband, who's doing a pretty good job where you failed. I play hockey, so I know what it's like to be a part of a team and to work as a unit and not just be one person. And I have an amazing, kind, caring, smart, and beautiful girlfriend who I'm amazed by every single day. So you didn't win. I'm broken and fucked up beyond my therapist's wildest dreams. I may still be learning how to let people love me but you didn't win because I'm ok." I jab my finger into my chest on those last words to emphasize my point as tears stream down my cheeks again.

His eyes are glassy and he just stares at me from across the table. He reaches up his hands and scratches at the stubble that lines his face.

"Elleri– Ryn, Ryn– sorry, I'm sorry, fuck– I meant Ryn." He seems genuinely worried about my reaction to his use of the wrong name so I don't say anything and just let him talk. "I never wanted to win." He takes a deep breath. "What I said to you when you and your mother left, well, there's really– there's no excuse for it. I can tell you that I was at the lowest point of my life and that I was the drunkest I'd ever been, which are all true things but that doesn't make it better." He sniffles and the tears start to build up in his eyes and for once in my life I don't recognize the man sitting across from me at all.

"I started drinking when you were just three years old." He looks at me deeply as he continues, "I had my own problems that I used the alcohol as a coping mechanism for and it just made them worse. But I couldn't see past my own ignorance to get help. You and your mother didn't deserve that and I'm so sorry. I don't deserve your forgiveness, I know that, believe me I know that. I don't even deserve you sitting here having this conversation with me." He pauses and looks thoughtful for a second, like what he's about to say he's mulled over more than once before. "Jail has been a– complicated– experience for me." That southern twang comes out again. "It forced me to get sober, left me with no other option. But that came at a devastating price for other people and the price of my soul.

"Getting sober has both given me the chance to fully realize everything I did to you and your mother and also sit in every ounce of deserved pain it causes me to know it. So no Ryn. I did not win. And on no planet, solar system, or universe, did I *want to win*." His voice cracks at the end and there are tears fully streaming down his face as he cries openly in front of me now and I don't know what to do with that. So I give him a quick nod, push my chair back and get up and look at the guard– who's been standing in the corner of the room trying to act like he doesn't exist and give us a relatively private moment– letting him know I'm ready to leave and practically sprint out of the prison.

I've been sitting out on the curb outside of the prison fences for five minutes now with my hand hovering over the button to call an Uber to take me back to the airport but I haven't been able to make myself press the button.

Part of me feels like I left the situation with him too soon but the other part of me doesn't know the man sitting at that table and I wasn't prepared to see a version of him that feels sorry for what he did. I wanted the man who was gonna fight me and yell at me and call me names. Someone I could feel vindicated hating.

The person in there is not that. Our conversation doesn't feel over but I can't bring myself to go back in there. But I also can't bring myself to fucking leave. I look over to the left and I see the guard sitting at the booth manning the entrance to the prison and I get up and walk over to him.

"Do you have a piece of paper?" I ask. "Oh, and a pen." The guard looks at me like I have two heads but still finds a piece of paper and a pen and hands them to me.

I sit back down on the curb and lean over like a child chalking on the sidewalk and begin writing on the paper.

Dad

Sorry that I left like that.
If I need you I know where to find you.

-Ryn

I get back up and ask the guard how I get letters to prisoners and he directs me back inside to someone who can help me with the process. He probably won't get my letter for another few weeks or something but at least he'll get it.

12:23 P.M (1:23 P.M Florida)

I've spent the last three hours just sitting in the airport waiting for my flight. I can't even begin to express
how boring it is to sit in an airport by yourself for three
hours. By hour two I was honestly a little ready to do
something to make the TSA take me into custody just
so I'd have someone to talk to but I knew that was the
last thing I needed on my list of problems, to be on a
"no fly list" or an FBI watchlist.

Just when I'm starting to lose all hope my phone
dings with a text from Liza.

Liza: How come I didn't see you at lunch? Where you at?
Me: now, now. is that proper grammar sweetheart

I really hope she can hear the sarcasm and falsetto I intended through the phone.

> *Liza: Oh well. I think I'm spending too much time with you ;|>*
> *Me: ... is that supposed to be an emoji*
> *Liza: Yes.*
> *Me: sometimes i think i'm dating an old lady*
> *Liza: Alright are you gonna tell me where you are or are you*
>> *just gonna insult me?*
> *Me: ...*
>> *I can't*
> *Liza: What do you mean you can't? That's really cryptic Ryn.*
>> *I thought we were done doing this kind of shit.*

I sigh because she's right. We are. We've moved past this. I owe her more than some Ryn 1.0 shit. I begin typing a response.

> *Me: youre right*
>> *im in florida*
>> *visiting my dad*
>> *in jail*

The dots indicating she's typing come up and go away several times before a response finally comes through.

Liza: Oh. Why did you decide to do that? Are you ok? I'm sure that's brought up a lot of unhappy memories.
Me: im ok. i needed to do it for me
    i already saw him. it went as well as it couldve gone.
    dont worry ill be back for the game.
Liza: You better. You're the best player on the team ;)
    I guess I didn't need to text your mother and ask
    her where you were.
    I was kind of worried you'd run off again.
Me: its ok. i dont blame you.
    wait what do you mean you texted my mom???

I don't even have time to wait for her response before my phone rings and the word **Mom** appears on the screen. Uh-oh. I almost want to decline the call but I know that that will put me in deeper shit with her if I do that than if I just get it over with and answer and let her reem me out.

"Hello?"

"*Elleri Ryn I wish you had more names for me to yell at you Bradford.*" Ok she already sounds pissed. "*Where the actual hell are you?*"

"Please don't be mad." I start. She growls on the other end of the phone and I recoil back in my seat as I try and mentally prepare for this conversation. I don't think she'll be mad I went to see him, but she's definitely gonna be mad for the way I went about doing it. "I'm in Florida." I hear something break on the other end, something that sounds suspiciously like glass and my eyes widen. "Are you ok?"

"*Son of a bitch– yea Elleri I'm fine.*" Oh shit. Full name, no nickname, full name. "*I broke a glass.*"

"Like dropped it?" I pray.

"*No, like I actually broke the glass. I cut my hand.*" She sighs.

"It doesn't sound like you're fine." I grumble, rolling my eyes, but slightly terrified of her strength.

"*What did you just say?*" She snapped through the phone. Immediately I shut up, my cheeks getting warm.

"Nothing."

"*That's what I thought.*" I can hear her moving throughout what I assume to be the kitchen if she was holding a glass, probably in the process of trying to clean up her mess and clean up her hand. I let her do whatever it is she is doing and sit here just listening to her before she speaks again. "*Why the hell are you in Florida?*"

"After my party yesterday I had another moment where I saw dad in my reflection." I pause, trying to somehow gauge her reaction through her breathing on the phone since I can't see her. "I decided I needed to come see him. To give myself some sort of peace of mind. Not closure necessarily. I don't know if I'll ever have closure since he'll always be a part of me, but the opportunity to face him and talk to him so that maybe I'll stop seeing him when I look at myself. He's in prison."

She doesn't say anything once I've finished talking.

In fact the other end of the line is eerily quiet and I pull the phone away from my ear to make sure I'm still connected, which I am. "Look, maybe it was a stupid idea and yea, I probably should have run it by you and Daniel before I did it. But I felt like I needed to do it for myself and I'm 18 now so I technically didn't have to run it by you." I scramble to add that last part and maybe it wasn't the best idea because she just sighs after I do.

"*I know I've said it before but you truly are going to be the death of me Ellie.*" I can picture her rubbing her hand over her face as she says that. I don't need to see her to know she's doing it. "*And I know he's in prison. Olivia told me when she flew in for your trial.*" Olivia told her– wait that's how I know her! Olivia was my mom's divorce lawyer. I never met her and only heard her name in passing but that's why she was so familiar.

She goes silent again for a few minutes before she says, "*How did it go?*" I'm sure this question must be hard for her. I can't even begin to imagine the complicated feelings she must have when it comes to him.

"Well I left without saying goodbye." It's the truth. I did leave without saying goodbye, even if I did end up writing him a note that he'll get in a few weeks.

"*That bad huh?*" She chuckles a little and I crack a small smile knowing she's starting to ease up since she knows where I am and that I'm safe.

"I've been sitting at the airport in Jacksonville for the past, like, three hours just waiting for my flight." She just hums in response and once again we sit in silence on the phone. I assume she went back to cleaning up the mess of her spilled drink and broken glass because I can hear a slight rustling of paper towels and some clinking.

"Hey mom?" I start.

She must stop what she's doing to give me her attention because the noises stop. "*Yea baby?*"

"He's sober now." She doesn't say anything, instead there's just a deafening silence for a few minutes before she goes back to cleaning. "He says he's sorry." I start again. "I'm not telling you this so that you forgive him." I stop and I hear that she's stopped cleaning and is listening to me again. "If anyone deserves to never forgive him and to hate his guts for eternity it's you. I'm telling you this because I think you deserve to let go of him. If you want to hate him forever you can and you have that right. But letting go of him would be so much kinder to yourself and so much more of what you deserve than being angry. You are one of the best people I know and more than any anger you deserve to have, you deserve *kindness*. For yourself." I take a deep breath so that I don't start crying in the middle of an airport. "So maybe think about forgiving him. But don't do it for him. Do it for yourself."

After a few moments of silence I hear a ragged intake of breath and I feel a little bad for making her cry.

"*Thank you Ellie.*"

Just then I hear the overhead announcement telling me it's time to board my flight. We say our good-byes and she tells me to be careful. I give her my flight number so she can track me on the way home and I hang up and get in the boarding line to get onto the plane back to Minnesota.

It's 6:15 and I'm still not off the damn plane.

First there was a delay with my connecting flight so that part took a lot longer than expected and now for whatever reason we're sitting on the damn tarmac and they aren't deboarding. The one thing I do know is that I was supposed to be at the arena fifteen minutes ago and I'm about forty away. The game starts at 7 and I've been receiving about a hundred different messages from the team and Coach asking me where the hell I am.

I'm already in deep shit for missing the parade and pep rally and I'm gonna be in bigger shit for missing warmups. But I swear to god I'm gonna get off this plane even if I have to break my way out of it and fight

TSA on my way out of the airport.

> *Your Grace: What do you mean they aren't letting you off the plane????*
> *Saliva: Ryn if you don't make it to this game I'm gonna cry*
> and have an asthma attack and I'm just starting to gain a little bit of street cred so don't take that away from me.
> *Plane: Do you need me to come bust you off the plane? I'll fucking do it. Say the word Bradford and it's done*
> *Camouflage Man: wtf Ryn. I'm gonna key the fuck outta your motorcycle if you don't make it to this game, just saying.*

Some of the messages have been encouraging, some of them not so much. My response to Hunter was a little graphic. Something along the lines of if he so much as lays a hand on my motorcycle I'll rip his testicles off, one at a time, and deep fry them in front of him and then feed them to a rottweiler while he watches. He apologized really fast.

Daniel is waiting at the airport to pick me up and take me straight to the arena. Everyone else is already there waiting for the game to start. Apparently it's packed. I'm not nervous about losing the game. I've never really cared about winning. I'm nervous about letting my team down because even if winning doesn't mean everything to me it does to a lot of them. And if there's anything I've learned this year it's that having people in your life to care about and who care about you is important and it feels pretty damn good. So if I can be there for them and help them try and win this game then I'm going to.

Just then one of the flight attendants comes on over the announcement system and lets us know we're about to begin deboarding in a minute or two.

"Sorry about the wait everybody, but we are happy to announce that we are moving to the gate now and will begin deboarding in just a few minutes. Once again, we apologize for the wait."

The plane starts moving and I shoot a text to Daniel letting him know it shouldn't be too much longer and I wouldn't mind if he broke a few speed limits on the way to the arena. He just sends an eye rolling emoji in response and I laugh a little in my seat, my leg bouncing relentlessly. I've been chewing my nails for the past fifteen minutes and clearly it's bothering the uptight, obnoxious, snob of a woman sitting next to me because when I first started chewing them she actually, out loud, went *"blech."*

It didn't make me stop, instead I just chomped down harder and made a pointed effort to grind my teeth in her direction. She uncomfortably shifted in her seat away from me after that and crossed her arms in a huff.

Finally the plane comes to a stop after having started moving and I move to get out of my seat in the aisle.

I make my way off the plane slowly and finally start

making long, quick strides through the airport. Thankfully I don't have to stop at baggage claim because I don't have any luggage so I can just weave my way through the crowds and get to Daniel as soon as possible.

After a few minutes of walking, I'm finally at the front of the airport and I spot him standing by the doors waiting, he keeps glancing down at his phone and then back out to the crowd looking for me, having not spotted me yet.

I wave my hand in the air as I speed up and keep making my way over to him and finally his eyes lock on mine and he makes a waving motion with his own arm to usher me over to him hurriedly. I start to run over.

"C'mon, c'mon. We've got no time to waste here. It's 6:21 already. You're gonna have to change in the car. I brought your gear." He says as we start speed-walking towards the car.

I practically dive into the backseat of the car that he had illegally parked in the loading zone and start digging through the bag he had set in the backseat.

"Don't use your rearview mirror." I threaten. As he peels out of the lane and starts making his way out of the airport parking lot.

I shrug out of my leather jacket and throw it on the floor and rip off my Converse one at a time and chuck them aimlessly, one of them hitting Daniel in the back of the head.

"Hey! Watch it kid." He feigns hurt and rubs at his head and slightly turns his head, while keeping his eyes on the road, so I can see the grimace he's making.

I roll my eyes and continue to wrestle on my gear in the back of the car. If there was ever a time for my athleticism to come in handy it's right now as I try to do fucking gymnastics back here.

After about thirteen minutes I've got all my stuff on and I'm stretched out across the back of the car seat trying to tie the laces on my skates.

"Ok I'm coming up." I tell Daniel.

"Ok– wait what do you mean you're coming up?" He asks suddenly.

I throw my leg over the middle console into the passenger seat and plant one hand on the driver's seat and the other on the passenger's and hoist myself up and over the middle space and squish my large frame through. Before he even has a chance to say anything else I plop down in the passenger seat with a puff of air that blows my hair out of my face.

"Seriously, what is wrong with you?" He laughs.

I just shrug and start parting my hair into two sections so I can dutch braid it.

The way Daniel's driving keeps messing me up, so by the time I'm done we've made it to the arena. I shouldn't be complaining because he cut a 40 minute drive down to 36 minutes but still.

Daniel doesn't even pull into a parking spot, just pulls up in front of the stadium and lets me get out of the car. I grab my bag and take off running, as best I can on skates. I go barreling in the front door and past the people trying to take money as they shout at me to stop and I just pull on my jersey and yell "I'm on the team," and keep running.

And like a wild animal being hunted I burst into the men's locker room where I know the team is dressed and ready, mostly because the game is about to start, and stand there panting while they all look like they've seen a ghost.

I made it.

It's come down to this.

Two minutes on the clock.

And Hunter's gotten his dumbass in the penalty box. We're winning by one goal. But for the next two minutes we're gonna be down a player and that means working twice as hard to keep them from scoring on us while we're a man down.

I stand at the ready in the face-off spot, staring down number fourteen before the ref blows the whistle.

"Phweet!" And we're off. I get to the puck first and pass it off to Spitz who's on my left side and the two of us go racing forward towards the other end of the ice. Spitz passes it back to me and it gets stolen from me as I go to make a shot and immediately we're racing right back down the other way. I'm neck and neck with the player who stole the puck from me when I check him into the wall, fighting to get the puck back. I only manage to knock it away from him and towards Jet who thankfully was skating over and intercepts the puck and passes it over to Spitz who starts taking it back down to the other end again. He makes a pass behind one of their defenders to Cliff but it never makes it to him and he falls flat on the ice as he gets bumped rushing to beat the other forward back to the net.

Jet misses the block and in a split second the season flashes before my eyes. All the practices where the guys and I had to do suicides on the ice. Sneaking into the arena to ride the zamboni around when we shouldn't and when we know Coach Maddox would kill us. All the nights we spent at Gino's after games, win or lose. All of them flashing through my mind as the puck sailed towards Duke, standing there in front of the net, the last line of defense before we go into overtime.

At the last second his knees buckle together and his hands come down in front of him and the puck slots right in between his knees and the buzzer goes off. The world stops moving in slow motion and the screams of the fans in the stands come crashing in in full force as the world starts moving around me. All my teammates on the ice stand still for a moment before they start skating around and hugging, some jumping up and slapping each other on the backs. Confetti falls from the ceiling, which is honestly really dangerous. I'm still standing in place, not moving when Duke and Spitz come crashing into me.

I look up and I see my mom and Daniel cheering and jumping around. Liza is waving wildly and screaming her head off. Maria is crying and Mrs. Kahn is shouting something I can only presume is in Ukrainian.

We did it! We won!" They shout. We won. We're state champions.

The locker room afterwards is insane.

Instead of heading to the girls' locker room to get changed, I go with the rest of the guys into the guys' locker room to celebrate the win for a few moments and to hear a few words from the coach.

Hunter had snuck in sparkling cider and popped it open like it was champagne and was now spraying it around the locker room. But none of us cared. We were all jumping around yelling and screaming our heads off taking it all in.

Finally Coach Maddox came in and he was slightly annoyed at the mess all over the floor and the fact that some of his players were sticky, but he couldn't help but smile to himself and shake his head as he stood in the middle of all of us.

"Listen up ya knuckleheads." He whistles and then shouts over the noise. Everyone starts to quiet down, some people stepping off the benches they were standing on, Hunter remains on the one he was on. I roll my eyes at him while chuckling.

"I don't want to take up much of your time because I'm sure you all have plans to go out celebrating either with each other or with family or both, but I wanted to say a few words before I let you guys get dressed and we officially call our season over." He looks around the room as he talks and everyone has gone completely silent, giving the floor over to him at this point.

"I have watched each and every one of you grow into amazing teammates, players, and people throughout this season. I am honored to be your coach and I am honored to be standing here, holding this trophy," he motions for the trophy from Duke who's been holding it for the last few minutes. At this point we've all been passing it around and taking pictures with it. We've got medals and we'll get rings paid for by the school but there's only one trophy and it'll stay at the school so we're all trying to soak in the most time with it that we can.

"I want to give a special shoutout to our seniors. For whom winning this championship might've meant a little bit more than the others. To our captain, Duke," He looks to Duke and raises the trophy and keeps it raised as he continues to name us one by one, looking each of us in the eye before moving on to the next, "Ryn. Jet. Cliff. Hunter." I have my arm around Spitz and hug him tight when he gets to me, knowing I'll be leaving this kid behind next year. I clench my jaw and try not to tear up. Coach continues his speech once he's done naming seniors, of which there's nine in total.

"Lastly, I just want to say that coaching you kids makes me a better husband, a better father, and a better man. And that's all I could ask for coming into this today." He sniffles a little and adds chuckling, "But man am I glad we won this." He shouts as he hoists the trophy higher in the air and we all start yelling and clapping and jumping around again.

"Look, all I'm saying is there's no way Sonic the Hedge-hog could beat Luigi in a 1v1." Hunter exclaims wildly as we all look at him with various emotions of disgust, shock, and amusement.

The entire gang is here including Liza. I guess she's probably officially a part of the gang now so it's safe to assume she'll be coming to the outings as well. I know Duke was friends with her before I was and I know the girls hung out with her at the games before we had our short split but it's nice that everyone else has seam-lessly let her in.

The people sitting here at this table in this honestly somewhat dingy establishment– I don't know why we love it so much– they're my family.

"Hunter, your talking privileges have been revoked for the rest of the night because everything you say is complete and utter bullshit." Amber pipes in, practically leaning across the table as she gestures wildly at Hunter.

We all laugh and I lean into Liza who's got her arm around my shoulders and slump down further into the booth. The raucous laughter around me carries through the small restaurant and if it wasn't so late and the owner didn't know us and like us at least a little bit we might get kicked out. Sitting here in the glow of the different neon signs and the soft light hanging low over the table, I finally feel like I'm not running from anything. The shadow I've been running from is staring back at me but it isn't scary. It just exists. It's a part of me. Maybe it won't always feel that way, but at least for right now, I feel lighter.

It's been a really really long day for me. In fact when I think about it I realize I haven't really slept in 24 hours and I've flown on two planes and played in a championship hockey game in those 24 hours so I deserve to be tired.

Upon that realization I snuggle in closer to Liza while the conversation carries on around me without any notice to me or what I'm doing. I close my eyes and just listen to the people I love most in this world argue about video game characters. I let their voices lull me into sleep.

Maybe this is happiness.
Maybe this is peace.
Maybe this is being loved.

It's not like it's extremely hot out right now. It's a good 72 degrees. But the sun is blaring down on packed bleachers and when you're wearing heavy cloth over your best ripped jeans and a skin tight black, short sleeve shirt, it gets a little sweaty. That was the nicest I agreed to dress up for this occasion. My mom's holding my leather jacket and vintage t-shirt hostage in the crowd. She told me I could change as soon as she got some pictures with all my friends of varying different combinations. That'll mean about fifty different pictures. I'm just glad to finally be graduating.

The last few months have been amazing. I've spent my time divided between the greenhouse, hanging out with my friends and family, doing my community service at the firehouse, and doing my therapy with Dr. Shaw. This past week I turned in my two weeks notice with Mrs. Kahn at the greenhouse which was a bittersweet moment. I hate to be leaving but I know I can't stay there forever. I don't want plants to be my job. It's my escape from reality and it won't continue to be my escape if I try and make it my career. Dr. Shaw says that's a very mature thing for me to realize. I rolled my eyes at her when she said that and she just laughed.

You know I vaguely remember all those months ago saying something about how if we hadn't met through therapy we would've met arguing over cereal at some store. Part of me still believes that's true. Except I've come to realize something since then. She would've always let me have the cereal. She may make me work for it, but at the end of the day she knows I need it, so she'd concede and let me have it.

I completed my community service hours yesterday and am officially done with that chapter of my life which means I'm free to start the next one. I learned a lot while working at the firehouse and one of the things I learned was that I actually liked helping people. That's what I want to do. I want to help people that can't help themselves, the way that I couldn't help myself through my dark time and needed others to help me through it. I want to be there for others in that way. I'm not smart enough to be a doctor or anything like that but I can do this. Plus I can take care of plants around the station and workout while we aren't out on a call so it's really perfect for me. I can read and practice all my hobbies all while being of service. I start at the fire academy in a week.

I'm pulled out of my daydreaming by the name of my girlfriend being announced. Cheers are made and she gets up from her spot down in the front, perks of being valedictorian. Her hair flows from behind her, curls loose and free with the sun shining on them and she looks stunning. She's wearing a light green dress that compliments her olive skin, not that anyone can even see her dress right now. But I know what she's wearing because I got to see it earlier before we all got to the school.

Liza's gonna be going to the University of Forthsworth studying pre-law with focuses in humanitarian stuff and equality shit. Lots of big words that I don't understand. She's gonna be a lawyer and I couldn't be more proud of her.

Once her speech is over the principal starts calling names and handing out diplomas. This part is gonna take forever. Our class is huge. Which is all the more reason I'm proud of Liza for being valedictorian.

He gets to the "B's."

"Elleri Ryn Bradford." I hear my name and stand up and make my way to the front of the stage. My section of family erupts in cheers and whoops as I walk across the stage and shake the principal's hands and smile awkwardly for my picture and take my diploma from him and continue walking as the next person's name was already called.

~~~

After the ceremony is over Liza and I are down talking with my parents, Arabella and Nakoa have already gotten the pictures they wanted and are wrangling their kids into their car and will see Liza later at the party my parents are throwing. I've got my arm around her when someone interrupts us.

"Excuse me." The voice says.

We all turn around and my eyes go impossibly wide. Liza looks dumbstruck as she stares at the figure in front of us.

"Mom?" She says. I gulp and look at Liza trying to gauge her reaction and my hold on her gets a lighter tighter trying to be as protective over her as possible from whatever might happen.

"Hi Liza." The woman I confronted months ago says.

"What are you doing here?" Liza asks. Her voice would seem emotionless to almost anyone else but not to me, not to someone who knows her inside and out like I do.

"Your fr– your girlfriend," she corrects herself and looks at me, "gave me the information." She says. Now it's Liza's eyes turn to go impossibly wide as she turns to look at me. I shrink in on myself and turn sheepish.
~~~

"Sorry?" I mumble, unsure of how to read the situation.

"I wanted to apologize." Her mom sniffs a little, already getting choked up. "I am so sorry for the way we treated you. There's no excuse and I will be spending the rest of my life regretting it. I was ignorant, and hateful. And I really wish I could take back how I reacted that night. You deserved love and acceptance and I'm so glad that you at the very least had Arabella even though your father and I should've been the first ones to give that to you. I know I can't undo the hurt I've caused you in just one apology but I want to get better. I want to learn to be an ally. I want you to teach me. If you'll let me. I watched your speech. It was beautiful. I'm so proud of everything you've become. And it looks like you picked a pretty good partner to share that with." She looks and gestures to me again. I've got tears in my eyes and I look at Liza and she's crying so I pull her into my side tighter.

Liza is quiet for a few moments and I notice Daniel and my mom have distanced themselves slowly from us to give us some privacy and I've never been so thankful for their self-awareness.

"You really did hurt me. All I wanted was my parent's love. That's all any child wants." She pauses and I'm not sure where she's going. "But if there's anything I've learned from watching Ryn it's that it's more important to forgive you than it is to hold on to that pain. So I'm willing to try if you are." A sob escapes my lips and both of them look at me shocked and I shake my head and wave my hands and Liza chuckles at me and kisses my cheek. Her mom smiles slightly and just stands there awkwardly.

"Where's dad?

Her mom's face changes to a grimace and I feel my blood heat up. "He's not quite there yet." It's all she says and she looks genuinely sorry to be hurting her daughter more.

I leave and let Liza and her mom talk for a little while and go back over to Daniel and my mom who have started cleaning up where they were sitting.

"Is she gonna be ok?" My mom asks, the ever worrying protector of those she cares about.

"Yea I think so." I look over to the two of them talking and see Liza with her arms crossed, protecting herself but see her face relaxed.

"What about you? You gonna be ok?" My mom looks me up and down in my open gown and vintage tee. I changed as soon as we got done taking pictures, not caring who saw my bra.

"Yea." I nod. I put my arm around her and we start walking towards the car as I send a text to Liza telling her where we are going. "Yea, I'm gonna be just fine."

Coming Soon...

Duke's Story

Acknowledgements

I wrote a book. Wow.

I've spent a lot of time trying to figure out how to say all of the following to all of the people in my life who have been by my side throughout this entire journey. It's hard to believe that this all started one February two years ago, because of a random sentence that popped into my mind, as I was walking home from taking care of a friend's dogs after it had just snowed five+ inches.

I want to start off by thanking Grace Waibel, without whom I don't know what this book would look like. Thank you for putting up with my endless late night text messages, tracking you down at work to pester you about when we could meet to go over edits, and my all-around over-eagerness when it came to this project. Thank you for all of your suggestions when it came to marketing the book and the people I should reach out to. Even if I didn't always take your advice exactly as you gave it, I still greatly appreciated it and used it in a way that worked for me.

I also want to thank the people who beta read my book for me and gave me critiques and feedback to make the book stronger. Andrew, Tammie, and Kelsey, thank you so much for your hard work and the thought you put into your notes and suggestions. I took each one into consideration and made many of the changes or additions you all suggested. Thank you all for putting up with my constant questioning of where you were in the book and how much longer it would be before I would have your comments. Parts of this book were made better because you guys pushed me to make it better, so thank you.

There are two teachers in my life who I want to thank as well.

First I want to thank Ms. Abby Schrantz. Thank you for fostering my creativity and teaching me to love writing and love creating poems and art with my words. Thank you for teaching me how to tell a story, for teaching me I could tell a story. The world seems so much bigger now than it did in that 8th grade classroom.

The second teacher I want to thank, the one I credit the most with my writing successes, both academically and in general, is Mr. Stephen Grabek. I still remember the way you helped me organize my thoughts in English class and worked with me to start my papers because my thoughts were so jumbled that I couldn't organize what I was thinking into a sentence without working through it with someone else. Not without great pain and struggle at least. And I remember the way you challenged me. You told me that great essays start every paragraph with a different word and that mine already did that. Even greater ones start every sentence in that paragraph with a different word. So you challenged me to do that.

That's still something I carry with me to this day when I'm writing academic essays. And sometimes when I'm writing for fun I'll try and see how long I can go without starting a sentence with the same word. But not only did you challenge me, which was not something many of my teachers often did, but you made class that year fun. It was always enjoyable which made it easy to learn and read as many books as I did that year. So from the bottom of my heart, thank you Mr. Grabek.

Up next on my list, I want to thank Megan Sims. (It's weird calling you that.) Can you believe I wrote a book? That was so not in my four year plan when I started high school. That also wasn't the plan when I started senior year. Thank you for being there for me throughout my ups and downs in high school and now throughout those even greater ups and downs as an adult. I don't know if I would've made it through high school without having you in my corner or having your office as a place to run to and I certainly know I wouldn't have made it through this book without having you in my corner to turn to to brainstorm either. Thank you for being one of four people to read it as I was writing it and for giving me all of the in-depth feedback I was looking for that I didn't get from some people, *cough* mom *cough cough*. I hope that you'll keep reading as I keep writing and that I'll still be able to brainstorm with you when I need to. Thank you for looking out for me even though I wasn't even your student to look out for.

I also have to thank Danielle Wheeler for reading the book as I was writing it and for being my best friend in the world since sophomore year of high school. We're family and I couldn't ask for a better pseudo sister to put me in my place when I need it. Thank you for doing just that for me throughout these entire past two years while I was living my life while also trying to go to school and write this book at the same time. As you know I'm a little impulsive and that can make me make some unwise decisions. But that's what I have you for, and that's what Ryn has Duke for.

It would be a crime if I went through this long spiel and didn't thank my mom, who's been there for me through so much these past two years when it came to this book and life in general and what I was going to be doing in it that it's not even funny. Even though you didn't always give me helpful feedback when you were reading the book, you still were always reading it every time I updated it, even at work when I would call you and say, "Can you read my book?" Thank you for being so invested in the characters and the lives and stories I created, so much so that you start crying at emotional scenes. And most importantly thank you for believing in your daughter's dreams to write a book that people will want to read.

And last but certainly not least, I want to thank my sister. My sister who is my rock and my best friend and has been since the day I was born. Thank you for believing in me and for reading my book even though you are the slowest reader I've ever met. I think you still have one of my books. Thank you for doing literally anything and everything I've needed and asked of you to do for me throughout this entire process. That includes everything from marketing and making schedules, to finding beta readers, to commenting, liking and favoriting all of my TikTok posts, to designing the beautiful cover on the front of this book. I can't thank you enough for everything you do for me. Bookwise, and lifewise. You are the best sister in the world and I'm reminded of that all the time. I'm sorry I don't text more. I really do try.

To my family, thank you, to my friends, thank you, and to anyone who I may be forgetting but am not so grateful for, thank you.